"About the Bennett case—
we have a problem."

Donna, his partner, stared at him. "Mike, I don't like the sound of this. You didn't kiss her again, did you?"

"Kiss her?" he muttered. "If only it was that simple."

"Tell me that what I'm thinking isn't true. For crying out loud, you can't be involved with this woman! Do you realize how crazy that is?"

He'd asked himself the same question plenty of times since awaking that morning. "We're not involved in the strictest sense of the word," he said. "She told me to go to hell before breakfast."

"There's more, isn't there?"

"She knows we're investigating her."

"Mike! You just blew the case."

"Except for one thing. I don't think Kim Bennett killed her husband."

ABOUT THE AUTHOR

Ever since winning a national short-story contest when she was in high school, Ellen James has wanted a writing career. *The Man Next Door*, Ellen's fifth Superromance title, is actually her thirteenth romance novel, so Ellen obviously has her wish. Ellen and her husband, also a writer, share an interest in wildlife photography and American history.

Books by Ellen James

HARLEQUIN SUPERROMANCE

613—TEMPTING EVE
641—FORBIDDEN
651—A KISS TOO LATE
685—MOTHER IN THE MAKING

Don't miss any of our special offers. Write to us at the following address for information on our newest releases.

Harlequin Reader Service
U.S.: 3010 Walden Ave., P.O. Box 1325, Buffalo, NY 14269
Canadian: P.O. Box 609, Fort Erie, Ont. L2A 5X3

Ellen James

THE MAN NEXT DOOR

Harlequin Books

TORONTO • NEW YORK • LONDON
AMSTERDAM • PARIS • SYDNEY • HAMBURG
STOCKHOLM • ATHENS • TOKYO • MILAN
MADRID • WARSAW • BUDAPEST • AUCKLAND

ISBN 0-373-70708-8

THE MAN NEXT DOOR

Copyright © 1996 by Ellen James.

This edition published by arrangement with Harlequin Books S.A.

® and TM are trademarks of the publisher. Trademarks indicated with ® are registered in the United States Patent and Trademark Office, the Canadian Trade Marks Office and in other countries.

Printed in U.S.A.

THE MAN
NEXT DOOR

CHAPTER ONE

SHE FELL IN LOVE the first moment she saw him. He had curly brown hair tumbling over his forehead, dark brown eyes and knobby knees. His hands were tucked into the pockets of oversize shorts, and his high-top sneakers engulfed his feet, giving him a gangly look. He appeared to be all of ten years old. The expression on his young face wavered between trepidation and defiance.

Kim was careful to keep her own expression dead-pan. She stood on the lawn beside her living-room window, studying the shattered glass. She waited for the boy to speak, figuring that sooner or later he'd have to explain himself. Surely it had taken courage for him to approach her; most kids would have run into hiding after breaking the neighbor's window.

"The ball wasn't supposed to do that," he said at last, making an obvious effort to keep his voice gruff.

"I see," Kim said. "It just sort of flew over here...on its own."

He shuffled from one foot to the other. Now he looked gloomy, as if determined to face the inevitable however much he dreaded it. Yes, he did possess a certain courage.

Kim supposed she could lecture him, but somehow she didn't have the heart. He seemed vulnerable in his baggy shorts and too-big T-shirt, as if lost inside his own clothes. Yet he would probably hate anyone thinking he was vulnerable—that hint of cocky defiance never quite left his face.

I should have had a son like this. The thought dismayed Kim, and she tried to battle the regret that swept over her. She reminded herself how impossible, how painful her marriage had become in the end. She ought to be grateful she and Stan had never had children. It would have been a disaster for everyone concerned.

But still the regret stayed with her, brought to life by this tousled-haired kid who'd broken her front window. She didn't want to feel like this, didn't want the inconvenient tenderness he seemed to inspire. She moved away from the window and picked up her garden shovel.

The boy watched her closely, as if he still expected a lecture and couldn't leave until it was over with.

"We only moved in two days ago," he said, perhaps hoping that would exonerate him.

Kim glanced across at the house next door. She knew she'd retreated inside herself these past few months...ever since Stan's death. She'd been only vaguely aware of new neighbors moving in. "I haven't met your mother yet," she said reluctantly.

The boy poked his toe at the ground. "My mom's not here. She's in England. *I* have to stay with my dad. But just for the summer."

From behind Kim, another voice spoke—a man's voice, deep and unfamiliar.

"Don't make it sound like a prison sentence, Andy."

The boy turned. "Dad," he mumbled with a marked lack of enthusiasm.

Kim turned, too, and studied the child's father. The family similarities were striking; this was the man the boy would become. He was tall, lean in a way that hinted at strong muscles. He had dark rumpled hair and brown eyes the color of toffee. But they weren't soft eyes; there was a hardness to them, something that put Kim on guard.

"Michael Turner," he said. "Your new neighbor. I believe you've already met my son." He gave only the briefest of smiles, just enough to hint at a few attractive crinkles around his eyes. Laughter lines, perhaps? Except that he didn't look like the kind of person who laughed readily.

Kim realized she was staring. But she didn't smile back at him. These past few months, she'd lost the knack of smiling.

"Yes . . . Andy and I have met," she said.

The boy's gaze traveled guiltily toward the broken window. Michael Turner stepped over to inspect the damage.

"Guess you'd better explain, son," he said calmly.

Andy's young face grew belligerent. "You can *see* what happened," he muttered. "What's to explain?"

Michael Turner drew his brows together and regarded Andy. His face was as expressive as his son's— Kim caught a glimpse of exasperation and puzzlement in his dark intent eyes. But she saw something else there . . . She saw the love. In that instant, she sensed that this was a man who cared very much for his son. In the same instant, she realized that Michael and Andy Turner didn't know how to talk as father and son. They stood warily apart, as if unsure how to take the first step toward each other.

Kim gripped her shovel. Why did she feel such protectiveness toward a child she'd only just met? And why did she want to tell Michael Turner that he ought to exercise his laughter lines a little more?

Kim pushed the shovel into the ground, wishing she could get back to work and forget about the two Turner males who had intruded on her life. But they would not be ignored. They remained in her yard beside the broken window.

"Andy," Michael Turner said, "you have an apology to make."

Andy stuffed his hands deeper into his pockets. Again he managed to look both stubborn and unsure at the same time. He didn't say anything, glancing covertly at his father now and then. Michael Turner gazed back steadily at his son. In the end, the man won out over the boy. Andy grudgingly addressed Kim.

"I'm sorry," he mumbled.

Kim leaned on her shovel and considered the situation. After a moment she shook her head.

"Apology not accepted," she pronounced.

Both Turners stared at her. For this moment at least, they seemed united in their surprise at Kim's words. Then Michael Turner frowned.

"Son," he said, "I think you'd better run along home."

Andy hovered for a second or two. Kim suspected it had become a habit with him not to obey his father right away—perhaps as a point of honor. But at last he began sidling across the yard. He seemed about to go sprinting off when he gave Kim a glance. She felt it more than ever—a quick unreasoning affinity with this boy. And, from the brightness in his eyes, she knew he felt it, too. Then he turned and finally did go sprinting off, his too-big sneakers thumping over the grass. He reached the house next door and promptly disappeared around the side.

Kim took a deep breath. What was wrong with her? The boy had a mother, whether or not she happened to be in England. Kim was just the neighbor lady. If she had any misguided maternal instincts, she ought to forget about them.

She gripped her shovel again, but it seemed she still had Michael Turner to deal with.

"So it wasn't the best apology in the world," he remarked. "But it *was* an apology."

"Not good enough," Kim said.

"I'll repair the window."

"Well, that's the point," she said. "Don't you think Andy should be the one who does the repairing?"

Michael Turner looked thoughtful. "Are you telling me I'm too lenient with my son?"

Kim shrugged. "I wouldn't know. I've barely set eyes on the two of you. I'm just telling you what my terms are."

He examined her with disconcerting thoroughness. "So we're negotiating," he said.

"Something like that." Kim paused. She didn't like the way her gaze kept returning to this man, drawn by some enigmatic quality in him. He gave a disquieting impression of restrained power. "Andy mentioned that your... uh, wife is out of the country. Maybe he's acting up because of that, who knows, but—"

"Ex-wife," Michael Turner said impassively. "And yes, Andy isn't too happy about being left with me for the summer. I think he made that pretty clear."

Kim wondered irritably why she was poking into Michael Turner's personal life. Against her will, she found herself studying him more carefully. She supposed you could call him handsome, what with his strong features, his dark eyes under dark brows. You could certainly call him virile. But surely that was another knack that Kim had lost somewhere along the way—the ability to appreciate a good-looking man. She didn't think she'd be getting that one back anytime soon. All she felt right now was the dull, heavy emptiness that had become too familiar.

Kim glanced away from him. She focused on the bush she'd been trying to unearth when that ball had come flying into her yard. Digging her shovel into the ground, she stood on top of it, centering her weight. Just a little more, and maybe she'd finally get somewhere.

"You're doing that all wrong," Michael Turner said. "The way you're tussling with that thing, you're liable to hurt yourself."

Kim wiped away a trickle of sweat with her gardening glove. "I can manage."

"Perhaps. But the bush can't."

She glanced at him sharply, unable to detect any humor in his expression. "I don't usually attack shrubs, if that's what you're thinking. But this is a special case." She regarded the bush once more. It was an evergreen, limbs shorn naked except for three round tufts of greenery on top. The thing had always made Kim think of a spindly cheerleader waving pom-poms in the air.

Michael Turner studied the bush, too. "Sure is ugly."

"Well, you understand then. It has to go."

"Understand?" he said, with a tinge of impatience. "I understand that whoever trimmed it had a lousy eye and even worse execution."

"My husband trimmed it," she said in a stern tone that surprised even her. "Yet another reason why the damn thing's got to go."

Michael Turner continued to study the bush in a brooding manner. "It's ugly all right, but what the hell... I'll take it off your hands."

"You can't possibly want it," she protested.

A flicker of dissatisfaction showed in his face, as if he'd had enough of both Kim and the bush yet a sense of duty impelled him to stay—perhaps because his son had broken her window.

"You're right," he said gruffly. "I don't want it. But I'll take it, anyway."

Kim was intrigued in spite of herself. "I've heard of people taking home stray dogs, but stray shrubs?" She glanced across at the rambling two-story house next door, impressive with its red-tile roof and carved balustrades—very upscale for all that it was a rental. The yard had long ago been turned into a neatly maintained rock-and-cactus garden. "You wouldn't have a place to put it over there. The owner doesn't like mess."

He nodded. "I'd already guessed as much. When I signed the lease, she threatened a lawsuit if I spill anything on the carpets."

Kim hesitated, but then she spoke. "The owner also happens to be my mother-in-law."

"She mentioned that, too."

Nobody could accuse Michael Turner of being loquacious. If he was curious about anything, he didn't let on. Kim suddenly felt a discontent she couldn't explain, and she jabbed her shovel into the ground again.

"For eight years, I've looked at this damn bush," she muttered. "That's about to change."

He didn't answer. With seemingly little effort, he managed to walk over to her and relieve her of the shovel. Kim felt a stirring of unease. Yes, there was an aura of power to this Michael Turner, as if he was accustomed to taking what he wanted.

She'd known, of course, that Sophie had been looking to rent the house next door. The last tenants had been a pleasant older couple, but they'd moved out more than a month ago. Her *new* neighbor, this Michael Turner, started digging around the shrub, every motion efficient and methodical. No show of brawn here; he was just getting the job done. Kim suspected he was the type of person who'd always get the job done, whatever it happened to be. As he worked, his dark hair curled a little over his forehead. The way it refused to stay properly in place implied a certain unruliness...

Silently she cursed Sophie for renting to this man and his son. Of course, she'd been cursing her mother-in-law for one reason or another these eight long years. Why should that change even now?

Kim felt a bitter sensation inside. She couldn't let herself think about Stan and all the rest of it. She couldn't let her anger out, that was for sure. Because if she ever started to let it out, who knew where she'd end up?

Meanwhile, this stranger was digging up a bush in her front yard.

"It was therapy," Kim said.

Michael Turner glanced at her, although he kept on working. It was remarkable how much progress he'd made in just a few minutes.

"Digging up the damn bush was therapeutic!"

He glanced at her again, his dark eyes unreadable. And then, silently, he handed the shovel back to her.

"Thanks for your help," she said.

He gave another faint smile. "Why say it if you don't mean it?"

"Something to do with being polite." She worked the shovel into the ground.

"Forget polite," he said. "You're not very good at it, anyway."

Kim wished she could start over with the man, maybe something on the line of "Hello, neighbor—goodbye." She dumped a shovelful of dirt beside her.

"Funny, but my mother-in-law has a similar complaint about me. Says I'm not nearly well mannered enough."

"Do you listen to her?"

Once again Kim couldn't detect any humor in his expression, just that hardness she'd already sensed. Michael Turner, a man of stony edges.

"Mr. Turner," she said, "it's been nice getting acquainted, but—"

"You're pretending to be polite again."

She'd scarcely met the man, but already he chafed at her nerves. It almost seemed as if he was doing it deliberately, to get a reaction from her. Kim wielded her shovel more forcefully.

"Not very many people rent in this neighborhood," she said. "Everyone here likes to think of themselves as the silk-stocking type. Pride of ownership, the whole bit. Pretty snobbish, unfortunately—"

"Why don't you come right out and ask what I'm doing here?" he suggested. The mildness in his tone sounded deceptive.

"Hey, nobody's too sure *I* belong in this neighborhood," Kim said. "I've lived here eight years, and they still don't know whether to accept me or not. But that's beside the point. I'm just saying you seem more like the home-owner type yourself."

"Really."

"Yes, really." She was lying. For all that he was a father, Michael Turner didn't look like the kind of person who would settle down behind a white picket fence. He had a watchfulness about him, like someone who always had to be on his guard, someone who perhaps wouldn't stay in any one place for very long. Certain details about him she couldn't seem to fit anywhere, such as that he was home in the middle of a weekday. Other men on this street worked long hours as lawyers or business executives to afford the life-style of the neighborhood.

"Okay," Kim said, giving in with a sigh. "What *are* your credentials, Mr. Turner? What's your... line of work?"

He paused just a second before answering. "I'm a writer."

He didn't look like a writer, Kim thought. It seemed too tame an occupation for him.

"What kind of writer?"

Again the slightest pause. "Mystery."

That made sense, anyway. "Well," Kim said inadequately. "Sounds...interesting. Not that I'm trying to be polite."

He remained inscrutable. "As long as we're swapping credentials, it's your turn."

Kim realized she'd forgotten to shovel, so she got to it again. "I don't have any credentials—unless you count my marrying into the Bennett clan. Not that the

Bennetts count that in my favor." She didn't want to talk anymore. She just wanted this wretched bush out of her life. She toiled away, exposing the roots. They looked stunted, shriveled, as if they hadn't found enough nourishment in the dry Arizona soil. Kim almost started to feel sorry for the bush, and that worried her. She'd always hated it—why change her mind now?

She was hoping Michael Turner would simply turn and walk away; surely she'd made it clear she wasn't one for cheery conversation. But he just stood there, observing her as if he couldn't believe this was how she handled a shovel. Kim was annoyed, yet she also felt something else—a skittering awareness along her spine. She didn't think she could ever relax around a person like Michael Turner. She certainly wasn't relaxing now.

The heat of the sun pressed down on her, and his gaze pressed on her, too. At last she stopped attacking the bush and stared back at him in exasperation.

"Let me guess," she said. "You're going to remind me that I'm doing it all wrong."

His expression was serious. "I just wondered if it was working—the therapy part."

"No. It's not." She jabbed the shovel into the ground and kicked it, stubbing her toe. She held in an expressive oath. So much for sneakers. Next time she worked in the yard, it had better be boots.

Michael Turner came over next to her, just as he had before, and took the shovel.

"Maybe it's time for a different tactic," he said.

His nearness was disconcerting. Not that it lasted long, though. He moved a few steps away and resumed his own shoveling.

"I was doing just fine—" Kim began.

"I don't think so," he said. "I'd say you were digging at more than this bush. Something's obviously bothering you. Maybe you should figure out what it is before you really hurt yourself."

His confident attitude was irritating, but what could he possibly know about her? "I'm not trying to get out my aggressions, if that's what you think," she protested. "It's not like that at all."

"Something's got you riled up." He continued deepening the trench around the bush. Kim frowned at him, wondering why she felt the need to justify herself to this man. But then she just let him dig. She sat down on the low adobe wall that surrounded her yard, pulling off her gloves and smoothing the damp hair away from her face. Boots weren't the only equipment she needed. A gardening hat might be in order, the floppy straw variety. Kim was learning as she went along. After Stan, it was all learning.

Again the anger stirred inside her, unpredictable and treacherous. Taking another deep breath, she centered her gaze on Michael Turner. He seemed comfortable working, in spite of the heat. He'd rolled up his shirt sleeves, his arms the natural tan of someone who didn't fear the sun.

"Shouldn't you be off writing a scene or whatever?" she asked.

"It'll keep."

She ran her hand over the rough surface of the wall. "What's it about? Your latest mystery, I mean."

He stopped shoveling for a minute, his dark eyes on Kim. "A woman," he said.

She wished his gaze wasn't so intent. "That's not saying much. What kind of woman? Who is she?"

Michael studied Kim for a long moment. "She has brown hair. Not just brown—there's some blond mixed in. Gold-brown, I'd say. And blue eyes... very blue. She likes wearing T-shirts and khaki shorts."

Kim stiffened. She didn't have to be a genius to realize Michael Turner had just described *her*. "Amusing," she said after a short pause. "But now tell me what your heroine *really* looks like."

"I did tell you." He went back to shoveling.

Kim thought about the way he'd looked at her just now—so analytically, yet with a spice of masculine appreciation. There'd been something else in his gaze, too, something she couldn't define. It sent a disturbing ripple through her.

"You can't just do that," she said.

"Do what?" He went on working imperturbably.

"You can't make your heroine look like... me."

He glanced at her. "You make it sound as if you have a patent on gold-brown hair and blue eyes. And freckles."

Immediately she felt self-conscious. "There aren't *that* many freckles."

"What's wrong with freckles?" he asked in a reasonable tone.

Somehow they'd gotten offtrack here. "Mr. Turner, you must be a peculiar sort of author. You're writing about some woman, and you don't even know what she looks like."

"I just described her. That should do." He sounded oddly grudging, as if he didn't want his heroine to give him too much trouble. By now he'd dug all the way around the bush. He began rocking it back and forth, chopping at the roots underneath with the tip of the shovel until eventually it came free of the ground. As he pulled it up, Kim saw the dirt clotted to the sickly roots.

"It needs to be put out of its misery," she said. "There's no point in trying to save it."

"Lost causes are my specialty," he remarked sourly.

The whole situation seemed absurd to Kim. She'd just wanted to get rid of the damn evergreen. Now, because of Michael Turner, she felt guilty, as if she hadn't given the bush a fair chance.

"Mr. Turner," she began, and then stopped herself. She didn't even know what she had to say to the man.

"Gardening *is* supposed to be therapeutic," he told her. "I don't think you have the hang of it yet, but if you need any tips... I'll be around." He started back toward his own yard, only to stop. "Don't worry about your window. I'll take care of it. *Andy* and I will take care of it," he revised. Then he did walk away, carrying the bush with him, its tufty green pom-poms wagging pathetically in the air.

Kim watched until Michael Turner disappeared around the back of his house, taking the same route Andy had earlier. When she could no longer see him, she surveyed the damage around her: the shattered front window, the gaping hole in her lawn. She wished the two Turner males hadn't moved in next door. Of course Kim had wished for a lot of things lately—like a divorce, instead of a murdered husband. Not that wishing had done her any good.

She stared at that raw hole left in her once-neat yard. It made her feel regretful, but only for an instant.

Surely the time for regretting—and wishing—was past.

CHAPTER TWO

MICHAEL SAT in his Jeep across from the public library. He took a sip from his Coke, but the ice in the cup had melted a long time ago. It was a hot, oppressive afternoon, nothing unusual for a Tucson summer. Idly he glanced at his watch again. Kim Bennett had been in the library for an hour and twenty-two minutes.

Michael considered what he knew about her so far: Kimberly Marie Lambert Bennett, born in Pinetop, Arizona. Her parents had owned a small restaurant, but her mother had died under questionable circumstances when Kim was twenty. Kim had moved to Tucson immediately afterward, taken a secretarial job at Bennett Investing, Inc., and married the boss three months later. Now, at twenty-nine, she was the very wealthy widow of Stanley Evan Bennett.

Those were only the dry, straightforward facts, of course. Michael had always been interested in the less tangible aspects of a case—the thoughts and emotions of a suspect. Those were hidden; you wouldn't find them on a computer data base or in a file on someone's desk. You had to speculate, use your imagination, ponder a little. And Michael had definitely been pondering Kim Bennett.

This morning he hadn't met her exactly the way he'd intended; your son's pitching a ball through the neighbor's window was one of those unforeseen events of parenthood. He'd had no alternative but to follow Andy across the yard and introduce himself. Right away he'd been able to tell that something was bothering the widow Bennett. She'd handled that shovel as if she'd wanted to bury something, not merely dig up a bush. There'd been a haunted look in her eyes. He didn't need to be a detective to have seen that much.

But the questions still remained unanswered. What was it that made Kim Bennett look tormented? Sorrow, grief over a dead husband? Or was it guilt? Had she killed him, after all?

Michael shifted position, taking another sip of Coke. Wealthy widow...murderer...maybe both. Not to mention loyal patron of the local library. She'd been in there almost an hour and a half now.

Michael pictured her: sun-streaked hair, vivid blue eyes, dusting of freckles across her pretty nose. An attractive woman, Kim Bennett. Very attractive. Maybe even beautiful...

He reminded himself that she was just a case he was working on. He didn't need to get carried away. Maybe he really could do with more of a social life. Since the divorce, he hadn't dated a lot. Okay, make that no dating. He was out of practice with women, and maybe that was why Kim Bennett looked so good to him. He sure as hell hoped that was the only reason.

Just then his partner's van pulled up; she was right on schedule. After a moment Donna climbed out, moving slowly. Her blouse billowed over the bulge of her stomach, and she walked with that telltale waddle of a pregnant woman—as if her back ached and her feet were made of stone. Opening the passenger door of the Jeep, she slid in beside him. She didn't say anything, just sat there for a second or two, her hands resting on the swell of her stomach. Then, with a grimace, she reached under her blouse, pulled out a small weighted pillow, alias baby, and tossed it into the back seat. Michael observed her gravely.

"So," he said, "still haven't told her, have you?"

Donna gave him a withering glance. "Does it look like I've told her?"

He didn't say anything. Donna let out an explosive sigh.

"What kind of idiot am I, anyway?" she muttered.

Again, silence was the only diplomatic answer. Donna gave another sigh, a heavy one.

"Think about it," she said. "Is this the act of a rational woman? Pretending to be pregnant for my blasted mother-in-law?"

Michael settled back in his seat. He'd been through this before.

"And for that matter," Donna said, "what kind of man did I marry? What kind of man, just out of the blue, tells his mother that his wife is expecting when she isn't?"

Michael almost felt sorry for Brad. The guy was going to pay for this one, big time.

"Okay, so she wants a grandkid. Is that any reason to *invent* one? Heck, why not just tell her I'm having triplets!"

Michael swirled the Coke in his cup. He sure could've used some more ice.

Donna groaned. "For crying out loud, I don't even know how pregnant I'm supposed to be. Four months? Five months? Three?"

Michael thought it over. "I'd say that pillow is a good five months along."

Donna scowled at him. "Oh, I could throttle Brad! 'Mom, guess what, we're pregnant.' Hah. What's this 'we' stuff? I don't see Brad carrying a pillow around in his pants, do you?"

"No," Michael said solemnly, "I don't."

She rubbed her hands through her hair. "Just tell me. What kind of idiot am I to go along with this for even a minute? I'd really like to know."

Michael finished his Coke. Perhaps it was time for a real answer. "I'd say you were just trying to be nice— in the beginning, at least. Trying to spare the feelings of an aging woman who dreams about grandchildren. As for now, though...I'd say you have a husband who doesn't know how to stand up to his mother. And I'd say you're starting to get into this pregnancy thing, too. You already have the walk down—that's a good touch."

She stared at him. "You can't possibly think I'm enjoying myself."

Michael wished he could stretch out his legs more. Such were the hazards of a stakeout—sore butt and muscle cramps. "Maybe you're just trying it on for size," he told Donna. "Trying to figure out what it really would be like to have a kid."

She looked peeved. "That's ridiculous. Brad and I don't want children. Not for a very long time, anyway." Suddenly she didn't seem to want to talk about it anymore. She snatched up Michael's log sheet and scanned it.

"Exciting day, I see. Ms. Bennett went to the grocery store...the bagel shop...the drycleaners...My, sure signs of criminal activity. And now she's at the library of all places. Scary, indeed. Should we call for backup?"

This was the Donna he knew best: sassy, sarcastic, outspoken. He settled more comfortably in his seat.

"You forget," he said, "we no longer have backup. It's just you and me."

Donna plopped her feet on the dashboard. "I do forget sometimes," she admitted. "You can't be a cop for ten years and not have it ingrained. Sometimes I actually miss the uniform."

Donna always had liked the uniform. Even after she'd made detective, she'd grumbled about having to give up her cap and her billy club.

Michael gazed across at the library. Maybe Kim Bennett liked to read. Or maybe she'd just wanted to get out of the heat. Either way, she'd been in there awhile.

"Sometimes it still seems strange," Donna said. "You and me private investigators. Doesn't it seem strange to you?"

The back of his shirt was damp, sticking to the upholstery. "It's a job," he said.

"We're self-employed, anyway. And the money's good. We make a whole lot more than we used to."

"Can't argue with that," he said briefly. People were willing to pay exorbitant sums to have their husbands or business partners or employees tailed.

"You know, Mike, you never talk about the old days," Donna remarked. "It's very annoying. Who else am I going to reminisce with?"

"There's no point in looking back," he said after a moment.

"You *do* miss being a cop," she persisted. "I wish you'd just admit it."

He moved restlessly. This was Donna, too: always wanting to dredge up memories. But he'd left the police department because it was the only wise choice. Now it was up to him to make his new life work. He'd damn well make it work—and that meant leaving a whole lot behind.

"Okay, so you're telling me to mind my own business," Donna said imperturbably. "But someday you'll have to talk about it. The good parts and the bad, too...."

"Give it a rest," he said.

"And people think *I'm* touchy." She swung her feet down from the dashboard and grabbed her pillow from the back seat. Clutching it to her, she glared at Michael. "Don't say anything. Just don't."

He lifted his hands. "Not a word."

Still glaring at him suspiciously, she opened the door of the Jeep. "It's time for me to clock in. I'll take over and do a wonderful job of following Ms. Bennett. Too bad she never goes anywhere exciting."

"Maybe she'll surprise us," Michael said. He had a feeling the lovely widow Bennett might be full of surprises.

Donna started to climb out, but then stopped. "Mike," she said, "do you really think she did it? Do you think she killed her husband?"

Again a picture of Kim Bennett materialized in his mind—her blue eyes the color of shadow over sea, the reckless tumble of her hair about her shoulders... but, most of all, the haunted expression on her face.

"I don't know," he said at last, reluctantly. "I sure as hell don't know."

A SHORT TIME LATER Michael pulled up at the community center. It was an older building in downtown

Tucson, adobe walls stuccoed a startling shade of lavender. The place wasn't easy to miss, you could say that much for it. Built onto the side was the new brick gym funded by the Police Athletic League. It seemed an unlikely combination—lavender adobe and redbrick—but Michael had been right in the middle of those fund-raising efforts, and he liked the way the place had turned out: oddball, perhaps, but sturdy. Maybe he wouldn't admit as much to Donna, but he'd missed being around here this past year.

He got out of his Jeep and walked along the border of palm trees until he reached the gym entrance. He hesitated for just a moment, then pushed the door open and went inside.

He saw Andy right off, sitting on the bleachers, in a huddle with a couple of his friends from the old days. Andy seemed distracted, as if only pretending to listen to the other kids. As usual, he wore a vaguely tense expression. But why should an eleven-year-old look tense? It was a question that had been bothering Michael more and more lately. He wanted his son to be happy... carefree. Wasn't that what childhood was all about? Perhaps Michael's own long-ago childhood hadn't measured up, but that was all the more reason he wanted something good for his son.

When Andy glanced over and saw Michael, his expression changed. It went from tense to guarded—not much of an improvement. He slid away from the bleachers and crossed the gym. He moved at a normal pace, but somehow gave the impression he didn't want to be walking toward his father. Maybe it was the way he dragged his duffel bag along the floor.

"Hey, Dad," he said when he reached Michael—not the most enthusiastic greeting a father had ever heard.

"How'd it go this afternoon?" Michael asked.

"It was okay... I guess." Again, Andy spoke with all the enthusiasm of Daniel to the keeper of the lions. Michael had the urge to reach out his hand and rumple Andy's hair, the way he'd done when his son was younger. But he knew instinctively to stay the impulse.

"You guys get in some basketball?" he asked, instead.

"I suppose so... if you wanna call getting our butts kicked forty-four-zip playing basketball. The court was tied up, so we had to play against four older kids. It really sucks, being short."

His son, a cynic at age eleven? "Butts... sucks... Your mother would have my head if she heard you using language like that when I'm in charge."

Andy looked embarrassed. "It's not, like, a problem or anything. I was just... you know, talking. Besides, you talk a lot worse than I do."

"So maybe we'll make a deal," Michael said reasonably. "I clean up my language, you do the same with yours."

Andy didn't seem particularly thrilled with the prospect, and he said nothing in reply. Still dragging his bag, he shuffled out the door of the gym.

Michael followed his son to the Jeep and watched him climb into the passenger seat. Then he went around and got into the driver's side. Starting the engine, he glanced over at Andy.

"Fasten your seat belt, son."

"This thing's got air bags, doesn't it, Dad?" Andy muttered. A second or two later he snapped the belt into place, but he managed to make it seem a gesture of defiance.

It hadn't always been like this. There'd been a time, before the divorce, when Michael and Andy had shared a quiet, comfortable camaraderie. So much had changed since then—too much. Michael felt the grim edge of regret. For Andy's sake, he would go back and do it over if he could. And he wouldn't make the same damn mistakes.

Michael pulled out into the traffic. Andy leaned toward the dashboard and turned on the radio. He switched from one frequency to another until he came to the "oldies" station. He cranked that one up on high and slumped back in his seat. Andy's logic was all too apparent: find Dad's favorite music, blast it through the speakers and hope it'd keep him occupied—anything to avoid the need for conversation.

Michael reached over and turned the music down. "How was it today, being back?"

"Nothing's different," Andy mumbled. "Doug's still a jerk. Eric's still a whiny ass."

"We have a deal, remember?" Michael reminded him. "Watch the language. Besides, you always used to like Doug and Eric."

"No, I didn't. I just had to hang around with them because their dads were cops, too. But *you're* not a cop anymore. So why do I have to go down to that sh— stupid community center?"

They'd reached a stoplight and Michael studied his son. He saw the belligerence in Andy's expression, but also the uncertainty. Andy was probably wondering if he'd pushed it too far this time.

"I thought maybe you'd have fun," Michael said.

"I'm not going again," Andy muttered.

The light turned green and Michael pressed his foot on the gas. He'd hoped that Andy would enjoy seeing some of his old friends, but maybe that was unrealistic. Andy had started a new life when he'd moved across town with Jill. Another school, another neighborhood—those were big adjustments. And Michael knew firsthand how difficult it was to try visiting a life you'd left behind. Whenever he dropped in at the station house, he felt like an outsider, even with guys who'd been his closest friends for years. Michael had taken to dropping in less and less.

"Maybe we'll join a pool," he said now. "Get in some swimming together."

"It's not like you have to entertain me or anything," Andy said in a low voice. "I can make do on my own."

"I've been looking forward to spending time with you," Michael answered. He paused, then went on, "Andy, I know things have been . . . difficult. But now that you're spending the summer with me—"

"It's no big deal," Andy said quickly. "The only reason I'm staying with you is 'cause Mom had to go on that lousy trip. It's not like it's *supposed* to be this way."

Michael wished he knew the right words—ones that would convince Andy exactly how much this summer really did mean.

"Your mom wanted to take you along," he said at last. "I'm the guy who convinced her you should bunk with me, instead. It'll be a whole lot better than just seeing you on the weekends."

"Sure," Andy said. "I'd much rather stay in this crummy town than be at some castle in England. Who wouldn't?" Again the defiance mixed with uncertainty. But Andy had to know he'd pushed it too far this time. And where the hell had he learned that sarcasm?

Easy, Michael told himself. He realized his son was testing him. The worst thing he could do right now was show anger. He and Andy would have to take this a little at a time, figuring things out as they went along. The answers just weren't readily apparent.

Michael grimaced to himself. When he'd been a police detective, he'd faced plenty of unanswered questions. It had taken a mix of imagination and careful procedure to chase down the answers. He supposed he used that same combination in his new work as a private investigator. But when it came to his son these days, Michael's imagination seemed to fail him, and he didn't know what procedures to use. He was damn well lost.

It had been almost a year since the divorce, a year of picking Andy up every three out of four Friday afternoons and delivering him back to Jill every three out of four Sunday evenings. An arrangement like that wasn't exactly conducive to father-son bonding. But then Jill, a graduate student in art history, had received a grant to study in England over the summer. She'd planned to take Andy with her, until Michael had suggested a different idea: Andy could live with him for the three months she'd be gone.

Jill, of course, had taken her time making a decision. But at last, with a great show of reluctance, she'd agreed to leave Andy in his sole care while she went off to England. Michael had taken her to the airport a couple of days ago, listening all the while to a litany of instructions. Jill had conveniently forgotten that during their marriage he'd been a capable enough father.

It was only more recently that he seemed to have lost the parenting knack.

But here they were now, he and his son. Their time together had only just begun, and already the discomfort between them had grown. Not to mention that Andy had already made it clear he was going to be a smart ass.

Smart aleck, Michael amended. He'd made a deal with Andy, and he'd damn well—darn well—have to clean up his own language.

After a short while they turned into the secluded neighborhood where they'd be spending their summer. Lush orange trees lined the streets, and the large houses were built in quaint Southwestern style, with thick plastered walls, deep-set windows, bright shutters, here and there a *ramada*—a rustic wooden porch covered in vines. Inside, however, would be all the modern conveniences. The people who lived around here weren't the type to do without walk-in closets, Jacuzzis and sunken tubs.

Michael pulled up at the house he and Andy were sharing. It was much too big for the two of them. Too big, too plush, too everything.

"Well, here it is again," he said, his jocular tone not quite coming off. "Home, temporary home."

Andy glanced at the place skeptically. "Yeah, right. What'd ya do, Dad, rob the First National?"

Michael knew he had to be careful about what he said next. There was only so much he could tell Andy, but he disliked lying to his son.

"It's only for the summer," he said. "You know I don't live like this all the time." Involuntarily his gaze went next door. Kim Bennett hadn't returned yet. Without her Jaguar parked in its usual spot, he had a clear view of her house and could see the cardboard she'd taped up over the broken windowpane. Michael had already checked around, trying to locate someone who could deliver just the right glass. So far no luck.

Andy followed the direction of his gaze. "That lady lives all alone," he said.

Kim Bennett definitely seemed the solitary type. "Maybe she likes it that way," Michael said.

Andy didn't say anything for a long minute. The two of them just sat in the Jeep, sharing the same space but nothing more. The tension between them remained.

"What the hell are we doing here, anyway?" Andy muttered.

"Andy—"

"What the *heck* are we doing?" He managed to sound surlier than ever.

"I thought I already explained all that," Michael said. "I'm house-sitting for an acquaintance. Meanwhile, you and I might actually have a good time together once you take off the boxing gloves."

Andy didn't look convinced. He just looked suspicious. Michael wondered what Jill would say if she knew he and Andy were living next door to a murder suspect. On second thought, he knew exactly what Jill would say.

But Michael had realized that if he didn't see Andy for three whole months, the distance between them might become irrevocable. That was a chance he just couldn't take. If it meant Andy getting a little too close to his work, that couldn't be helped. After all, one of the reasons Michael had quit the police department was so he could spend more time with his son.

"Andy," he said now, "it really can be a good summer. Just give me a break now and then, and I'll do the same for you. And . . . be careful, like we discussed."

"I know the routine," Andy muttered. "I'm not supposed to tell anybody you used to be a cop or that now you're a spy."

"Private investigator," Michael amended.

"Yeah, well, what does it matter, 'cause I can't tell anybody." Andy made it sound as if he wished his dad had an ordinary job, like an accountant or a salesman.

"Andy, I want you to be careful in other ways, too."

"Like what?" he asked, looking more skeptical than ever. Michael considered telling him the truth. Don't get too close to the pretty lady next door, because she may very well be a murderer. But for Andy's own protection, Michael couldn't go that far.

"Just stick close to me and do what I tell you without putting up a fight all the time."

Andy had that expression on his face again: willfulness, perversity and, underneath, an undeniable wariness. Why should any kid be wary around his own dad? That was what got to Michael the most.

"You know," he said quietly, "you could try at least a little, Andy. I'm not the bad guy here."

Andy kept his mouth clamped shut. The belligerence didn't leave him, but he truly was small for his age, and at this moment he looked much too fragile—all spindly arms and legs, ears poking out beneath his curly hair, an undersize kid struggling to protect himself with a cheeky attitude he couldn't quite pull off.

At last Michael could no longer resist. He reached out and placed his hand protectively on Andy's shoulder.

"I'm on your side, son."

Andy pulled away. He still didn't say anything, just stared straight ahead with that stubborn tilt to his chin, but the message came through. At eleven years old, he didn't want anything to do with his father.

CHAPTER THREE

BEFORE SHE COULD LOSE her nerve, Kim walked right up to Michael Turner's front door. She rang the bell not once, but twice, as if to demonstrate her own courage. Unfortunately she didn't feel courageous. She just felt foolish.

No answer came—no Michael Turner appeared. Maybe it wasn't too late for Kim to change her mind, after all. She hovered on the porch, considering the possibility of dashing back to her own house. She'd actually started down the porch steps when she heard the door open behind her.

She turned around slowly. And there he was, leaning against the jamb, his pose relaxed yet still managing to convey a certain watchfulness. She'd met him only this morning, yet she found herself learning his features all over again. Her gaze lingered on the stern line of his brow, the firm set of his mouth, the dark hair curling over his forehead.

"Ms. Bennett," he said. "Let me guess. You want your bush back."

Kim flushed. "Of course not. Although I don't know why on earth you took it or what you're going to do with it."

Apparently he didn't care to enlighten her. He just stood there leaning in his doorway, observing her with subtle amusement. He didn't smile—nothing so overt as that—but still she had the uncomfortable suspicion he found her humorous.

She heartily regretted the impulse that had brought her over here. She knew she ought to make up some excuse or other and then return as quickly as possible to the safety of her house. But a contrary pride made her stay where she was. At last Michael stood aside from the door.

"Come in," he said.

Kim hesitated only a second or two. If she was going to make a royal fool of herself, she might as well go all the way. She brushed past him, stepping inside the house.

Evening light spilled over the Mexican tiles of the entryway and burnished the oak floors of the living room beyond. Kim had been in the place a few times before, calling on the previous tenants. The furnishings were the same—sofa and wall hangings in desert hues of sage and sienna—but already Michael and Andy had managed to leave their own imprint: books scattered on the carved chest that served as a coffee table, a single shoe cast off by itself in a corner, a shirt dangling from a chair post. It seemed the two bachelors were settling in.

"Where's Andy?" she asked.

Michael gave her a look of mock disappointment. "You only came to see my son?"

"Not exactly," she said, feeling even more ridiculous about coming over here. What had gotten into her? Usually she was so much more self-assured. All those years of playing hostess at Stan's dinner parties had at least taught her to pretend sophistication. Why was she unraveling now?

Michael spoke. "After supper, a few kids from the neighborhood came by and invited Andy for a game of kick-ball. Maybe he'll make some new friends."

Just as she had that morning, Kim sensed Michael's concern for his son. She heard it in his quiet tone and saw it in the troubled expression that crossed his face.

"Some nice kids live on this block," she said. "I'm sure Andy will do fine."

"Parenthood doesn't make you sure of anything," he answered.

"I guess I wouldn't know." Kim tried for a light tone and failed. "Stan and I—we never had children." Now her dead husband's name seemed to weight the air. It brought too many memories with it, such as the humiliating reason she and Stan hadn't become parents. Futilely Kim tried not to remember all the secret shame. The silence only grew heavier.

Michael Turner didn't make things any better. He didn't ask for explanations, didn't try to cover up the empty spots in the conversation. He stood there, regarding her silently. But that couldn't be a hint of compassion in his eyes—surely not.

"Do you know about Stan?" she asked, her throat tight. "About the way he died... When my mother-in-law rented the house to you, she must have said something. She can't stop talking about him."

Michael didn't speak for a moment. Then he nodded, almost with reluctance. "Yes. She told me."

Maybe it was pity she saw in his expression. She couldn't tolerate that, and she needed something—anything—to distract her. Operating on a hunch, she crossed the living room, found a button under one of the wall hangings and pressed it. Smoothly and soundlessly, a portion of the paneling opened up to re-

veal a bar, complete with pitchers, decanters, ice bucket
and tongs. She glanced at Michael.

"I have one just like it," she said. "Both these
houses were built at the same time, and I always wondered ... Well, the people who lived here before were
a very sedate older couple. I couldn't very well ask
them if they were hiding liquor behind the wall." Kim
listened to herself, feeling more absurd than ever. "I'm
trying to say that I don't usually go snooping around
the neighbor's—"

"Don't let me stop you," Michael said. "Your
mother-in-law said something about a bar, but I never
did find it." He stepped next to her and picked up a
bottle of vermouth. "Care for a drink?"

"That's not why I came," she said.

"Have one, anyway." He took ice from the small
fridge, mixing vermouth and whiskey. Kim's gaze lingered on him again. This evening he wore a polo shirt
and jeans, and they subtly emphasized his lean yet
powerful build. He finished the drinks and offered her
one—a Manhattan. Automatically she reached out and
took it from him. As she did so, her fingers brushed
his. That accidental touch evoked a flicker of warmth
inside her, like the quick flare of an ember before it
died. Kim had to remind herself that she'd lost the talent for appreciating a good-looking man. That wasn't
going to change just because Michael Turner had
moved in next door.

She held her drink without sipping it and examined
the well-stocked bar—gin, scotch, sherry, tonic water,
even a jar of stuffed olives.

"How very thoughtful of my mother-in-law," she
said. "She's supplied you with everything. What did
you do to get her approval?"

Michael was impassive. "Can't say, but I refused to flatter her. Perhaps that did the trick."

Kim shook her head. "I never flatter her and it gets me nowhere. Must be something else." She paused. "Are you a friend of Sophie's?"

Michael appeared to think this over. "Would it matter?" he asked as he sipped his drink.

"Sophie is particular about her tenants. She won't rent to just anyone. Either you'd have to be her friend or come with damn good references." Suddenly restless, Kim wandered to a window and gazed out at the courtyard, where a native garden flourished—asters, poppies, devil's claw. But she couldn't delay any longer.

"Mr. Turner," she said, facing him, "let me get to the point. The reason I'm here is that...well, I need a date. For tomorrow night." How ludicrous the words sounded once they were out. Michael looked slightly surprised at first, then intrigued. My, he did have an expressive face. She also saw that glimmer of amusement in his eyes again.

"No doubt you're thinking it's a very peculiar request," she said stiffly. "I don't even know you. I mean, I only met you this morning. Of course it seems peculiar." She took a sip of her drink. It was inescapable: she really was making a colossal fool of herself.

"Have a seat," he said in a solemn voice. "I'm all ears."

She went to the sofa, sat down, then realized that wasn't going to help at all. She stood up again.

"I need a date for a business function," she said defensively. "Very well, a family function, too. The Bennetts always mix business and family. It's a volatile combination, but I suppose that's beside the point."

Michael continued to look both interested and quietly amused. He sat down in an armchair across from her, appearing completely at ease. To remain standing would only put Kim at a disadvantage. She perched on the edge of the sofa again.

"Perhaps 'date' is the wrong word," she said. "What I need is...an escort." That sounded even worse, and she hurried on, "It's a tradition, in a way. At these Bennett affairs, you never show up alone. You gather your forces, so to speak. But you're probably wondering why I don't ask someone else. Some male friend. Nonetheless...I thought of you. I mean, you don't seem the sort to be eyebrowed under the couch by a roomful of pompous, insufferable Bennetts. That was the deciding factor."

Michael inclined his head. "I'll take that as a compliment, I suppose. So I'm your last-ditch choice?"

She gazed back at him as resolutely as possible. "It's just that...after eight years of marriage, I find I don't have a whole lot of male friends." Oh, Lord. As long as she was confessing humiliating details, why not to ahead and tell Michael Turner what a miserable travesty her marriage had been? Why spare herself? "Anyway," she continued more forcefully, "the Bennetts thrive on despising each other—and everyone else. Family get-togethers aren't exactly restful."

He swirled his drink reflectively. "Sounds like this thing could be entertaining."

Kim wondered if his answer qualified as a yes or a no. Either way, she'd disgraced herself enough for one evening. She set down her drink and rose from the sofa.

"I'll understand if you want to pass. It's very short notice, and it's true that I hardly know you, and—"

"Tux?" he asked.

She frowned at him.

"Tux," he repeated. "Do you want me in a tux?"

Kim felt an idiotic sense of relief. "Nothing quite so formal," she said. "The Bennetts pretend to be casual. Mr. Turner—"

"If I'm going to be your date," he interjected seriously, "don't you think you'd better start calling me something else? Something less . . . formal."

After a second or two she tried his name. "Michael." It had an intimate sound to it, and she wished she could go back to calling him Mr. Turner. But unfortunately he was right. If they were going to get through tomorrow evening with any aplomb, Michael it would have to be. "Eight o'clock," she said briskly. "And if you need a baby-sitter for Andy, I know someone."

"It's a good thing Andy didn't hear you say that. He hates that word—baby-sitter. He's much too old for baby-sitters. But I have a friend he can stay with."

"Well. Then it's settled." There didn't seem any more to say. Except one thing perhaps. "Thank you for doing this. I know the whole thing's rather awkward and silly, but—"

"Kim," he said. "Quit while you're ahead."

She gazed into his brown eyes just a trifle too long. But at least now she had the sense to keep her mouth shut. She left his house without saying another word.

THE FOLLOWING EVENING, Kim stared disgustedly at the contents of her dressing room. When you were a widow of only a few months, how did you dress for a date that wasn't a date? She wondered if any of the etiquette books covered this particular situation.

There'd been a time when she had actually accumulated etiquette manuals with naive enthusiasm. She'd been newly wed, overawed that she'd married into the wealthy Bennett clan. She'd wanted so much to make Stan proud of her—to make the whole family proud. That was before she'd really come to know Sophie or the rest of the Bennetts. Her etiquette books had been gathering dust for quite some time now.

But it was seven-forty-five, and Kim still hadn't decided what she was going to wear for this evening's ordeal. She stood in the dressing room—all mirrors and strategic lighting designed to soften any reflection—and sorted through the gowns hanging against one wall. There were so many of them, in silk, tulle, velvet, brocade. All that entertaining in the past had required an extensive wardrobe. But these days Kim had given up entertaining—or being entertained. If she was showing up at the family enclave tonight, it was strictly as a stockholder in Bennett Industries. She'd do what was required, nothing more—on the arm of Michael Turner of course.

Kim rejected one dress after another. Too elegant, too fussy, too frivolous. Part of her heartily regretted that she'd ever gone over to Michael's house. The other part was grateful that he'd accepted her invitation. She scorned herself for being a coward, but she wasn't up to facing the Bennetts on her own. Not tonight, anyway.

Seven-fifty-two. She had all the clothes in the world and couldn't decide what to wear. At last Kim pulled a black dress from its hanger. She slipped into it and observed herself in the overabundance of mirrors. A low scooped neckline and slinky fit in satin and lace—widow's weeds with a vengeance. But it was too late to try anything else. Feeling out of sorts, Kim slid on a pearl bracelet, brushed her hair one more time and picked up her black pumps. She carried them with her as she started down the thickly carpeted stairs. But shouldn't she be wearing perfume?

She retraced her steps and examined the selection on top of her dressing table. Here was every fragrance a woman could desire, yet once again she couldn't choose. She knew that whichever bottle she opened, it would remind her of Stan. Suddenly the very thought of perfume seemed too cloying, too oppressive. The scent of fresh soap and water would have to do. Besides, it wasn't as if she was trying to attract Michael Turner. This wasn't really a date.

She'd reminded herself of that a dozen times already. She reminded herself again as she went downstairs and moved through rooms that seemed silent and empty. It wasn't a date. She'd merely asked her next-door neighbor for a favor. He'd obliged. And that was that.

The doorbell rang. Suddenly flustered for reasons she couldn't explain, Kim peered at herself in the hallway mirror. She was no more reassured than she'd been upstairs, facing those myriad reflections of herself. This mirror told the same story: her expression was severe and unsmiling. It didn't go with the damn dress.

Too late now. The words echoed through her mind as she went to open the door. Michael stood on her porch just as she'd expected, but she wasn't prepared for how good he looked. He wore casual gray trousers and a linen jacket that was well tailored but ever so slightly rumpled. His dark hair curled over his forehead, slightly damp as if he'd just taken a shower. He gazed thoughtfully at Kim.

"I should have gone for the tux," he said.

She felt unaccountably warm with his gaze on her, but at last she managed a shrug. "Trust me, you look fine. I'm the only one who'll be this dressed up tonight. This fancy. Don't ask me why I'm doing it."

He continued to observe her and she saw the subtle appreciation in his eyes. "Maybe you want the Bennetts to sit up and take notice."

"They'll take notice, all right," she said. "And when they do—watch out."

"Don't let them get to you," he murmured. "Because you look . . . fine."

Now Kim felt the color heating her cheeks. It had been a very long while since a man had gazed at her in just this way. She didn't know how to react. Whatever she'd learned from her once-precious etiquette books seemed to have flown right out of her head. All she could do was stare back at Michael, that unfamiliar warmth suffusing her skin.

Belatedly she remembered that she was still holding her pumps. She bent to slip one of them on and then realized that might seem consciously provocative. Quickly she stuffed her feet into both shoes.

"They pinch," she said. "I hate wearing them for very long."

"It's one of the things I've always wondered." He smiled slightly. "Why do women wear uncomfortable shoes?"

"Because we have no sense at all. Well . . . I'm ready," she added unnecessarily. "Shall we go?"

He escorted her down the walk. Even though he'd only come from next door, he'd driven over and parked behind her car—a considerate gesture. Perhaps this didn't officially count as a date, but Michael was observing the courtesies. Although his midnight-blue Jeep was a rugged vehicle, it looked freshly washed and waxed. He opened the door for her, waiting until she'd settled into the passenger seat before going to his own side. A few moments later he'd backed out of the drive and they were on their way down the street.

Kim searched for conversation and found none. It was Michael who spoke, glancing at her with that quiet amusement of his.

"I hope you have directions for me. Where are we headed?"

She felt foolish, apparently not an uncommon reaction when she was around Michael Turner. "To the Bennett family stronghold... my mother-in-law's very exclusive spread. Where else?"

CHAPTER FOUR

MICHAEL FOLLOWED the instructions Kim gave him: left on Vernon, right on Solano, head toward the foothills. He had to admit he was curious. In spite of his dealings with Sophie Bennett, he'd never been to her spread. Apparently Sophie was careful that way—never let the hired help get too close. She was in for a surprise tonight.

As he drove, Michael glanced at Kim now and then. She sat staring ahead, only her profile revealed to him. It was an intriguing profile, all feminine strength. There was nothing weak about Kim. Take now, for instance. She was obviously tense, obviously not looking forward to this little family get-together of Sophie's. But she wasn't talking about it. She was just sitting there, staring boldly ahead, her face beautiful yet unsmiling. That dress she wore conveyed boldness, too. Hell, it conveyed more than that. It showed that Kim Bennett was womanly and desirable, regardless of the "don't mess with me" attitude.

Michael reminded himself to watch the road. Maybe Kim Bennett was wearing a sexy dress, but that didn't stop her from being a murder suspect. He was on the job tonight. He couldn't forget that.

They traveled in silence, and at last they turned along a secluded, winding street where the houses were hidden behind foliage and high walls. This neighborhood was even more exclusive than Kim's. The people who lived here had gone beyond flaunting their wealth; they craved privacy more than anything else.

Sophie Bennett's two-story brick house, although large, was carefully unpretentious—no embellishments, no turrets or towers added for effect. Maybe that was supposed to be tasteful, but to Michael the place looked bland and impersonal, like a hotel. He parked on the drive behind a Rolls and a Jag, but he didn't get out right away. Kim didn't, either. She just went on sitting there, hands clenched tightly in her lap.

"Nice wheels," he said after a moment. "The Bennetts can't be all that bad."

She glanced over at him almost as if she'd forgotten his presence. "The Bennetts," she said with a hint of disdain. "They're nothing I can't handle. It's just that sometimes I'd rather not have to handle them. I can think of better things to do with my time."

"Such as?"

She didn't answer. "Well, we're here, so we might as well get on with it." She reached for the door handle, but Michael didn't want to go inside just yet. He couldn't explain why. He just knew he liked being alone here with Kim.

"If you could do anything you wanted right now, what would it be?" he asked.

She looked exasperated. "Mr. Turner—Michael, that is. You're choosing a very strange time to play twenty questions—"

"What would it be?" he asked again.

She slumped back against the seat. "This is ridiculous," she said, but she no longer made any move to leave the Jeep. After a silence, she spoke, her voice extra soft as if she was talking only to herself. "Perhaps

I'd go for a hike in the mountains. And perhaps I'd just keep walking. For hours..."

He thought it over, choosing his next words carefully. "Did you do a lot of hiking when you lived in Pinetop?"

The effect was immediate. Kim twisted in her seat to face him. "How did you know—"

"Your mother-in-law isn't exactly closemouthed. Seems she finds you a fascinating subject." That was the truth. But Michael saw the way Kim tensed, the distrust in her expression.

"Sophie always *has* liked to bad-mouth me, especially to her friends. You never did make it clear. *Are* you her friend?"

Again he considered his words. And again he told the truth. "No. I'm not."

That did nothing to ease the doubt in Kim's expression. And Michael knew he'd deliberately made her skeptical of him. It hadn't been the professional thing to do—but that was the problem; he didn't feel professional when it came to Kim Bennett. He just felt impatient with his job. Deception, secretiveness— those weren't his style. He would've disliked being an undercover cop, and he'd always been smart enough to admit it. So why the hell was he working undercover now? Lovely, haunted Kim Bennett made him ask that question.

"As a matter of fact," she said, an edge to her voice, "I did hike a lot when I was growing up. Most of the time by myself, but sometimes...sometimes my dad managed a day off and we went together. Sophie couldn't have told you *that*. She'd never want to admit I have rosy childhood memories. It would make me seem too...normal."

Kim had one thing right—her mother-in-law would probably never say anything favorable about her. Michael reviewed everything Sophie had told him about Kim and everything he'd been able to learn through his own investigation. Kim's parents had owned their own small diner in Pinetop, Arizona, but for years they'd struggled on the verge of bankruptcy. It had been difficult for them to keep employees, and Kim herself had worked in the restaurant all through her teenage years. Michael was willing to wager that neither Kim nor her father had been able to take off many days for leisurely hikes.

"How many of them do you have?" he asked. "Rosy childhood memories, that is."

Kim turned away so that once more all he could see was her unyielding profile. "Enough," she said tersely. "I have enough of them."

He wondered about that. He'd been doing a lot of wondering since meeting Kim yesterday. Having a case file on her was one thing. But actually sitting here next to her, sensing the vulnerability underneath her caustic demeanor, that was something else entirely.

He reminded himself that maybe she wasn't vulnerable at all. Maybe she was coldhearted, cold-blooded, and she'd actually killed her own husband. She certainly had motive: as a widow, she had become a very wealthy woman indeed.

Michael rubbed at a kink in his shoulder and silently cursed.

"You don't want to be here any more than I do," Kim said, glancing at him. "You look...disgusted."

"The Bennetts aren't anything I can't handle," he said, his tone only slightly mocking.

Now she gave him a challenging look. "Let's make this fair, Michael. What would *you* be doing right now, if you had the choice?"

Somehow that didn't take too much thinking. Michael's gaze dropped to her mouth. He noticed that her lips had a determined set, but he suspected they could be soft and inviting, too....

He saw the faint blush tingeing her cheeks, and that only made her dusting of freckles seem more appealing than ever. When he captured her gaze, she didn't look away. Almost against his will, he kept imagining what he'd like to be doing right now. It was a pretty safe bet she knew what he was thinking. Her flush deepened as she stared back at him. The atmosphere between them seemed to grow taut, suspenseful. Michael kept imagining.

"Stop," Kim murmured, her voice just a little unsteady. And then she turned, opening the door and sliding out of the Jeep. The moment was broken almost before it had begun.

Michael felt dissatisfied in a way he couldn't explain, but he came round to escort Kim up the walk to the house. They reached the portico and Kim rang the bell decisively. She held herself stiffly, as if preparing to fend off some sort of assault. Who were these Bennetts that they could produce such a reaction in her? Michael gave in to another impulse he couldn't explain, and for just a second placed his hand on Kim's arm. She gave him a skeptical look, but maybe she accepted the unspoken support he was offering her. Now he just had to figure out why he was offering it.

A maid finally opened the door, ushering them into a rather cavernous living room. The few people standing about only emphasized the space. Michael saw the pride in Kim's expression, the unabashed tilt of her chin. No matter what she might be feeling inside, she knew how to disguise it with a haughtiness that was surely worthy of any Bennett.

From long experience, Michael knew how to assess a situation quickly. He did so now, observing that the people in the room were divided in two separate clusters; no easy mingling seemed to be taking place. Faces turned with covert interest, but no one made a move to come forward in greeting.

Sophie Bennett, however, materialized from another doorway and walked purposefully toward them. If she was displeased to see either Michael or Kim, she gave no sign. Then again, if she was pleased, she gave no indication of that, either. She was a plain woman, with resolute features, but clearly she knew how to work with her looks. Wisely avoiding frills of any kind, she wore a simple yet sophisticated black dress. Although high of neck and long of sleeve, it discreetly emphasized the fact that, at sixty-odd years, Sophie had kept her figure. Her thick red hair waved artfully around her face. It seemed a natural shade, almost too natural, perhaps, as if Sophie Bennett watched vigilantly for gray hairs and obliterated them as soon as they appeared. And so, although she didn't possess beauty or any real charm, she had nonetheless cultivated a striking elegance that seemed to defy time.

"Kim." Sophie approached her daughter-in-law. "I was beginning to think you wouldn't come."

"Here I am," Kim said, still with that edge to her voice. "Of course you know Michael . . . your new tenant."

"Of course. How convenient that you could join us, Mr. Turner." She made the word "convenient" sound distasteful, as if he had done something underhand to get here. So far in his short acquaintance with Sophie Bennett, Michael had figured he could either be amused or irritated by her. Amusement took less effort.

"I hope you're finding the house satisfactory," she went on.

"It's adequate," he said, and Sophie's forehead creased a fraction. It probably wasn't good form to tell Sophie Bennett that something she'd provided was merely adequate. But Michael never had been one for good form. He caught Kim's eye and wondered if he saw a hint of approval.

"If anything is . . . unsatisfactory, I trust you will let me know immediately," Sophie said. Then she turned to Kim. "Will you introduce Mr. Turner around, or shall I?" It sounded like a command, not a question.

"I'll do the honors," Kim answered. "He's my guest, after all."

Sophie stared hard at Kim, as if looking for signs of insurrection. Kim stared right back at her.

"Very well," Sophie said. "Make sure he meets everyone. Have a pleasant evening, Mr. Turner." And with that, Sophie turned and walked purposefully off again.

Kim watched her go. "You really must be on Sophie's good side," she said in a low voice to Michael. "She actually put out the welcome mat for you."

"That was the welcome mat?" he asked dryly. "She kept looking at me like I was last night's garbage moldering on the stoop."

Kim almost smiled. Almost, but not quite. "I guess you don't know Sophie very well. She wouldn't bother to play hostess if she didn't like you."

Sophie Bennett's idea of playing hostess was a little limited. She was throwing this party, or whatever the hell it was, and yet she seemed to have made no concessions to her guests: no music playing in the background, no drinks being served, no plates of hors d'oeuvres being handed around. Apparently Sophie didn't even find it necessary to be present in the room. She'd made that brief, regal appearance of hers, then simply gone off somewhere else.

"We might as well begin," Kim said. "Which of the two sets of Bennetts do you want to tackle first?"

"Is that how they're arranged—in matched sets? You make them sound like plates of dinnerware."

She gave him a keen glance. "Actually the Bennetts do travel in sets—when they come to this house, at least. They know there's safety in numbers. You'll rarely find one of them alone—not while Sophie's anywhere near."

Sophie Bennett appeared to be a formidable woman, but did she really inspire such trepidation in her family? Perhaps Kim was simply exaggerating for reasons of her own. Michael already sensed that the undercurrents between Kim and her mother-in-law were murky and complex. Add the rest of the Bennett clan, and who knew what you'd end up with.

But Michael didn't want to think about Bennetts right now. He was still distracted by Kim, by the way she looked tonight. The sun-streaked ripples of her hair falling to her shoulders, the warm creaminess of her skin, the shadowed blue of her eyes...

She gazed back at him, consternation flickering across her face. "You're doing it again," she whispered fiercely.

"Doing what?" He imagined reaching out to touch her. Kim Bennett was the kind of woman you wanted to touch.

"You know. You're looking at me...that way." Her fingers tightened around the small black bag she carried. But he went on looking at her. He couldn't stop.

Her eyes seemed to darken as she went on gazing back at him. Now they were the color of blue just at sundown. Her lips had parted slightly, as if she meant to catch her breath. He didn't take a step closer to her, didn't make a move toward her. He didn't need to, as long as they were together like this, alone in their own private corner of the room.

He heard Kim utter something under her breath, something he couldn't quite hear. Then she turned abruptly and walked away. He followed, his gaze lingering on her. The dress she wore was cut daringly low in back, revealing more creamy skin. And more freckles.

Lord. Was he to be undone by freckles? Michael reminded himself that he hadn't been out with a woman in a while—that was the problem. After fourteen years of marriage, he'd forgotten what it was like to be on a date. Except that Kim had made it very clear this *wasn't* a date. And that led him to another question. Why was he acting like a damn fool around her?

He didn't have any time to ponder the matter, because they'd reached the first Bennetts: a man and a woman who made room for Kim and Michael, but only with an air of reluctance. Kim was very businesslike.

"Diane, your mother wants you to meet her new tenant. Michael Turner."

She could have simply introduced him as her next-door neighbor, but instead, she'd brought Sophie into it. Michael wondered why that bothered him. Meanwhile, he shook hands with Diane Bennett. She was obviously Sophie's daughter. The family resemblance was striking: heavy reddish hair, intractable features. But Diane at least was animated.

"So you're Michael Turner," she said with interest. "Mother told us all about you. She said she was interviewing tenants, and that it was very discouraging. She didn't think she could find anyone trustworthy to rent the house. Are *you* trustworthy, Mr. Turner?" Diane asked, apparently in all seriousness.

He reflected on the question. If Kim knew the truth about him, she probably wouldn't find him trustworthy by any definition. He caught her looking at him again, and he saw the doubt clouding her eyes. She was right to doubt him unfortunately.

Diane Bennett was veering off on a different tack. "You haven't met Jack yet," she said importantly. "Mr. Turner, this is my friend Jack Hutchinson." She sounded as if she was announcing royalty, and gazed at Jack with reverence. He seemed a normal enough guy, balding on top, spreading around the middle but clearly doing his best to suck in his gut. He looked like the kind of person who'd be happier in a pair of roomy overalls than in the suit he wore.

"Anyway," Diane went on, "Mother was saying maybe she just ought to sell that house next to Stan's— next to *Kim's*." Diane corrected herself deliberately, with an oddly put-upon air. "Mother said it was very discouraging, after all the trouble she's had with tenants—"

"The Harveys were a perfectly nice couple," Kim interrupted with that edge to her voice Michael was starting to recognize. "They never gave Sophie any trouble at all."

"Oh, well, the Harveys," Diane said dismissively. "I wasn't thinking about them. You know...it was the people before."

"The Millers?" Kim asked in a skeptical tone. "They were nice, too."

Diane Bennett was starting to look peeved. "The whole point is that Mother was getting very discouraged about having to rent the place again, and then Mr. Turner came along and solved Mother's problems."

They all studied him now, silently, as if contemplating the peculiar fact that someone had actually met Sophie Bennett's standards. Diane had a particularly knowing expression on her face. How much had Sophie told her? Did she suspect the real reason Michael was "renting" a house next door to Kim?

Subterfuge, deception—definitely not his style. He tried to remind himself of all the reasons he'd become a private investigator: a chance to get away from bad memories, a chance to spend more time with his son, a chance to pick his own cases. The only problem was, he regretted this case more and more all the time. Especially when he looked into Kim Bennett's eyes and saw the distrust there.

"If you'll excuse us," Kim said a bit forcefully, "I have to introduce Mr. Turner to the others."

There was an awkward pause. "Nice to have met you, too," Michael said to their pointed silence. He didn't bother to keep the irony from his tone.

Kim was already headed toward the remaining set of Bennetts, but Michael took her elbow and steered her outside, instead, onto a veranda. Night had fallen. The air still held the summer heat, but it was no longer oppressive. Michael preferred it to the artificially cool room they'd just left behind.

"We shouldn't be out here," Kim said.

"Do you think it will make them wonder about us?"

"They're wondering about you," she returned. "They've already made up their minds about me—they did that long ago. But you're someone new. They haven't figured you out yet."

He knew what she meant to say—that *she* hadn't figured him out yet. Too bad he couldn't help her with that.

"Let's just get it over with," she said impatiently. "You can meet the others, and hopefully Sophie will get on with this ridiculous thing." She turned back toward the room, but Michael clasped her hand to stop her.

"They can do without us for a few minutes."

Kim's fingers moved restlessly in his, and then she slipped her hand away. There was no porch light, and he could see only the outline of her face.

"There's no good reason for us to be here..." He heard the uncertainty in her voice.

"You can give me your take on Diane and Jack."

"You've just met them. Isn't that enough?"

"I'm curious," he said.

"Why?" Now the uncertainty was gone, replaced by outright challenge. He wished he could read her expression. He also wished he could tell her the truth, the reason he needed to know more about the Bennetts.

Smart, he told himself. *Confess everything to the woman who may very well have killed her husband.*

"Just curious," he repeated.

Kim hesitated, then gave a shrug. "*I'm* no authority on the almighty Bennetts. I'm not allowed in the clique."

"Maybe you don't allow them in *your* clique."

She seemed to consider this. "You think it's my fault I'm not a cozy part of the family? Once upon a time . . . all I wanted was to belong." Her words sounded brittle on the night air. "Anyway, what can I tell you that would possibly be of interest? Diane—she keeps talking about how she admires Jack, but she doesn't even realize yet that she's in love with him. She'd better figure it out soon, though, before Sophie ruins things again—and that's really all I have to say." She sounded chagrined, as if wishing she'd stopped earlier.

He thought over what she'd said, searching for anything that might be of use. Diane Bennett, for all her attempts at perkiness, was as peculiarly devoid of charisma as her mother. It was a strange lack, as if some essential gene had been left out of the family makeup.

"So you think she's in love with Jack," Michael said gravely.

"Anyone can see it—except Diane. And possibly Jack. For a physics professor, he can be remarkably dense. But do you really want to know about Diane Bennett's love life?"

He couldn't honestly say that he did, but he knew any detail might be important. One thing was certain—he never would've pegged Jack Hutchinson for a physics professor.

"You make it sound like Sophie's botched things for Diane before."

"And you make it sound as if you're very interested in the Bennetts." Kim spoke coolly, but he sensed an anger in her. Somehow he'd touched a nerve.

"If you despise them so much, why did you come here tonight?" he asked.

She paced a few steps back and forth, as if she couldn't bear to stand still. "When Sophie convenes the family, you know you'd damn well better be there—to look out for your own interests, if nothing else. That's one thing I learned from Stan at least."

Stan. The dead husband. Kim had given Michael the perfect opening, but he took it reluctantly.

"I'm sorry about what happened," he said.

"That's right—you know all about it, don't you? Courtesy of Sophie."

Again he chose his words carefully. "I know your husband died in a car accident. No real evidence of foul play, but the autopsy showed a high level of blood alcohol, and he wasn't known to be a heavy drinker."

Kim had averted her face as he spoke. "My, Sophie was thorough in her briefing," she said in a caustic tone.

Sophie had indeed been forthcoming on the subject, but the police report had provided all the pertinent details. Michael disliked what he had to ask next. He disliked a lot of things about his job lately. "Do you think it was murder, Kim?"

Standing there before him in the darkness, she was very silent. But then finally she spoke, her voice tight.

"Mr. Turner, you're a damn sight too curious. About Stan, about the rest of the Bennetts...about everything. And I can't help wondering why."

He wanted her to wonder. It was the closest he could come to being straight with her. He felt an unreasonable urge to protect her—from what, he couldn't have said.

"Yes," she said at last, her voice so low he barely caught the word. "Yes," she repeated a few seconds later. "I do think someone killed him. That was one of Stan's few virtues—he hardly ever drank too much. So why that night?"

She sounded innocent—convincingly so. But a person could perfect the art of sounding innocent.

"Any idea who the culprit might be?" he asked, though still reluctant to pursue the subject.

She stared at him in the darkness. "Not that it's any of your concern, but no, I don't have a clue who might have killed my husband. Satisfied?"

The last thing he felt was satisfaction. But he'd already noted the tension in her every time she spoke about her dead husband—and then the way she grew silent. Michael wondered about Stan Bennett. Had the guy appreciated his beautiful wife?

"It was a mistake," Kim said now. "I never should have asked you to come here with me. What was I thinking?"

"I should be here." Once more he clasped her hand, drawing her near. He felt her stiffen. They gazed at each other, but even the light spilling from the room beyond didn't chase the shadows from this secluded alcove. He couldn't read Kim's expression, knowing only the warmth of her fingers curled in his.

"You're doing it again," she said almost in a whisper. "You're looking at me...that way."

"It's dark. How can you tell?" His own voice was low.

"I just can. And you have to stop."

Michael forgot that he was supposed to be on the job tonight. He forgot about the Bennetts. He forgot everything but Kim's loveliness. He brought her even nearer to him. Their bodies didn't quite touch, yet still they gazed at each other in a darkness that both obscured and enticed. And then, at last, he bent his head to hers.

CHAPTER FIVE

MICHAEL'S CHEEK brushed Kim's. Her skin was as soft as he'd imagined it would be, her scent alluringly feminine. But she stood motionless, self-contained in her silence. He wanted her response and he courted it, bringing his lips to the corner of her mouth. Did he feel her tremble or was it only his imagination?

She allowed no more, stepping away from him. He experienced an immediate sense of loss. He knew he didn't have any right to touch her, but that didn't stop the wanting.

"I can't," she said after a moment, the darkness still cloaking her. He didn't ask her what she meant, just waited for her to say the rest of it.

"I can't do *this*," she went on, a turbulence underneath her words. "It's all a mistake. Bringing you here and pretending everything is normal. In this house, of all places—" She broke off abruptly. Slipping past him, she went back inside.

He stood on the veranda another second or two. Maybe he thought if he stayed out here, she'd return to him. That was wishful thinking of course, the kind of thing he should have left behind a long time ago.

Finally he walked back into that lofty, oddly bare living room. There was minimal furniture scattered about, and he supposed it was the kind of place where architectural details were supposed to take precedence: exposed ceiling beams, high arched windows, carved moldings. The overall effect was that of a drafty church with too few worshipers. The Bennetts remained in their separate little clusters, but again faces turned toward him in interest; Diane Bennett looked particularly alert. No doubt they were speculating about what he and Kim had been doing on the veranda. He couldn't say he cared.

Kim had taken up a position alone some distance from the others. She didn't do anything to minimize her solitary status, didn't pretend to be looking at the paintings on the walls, didn't indulge in any other ruse to appear occupied. She just stood there, back straight and chin up, holding her small black bag as if it were a weapon. She couldn't have made it clearer that she wished to go on being solitary.

A reluctant admiration stirred in Michael. She might as well have been wearing a sign that read No Bennetts Allowed. But did the warning extend to him? He walked over to her. The stern expression on her face told him she still regretted inviting him.

"Lively party," he remarked. "When does the conga line start?"

His stab at humor obviously didn't impress her. "Sophie has her own way of doing things," she said. "I wish you had some way to entertain yourself, Michael."

"I'm entertained."

She gave him one of her skeptical looks. "I'm sure you'd much rather be home working on your novel."

"I'm a little stuck," he said. In a manner of speaking, that was true.

"I've heard about writer's block. Is that your problem?" She glanced at her watch as if hoping he wouldn't answer.

"I'm having trouble with my storyline."

"Really." She didn't look sympathetic.

"My heroine won't open up much. She keeps everything bottled up inside. Anger...frustration...who knows what else. She's hard to get to know."

He saw the flush that made Kim's freckles so beguiling. She gazed back at him steadily. "Maybe you should write yourself another heroine."

"No. Sorry...won't do. This one's too intriguing."

"But you're not getting anywhere with her," Kim said.

"Not yet."

A flicker of some unnamable emotion showed in her eyes. But neither one of them had a chance to say anything more. Coming toward them was the second set of Bennetts: a fortyish couple, the man distinguished in bearing, the woman a pale blonde—too pale, maybe, her prettiness seeming almost bleached away.

"Hello, Kim," said the woman, smiling a little hesitantly. "I'm glad you came tonight. You know I hate it when I'm the only wife—" She stopped, looking flustered, but then rushed on. "I mean, I'm glad you came. You haven't been over to visit in so long, and the kids are always asking about you—after all, you're their favorite aunt...." Her voice trailed off uncomfortably.

"I miss seeing the kids, too," Kim said, although her tone was guarded. "Norie, Thad, I'd like you to meet Michael Turner—"

"Mother's new tenant," finished the man, shaking hands solemnly with Michael. The family resemblance was once again unmistakable; it seemed that Sophie had imprinted herself irrevocably on each of her children. Thad Bennett, however, possessed a preoccupied manner, as if too many important concerns filled his mind.

"How's the house?" he asked Michael.

"Fine."

Apparently even this brief answer gave Thad Bennett something to ruminate on. He had the air of a man weighed down by the significance of his own thoughts. While he was busy thinking up his next approach, his wife, Norie, jumped in.

"How nice you could come tonight, Mr. Turner. These family gatherings can be so tedious. Sophie hardly ever allows any outsiders, and—" She stopped herself once more, looking dismayed. "I mean—"

"Don't worry. I don't mind being an outsider," Michael said.

She gave him an embarrassed smile. "Believe it or not, Mr. Turner, I'm usually not such a blatherer. It's just my mother-in-law's proximity that...throws me off."

"Norie," said her husband on a warning note.

This, however, only seemed to inspire her. "Well, why try to hide it? *None* of us enjoys coming here, but we all put up a front. We ought to admit it for once." She glanced at Kim for confirmation.

Kim shrugged. "You wouldn't be offending Sophie. She loves to keep everyone off balance."

"That's it exactly," said Norie. "She orchestrates these command performances and she won't tell anyone what they're about. It's very disconcerting."

"Norie," her husband said with exaggerated patience.

She glanced defiantly at him. "I don't see *you* standing up to her, do I?"

Kim looked beleaguered, as if she had been through scenes of this kind often before. Michael surmised that Norie and Thad Bennett were the type who had been married so long and quibbled so frequently they forgot to be restrained in the presence of other people.

"Well," Norie said, "who knows why Sophie's dragged us all out here tonight? I've been guessing, but I don't have a clue." When no one responded, she glanced at Kim. "Any ideas?" she asked brightly. She behaved as if it was her duty to keep the conversational ball rolling. Something about the woman seemed just a little off to Michael. One minute she gave the impression of being overly timid, the next she was on the verge of arguing with her husband—and the next she was forcing the conversation. She appeared to be trying on different roles, different attitudes, to see which one fit.

"Sophie will let us know soon enough what she wants," Kim said after another awkward pause.

"That's just it," Norie said, speaking too quickly. "Sophie always *wants* something from us. Something that usually leaves bad feelings afterward. You'd think at least now and then she could invite us over to enjoy some family togetherness, nothing else."

"Norie," said her husband in a long-suffering tone, "I don't think Mr. Turner wants to know about our family squabbles."

"I'm sure he can speak for himself." Norie turned her attention fully on Michael. "Mr. Turner, we could use an objective opinion. Do you find us Bennetts dull . . . or interesting?"

The woman had taken on yet another pose. All of a sudden she appeared subtly provocative, but with a hint of anxiety underneath. She seemed to be asking for reassurance of some type—as if she wanted Michael to tell her she wasn't ordinary. In a way he supposed she was flirting with him. Her husband seemed to have the same impression, and he was beginning to look vaguely disturbed. As for Kim, she had arranged her features in a carefully neutral expression, and she seemed to find it necessary to check her watch again. Michael would have given a great deal to know what she was thinking at this moment.

"I'm just along for the ride tonight," he said finally.

Norie Bennett seemed disappointed. "That's a nonanswer, Mr. Turner. Very diplomatic, I'm sure, but I expected something more from you."

The woman had just met him—what could she have expected? But already she was glancing about discontentedly as if seeking another audience. She no longer seemed to care whether or not the conversation kept going. And meanwhile, Thad Bennett seemed to retreat once more into the protection of his own ponderous thoughts.

Michael caught Kim's eye and smiled a little. She didn't smile back, although he saw that hint of turbulence in her gaze. Was she more disgusted with him or with the Bennetts? It was difficult to tell.

Just then Sophie appeared beside them—somewhat eerily, because she hadn't made any noise, seeming to materialize out of nowhere. She proceeded to commandeer the group.

"Thad, please go call Roger and find out what's holding him up. Kim, Norie, I'd appreciate your pop-ping into the kitchen to reassure Yolanda about her soufflé. You know how she is when I have her try a new recipe. Go along—I'll take care of Mr. Turner.'' Sophie had deployed her troops. Thad Bennett went off toward the phone, and Norie hurried in the opposite direction. Only Kim refused to budge.

"Michael is my guest," she said firmly. "I'll keep him entertained."

"No doubt," Sophie said with the slightest hint of irony. "But he also lives in one of my houses. I have a few matters I wish to discuss with him."

Kim waited another second or two, studying Michael doubtfully. Perhaps she decided he could handle Sophie on his own, for she gave a shrug, turned and walked away. Michael watched her. As always she moved proudly, taking her time crossing the large room, refusing to rush for anyone—even her mother-in-law.

"Mr. Turner," said Sophie, "I hadn't expected you here tonight. Nonetheless, I commend you for working so quickly with . . . her."

Michael didn't care for Sophie Bennett's so-called approval. She made it sound as if he'd done something slick to be here with Kim.

"Don't rush to any conclusions," he said.

She raised her eyebrows just a fraction. "Mr. Turner, however you choose to . . . get close to her is no concern of mine. Just so long as you learn what is necessary."

Michael disliked this case more and more. He also disliked Sophie Bennett and her unsavory implications. If he was getting close to Kim Bennett, it was against all his better judgment.

"There's a lot I need to find out," he said grimly.

"No, Mr. Turner," Sophie returned. "You need to find out only one thing. How she did it. How she...killed my son." The words were stark, more so because they were spoken so dispassionately. Michael noted that she couldn't even seem to say Kim's name.

But Sophie couldn't disguise the pain that flashed in her eyes for just a moment. That she had genuinely loved her dead son there could be no doubt. Michael had sensed as much from the first time he'd met her. But Sophie was tough. She'd already made it clear that no amount of pain or sorrow would get in the way of anything she intended to do.

"What if Kim didn't kill your son?" he asked quietly. "What if it was someone else—or no one? What if it was just one too many and a winding road?"

This time she betrayed no emotion at all. She might have been a statue of mourning, her grief so deep that it had turned her face to stone.

"My son *was* murdered, Mr. Turner, and no one else had a motive to kill him," she said with absolute control. "No one else profited by Stan's death. Now, I hired you because you came highly recommended. I assume you will live up to my expectations."

It seemed he was hearing a lot tonight about expectations. "I'll do my job with an open mind," he said. "That's the way I work. Take it or leave it, Mrs. Bennett."

Still she maintained that implacable control. "As I said, you came highly recommended. I see no reason to question your capabilities—yet." With apparently nothing further to say to him, she left again. There always seemed a convenient doorway near at hand where Sophie Bennett could vanish.

Michael remained by himself, thinking that he could use a drink about now. Too bad there didn't seem to be any in the offing. He scanned the place. Diane and Jack still huddled together, although Diane periodically craned her neck to get a look at Michael. Thad was off in a corner, using the phone. Kim and Norie were still in the kitchen, it seemed, reassuring Yolanda about her soufflé. At least that boded well for food.

The doorbell rang, the sound resonating through the lofty room, and everyone seemed to crane their necks in unison. The maid came through on her way to answer the door. A few seconds later she could be heard murmuring to someone in the foyer, and then came the sound of a man's easy laughter. Finally a man came striding into the living room. He was unmistakably another Bennett—solid head of hair, those seemingly invincible features. Yet this Bennett possessed what all the others in his family lacked: charisma. It showed as soon as he spoke.

"Sorry I'm late," he said carelessly to no one in particular. "You know how things go."

Thad stepped forward, looking displeased. "Roger, I was just calling your place. If you're going to keep us all waiting, the least you could do is—"

"You should have started without me," Roger Bennett said, his inflection making it clear no one ever started anything without him. He scanned the room, his attention focusing on Michael. He came over to shake hands.

"Say, you're new, aren't you?" He gave an engaging grin, the kind that was second nature to people who assumed they were welcome anywhere, by anyone.

"Michael Turner."

"Of course—our new tenant. Glad to meet you," said Roger. "How's the place? Any problems?"

"Not so far." Throughout the evening, Michael had been referred to as "Sophie's tenant," but Roger spoke of him as "our tenant." A subtle distinction, perhaps, but it stirred Michael's curiosity.

"Property management isn't a family specialty, I'm afraid," Roger went on. "We've held on to the house for sentimental reasons. Were you aware of that?"

It wasn't the type of question worth answering. And Roger was already going on, obviously more interested in what he had to say than in any response of Michael's.

"It was the first place my parents ever lived together." Roger looked appropriately reflective. "They were so happy with it they bought the house next door, too, hoping to create a sort of family enclave. It didn't work out that way unfortunately. My father died, and my mother couldn't bear to live there with the memories. But she hung on to it, and Stan, at least, ended up living in the house next door. Poor unlucky Stan." Roger sounded just a little smug, as if congratulating himself for not ending up like poor unlucky Stan. Then he glanced at Michael again.

"You'll have to forgive us for being gloomy tonight. Stan's accident only happened a few months ago. You know about that of course?"

Another question not worth answering.

"It hit all of us pretty hard," Roger said. "Mother especially, although she doesn't let on." He looked wistful. "Stan was the youngest."

Michael never lost the impression that Roger Bennett had taken center stage in the room and was perfectly comfortable there. He didn't seem to be speaking so much about his dead brother as about himself—the grieving but irrepressible survivor. And all the while, he conveyed that relaxed charm.

Michael never had been easily swayed by charm, and for now, he was reserving judgment on all the Bennetts. But this time it didn't surprise him when Sophie materialized suddenly.

"Roger," she said in a chiding tone, "we've been waiting for you."

"Good to see you, too, Mother." He gave her a kiss on the cheek. Michael reflected that this was the first time he had seen any gesture of affection toward the Bennett matriarch. Sophie appeared merely to tolerate it. Maybe she wasn't easily swayed by charm, either.

"I want to get started," she said. "Come along." She headed out of the room, and everyone else fell in behind her. Michael wasn't sure the invitation included him, but he brought up the rear, anyway. He was on the lookout for Kim.

The procession led by Sophie ended up in a dining room with its own lofty ceiling. The vast polished table in the center was obviously a valuable antique. It had been laid with place settings and everyone gravitated toward a particular chair; Michael had the feeling that once you were assigned a seat by Sophie, you stuck to it. After a moment Kim and her sister-in-law, Norie, came into the room and took up their own posts. That left only a slight problem: no place setting had been laid for Michael.

He found it an interesting situation. The entire Bennett clan, including Kim, sat around the table, while he remained standing on the outside. Sophie didn't appear to find anything amiss; he suspected she didn't entirely approve of his intrusion tonight and wanted to make him pay for it in some way. But Kim stood again, pushing her chair back.

"I'll ask Yolanda to bring in another plate," she said, frowning at her mother-in-law.

A few minutes later, after a clatter of dishes and silverware, Michael was seated at the table with the rest of them. He'd ended up at one corner, with Kim directly across from him.

He'd gone without seeing her for five minutes, and somehow that meant he couldn't keep his eyes off her. He really was a damn fool. He tried to concentrate on something else and ended up analyzing the seating arrangement. It told him something about the Bennetts.

At either end of the table sat Sophie and Roger. Which of them was at the head and which at the foot? Maybe that question wasn't supposed to be answered, but it made one thing clear—Roger Bennett was Sophie's heir apparent. The other brother, Thad, was sidelined. Roger occupied the real power position.

Michael sat between Roger and Norie. Norie seemed to have taken it upon herself to be Michael's tour guide for the evening.

"Thank goodness we already have our salads," she murmured to him. "That's an encouraging sign. It means Sophie is going to let us eat before the ax falls."

Michael studied his serving of endive and watercress—not exactly his idea of substantial. "What makes you so sure the ax is going to fall?"

"Believe me, it always does at these things. Which of us is the target—that's the only question. I just hope it isn't me." She sounded nervous as she picked at her greens, perhaps running possible transgressions through her mind.

"What are you telling our guest, Norie?" Roger asked. He lounged back in his chair, and one thing was clear. Whether or not anyone else thought he was sitting at the head or the foot of the table, *he* had decided it was the head.

"Oh... it's nothing important," Norie said, poking at a mushroom.

"Don't sell yourself short," Roger murmured.

Norie brought her head up quickly and stared at her brother-in-law.

"What you say is always worthwhile," he went on encouragingly, as if giving Norie confidence was truly important to him. And Norie seemed to be swayed.

"Well," she said, "I was just telling Mr. Turner that someone's head is bound to roll, what with the family gathering and all. Oh, it's a ghastly image, but it's how I feel."

Roger's comforting expression subtly melted away. "Well, now... Michael, as you see, my sister-in-law can be quite melodramatic. Don't pay any attention to her."

The effect was immediate: Norie looked painfully embarrassed and ducked her head again. Maybe it was an act, or maybe this was the real Norie—timid, unsure, easily crushed. Either way, Roger Bennett had just been deliberately cruel, attempting to play with Norie's emotions. And Kim had obviously picked up on it, too.

"The Bennett men," she said forcefully. "All those years, being raised by a strong mother—yet you can't accept a woman with a mind of her own."

"Don't lump me in there with the others," Roger said. "You know I'm different." He gave an indolent laugh, as if inviting her to join him in a secret joke.

Kim didn't bother to respond. She just pushed her salad away, uneaten.

Norie had given up on her own salad and was glancing from Roger to Kim. The expression on her face was a disturbing one—a mixture of unhappiness and jealousy.

"Enough about the Bennetts," said Roger. "Michael, I'm sure you're far more interesting than any of us," he went on in a condescending tone. "I understand you're a mystery writer."

Yet another remark not worth answering. Michael's gaze once more lingered on Kim, but she refused to give him even a glance.

"I've thought of doing some writing myself," said Roger. "When I find the time, maybe I'll have a go at it. What do you think?"

Obviously Roger Bennett didn't give a damn what Michael thought—but for some reason the guy found it necessary to be patronizing.

"Maybe you can share some pointers," continued Roger. "What got you started with mysteries?"

"Curiosity," Michael said. "Too much curiosity."

"Really. So to be a writer, you have to be...curious."

"You tell me."

Roger chuckled. "I'm not the expert. But someday, Mike, I think I'll write a book. Something along the adventure line. That is, if I can find the spare time."

"Send me a copy," Michael said. "When it's published."

"Yes, certainly I will." Roger gave his cordial grin, but it seemed a little artificial this time around. Michael could tell that both he and Roger were on the verge of losing any pretext of civility. That would be fine with him.

Just then, however, the main course was served: some small pathetic bird, partridge perhaps, surrounded by an artistic arrangement of vegetables. Michael reflected irritably that if you were going to kill a defenseless bird and eat it, the thing ought to be at least big enough to fill the plate. He seemed to have lost his appetite. From the look of things, so had Kim—she barely touched her food. She resisted all of Roger's efforts to draw her into conversation and she also resisted looking at Michael. She seemed to have withdrawn into some remote place no one could touch.

Michael glanced discontentedly around the rest of the table. Diane Bennett was seated next to Jack, and she whispered to him occasionally in a self-important manner. He appeared glum—perhaps he'd attended one too many of these Bennett get-togethers. Michael still couldn't picture him as a physics professor expounding in front of a classroom of college students. He seemed more like someone who'd be happy outdoors pulling up weeds or tinkering with an old car. Meanwhile, Thad Bennett consumed his dinner methodically, carefully, lost in his own cumbersome thoughts, whatever they might be.

Michael couldn't forget Sophie, up there at the head of the table—*one* of the heads of the table. Nothing seemed to have disturbed her appetite. She ate fastidiously, not seeming to drop a crumb. When she was finished, she set down her fork and stared at each member of her family in turn.

"It's time for business," she announced.

"Here it comes," muttered Norie. "And before dessert. You *know* when she gets started before dessert, we're in trouble, big time."

Sophie's gaze riveted on her daughter-in-law. "Do you have something you'd like to share with all of us, Norie?" She sounded like a schoolmarm who'd just caught someone whispering.

Norie stared at her plate. "No," she said quite distinctly. "I do not have anything to share." Surprisingly she sounded almost insolent. Thad peered down the table at his wife.

"Norie..." he said in the warning tone he used with her.

"Please do not interrupt, Thad," instructed his mother. "Now, I have called all of you together as the stockholders in Bennett Industries." Michael already knew that the Bennetts had made their fortune in the health-food market back when the idea was still a novelty. These days Bennett Industries shipped its well-known products to grocery stores, restaurants and health-food chains across the entire country.

"Here comes the ax," whispered Norie Bennett. "I wonder whose neck it's going to be."

"Hush, Norie," said the matriarch, "and listen. All of you listen. We are here tonight so that we can discuss...Kim."

CHAPTER SIX

MICHAEL WANTED to reach out to Kim, give her some of the reassurance that so far she'd refused from him. She seemed much too alone right now, sitting there with every Bennett eye on her. But she was handling it well, her expression cool and self-contained.

"How flattering," she said. "I'm pleased to know I'm a subject of such interest to you, Sophie."

"No need to be flippant," Sophie answered with surprising mildness. "This is simply a matter that is long overdue. It concerns your shares in Bennett Industries."

"The shares I inherited from Stan," Kim said in a steady voice.

"Yes, of course—and your original shares."

"The ones Stan gave me when we married. Let's be precise, Sophie. Those original shares, combined with my inheritance, mean I now have quite a substantial holding in the company."

"Substantial, indeed," murmured Roger.

Kim didn't bother to answer, and Michael felt that stirring of reluctant admiration. She wasn't letting the Bennetts intimidate her in any way.

"In all honesty, Kim," said Sophie, "you have never expressed a great deal of interest in the business. And Stan..." Her voice almost caught on her dead son's name, but she went on with that relentless control of hers, "Stan was never interested in the business, either. He chose to go his own way. But it was careless of him to give you all those shares. Certainly it's unreasonable for you to own such a large portion of the voting stock. I am proposing that you sell it back to the family."

Sophie couldn't have made it clearer: she didn't consider Kim part of the family. Michael saw just the slightest flicker of hurt in Kim's expression. More than ever, he wanted to reach out to her. But it was still her battle and she had to be the one to fight it.

Michael knew all about the way Stan Bennett had declared his independence from the family business by founding his own investment firm. Apparently, though, he'd continued to rely on the family money. It seemed that he'd alternated between rebellion and dependence when it came to Sophie. Maybe giving all those shares to Kim had been one of Stan's little rebellions.

Roger was speaking now, addressing Kim in a smooth voice. "We'll make you a generous offer," he said. "Ten percent above market."

Kim stood. Her gaze swept the table.

"You wish to be rid of me," she stated flatly.

Silence met her challenge, except for the startled *ping* of Norie's fork dropping onto her plate.

"The Bennetts, closing ranks as usual." Kim gripped the back of her chair.

"Don't be ridiculous," Sophie said. "We are discussing business here, nothing more. A great deal of money is at stake—"

"It's not about the money and you know it." Kim's voice was still remarkably steady.

Sophie stared at her daughter-in-law. "We have made every effort to accept you into this family. Efforts that I must say, you have rejected. I don't know how to explain your attitude. I can only assume that unfortunately you are still influenced by your mother's...problems."

Kim's face went taut. "I'm afraid that it won't work this time," she said, her voice almost too calm. "You can bring up all of it, every detail, but it won't hurt this time." She paused. "The shares are mine. And you—all of you—can go to hell." Kim walked out of the room.

Michael pushed back his own chair and stood, his turn now to glance around the table.

"It's been a lovely evening, folks," he said. "A regular Bennett hayride, no doubt." And, with that, he turned and left.

THE NEXT MORNING Kim sat at her desk in the upstairs study. She pulled a stack of library books toward her, opened the first one and began reading, making notes as she went along. Surely if she went through the motions, doing something productive like this, the turmoil inside her would abate.

She skimmed several pages, set down the book and picked up another. She was making no progress at all, and the emotions inside her still churned.

Sighing, she propped her head in her hands, trying to rub away the tension. Scattered fragments from last night collided in her mind: telling the Bennetts, each and every one, to go to hell...Michael Turner, almost kissing her there on the veranda...Sophie, bringing up the wretched past all over again...Michael, brushing his lips so close to hers...

She moaned. The evening had been a disaster in every way imaginable. She never should have asked Michael to go with her. It had been a weakness, one she could not afford to repeat. Of course she doubted the Bennetts would be inviting her to any more of their family get-togethers. Last night they'd made it obvious that after eight years, they still considered her an outsider, someone unwanted. Their only intent now was to get their hands on her shares of Bennett Industries.

So why didn't she just sell the damn shares? That way she could be done with the Bennetts. She'd never have to see any of them again. The thought definitely had its appeal.

But in a way Kim couldn't really explain, her instincts told her to hang on to those shares. If she sold them now, she'd be giving in to the Bennetts, to Sophie and Roger and all the rest of them. She couldn't do that. She'd already given in too much where the Bennetts were concerned.

Kim took another book from the pile in front of her. She made every effort to concentrate, taking notes as she read. One step at a time, that was what she kept telling herself.

She also kept telling herself not to think about Michael Turner—and it did her no good. Once again she remembered the way he'd gazed at her last night.

Kim cursed, pushing away her books and standing. She'd only just met Michael Turner, and already her imagination seemed caught up by the man. How could this be happening to her so suddenly, so unexpectedly? What did she even know about him?

She felt a ripple of unease. Michael seemed just a little too interested in her. What was he looking for? A quick romance with the next-door neighbor?

"Don't be ridiculous," Kim murmured to herself. But she didn't feel reassured and the fact remained: Michael Turner made her uneasy.

Unable to keep still, she crossed the hallway to her bedroom. But that was a mistake. She faced the large, king-size bed where she slept alone these days. Not that sleeping alone was anything new; more and more during her marriage she'd done exactly that. She hadn't been able to entice her own husband into making love. What a sad joke! Stan had been able to perform with other women, but not with her. What would Michael Turner say if he knew about that? The humiliation flooded Kim, the old, painful sense of inadequacy. What was it about her that had so repelled her husband? Over and over he had blamed her for his impotence in their bedroom. And then, eventually, he had made sure she knew about the other women—the ones who could satisfy him.

She wouldn't think about it anymore. She wouldn't remember all her foolish attempts to win her husband back.

Kim escaped to her study across the hall. She sat down at the desk and opened another book at random. She forced herself to read the words in front of her, no matter how meaningless they seemed. She'd almost managed to immerse herself when she heard an odd clunking noise coming from downstairs. She stopped, listening. There it came again—*clunk-clunk-CLINK*. Had someone broken into the house? She'd turned off the alarm system because it was the middle of the day—and because she hated the alarm for being just one more evidence of Bennett wealth. But maybe it was foolish not to be more careful.

She slipped out of her chair and tiptoed from the room. Halfway down the stairs, she realized that she ought to have some type of weapon in hand. After another few steps, however, she was able to peer into the living room and see who her intruder was: young Andy Turner, standing outside her broken front window. He'd pulled away the cardboard she'd taped up and was prying at the frame with a screwdriver. He was so engrossed in his task it took him a moment to glance up and see her. His expression was serious and intent, making him look very much like his father.

"Hello, Andy," she said.

"Hi." He gave a nod in Kim's direction, then got back to work with his screwdriver. Obviously he didn't think explanations were necessary. Kim felt otherwise.

"Mind telling me what's up?" she asked.

"I'm fixing the window," he said. "And I know how to do it. You take out the molding around the edges here, and then you put in the new glass." He was trying to sound very competent and adult. Once more Kim felt that inconvenient tug of poignancy, the sense that if she'd had a son, he would be just like this—earnest and gawky and more than a little defiant.

She stepped closer to the window, examining the jagged edge of glass now left exposed. So far Andy had been undeniably proficient at his job, neatly prying away a section of molding. But Kim still didn't like to see him working next to that sharp glass with his screwdriver.

"Andy, does your father know you're here?"

His gaze was inscrutable. "It doesn't matter," he said.

"There's a yes or a no in there somewhere."

Andy looked impatient, as if he couldn't wait to get back to his job and be done with unnecessary talk. "My dad said we were going to fix the window. We even came over and took measurements when you weren't around. We bought the glass, but we never put it in. So I'm taking care of it."

"I'm sure he'd prefer the two of you to work together. Why don't you get him and bring him over here with you." The last thing Kim wanted, of course, was to see Michael Turner this soon. He'd dropped her back home last night after the fiasco at the Bennetts. She'd given him a thank-you that was awkward in the extreme, and then she'd escaped behind her own door. Somehow she didn't think the light of morning would make her feel any more at ease with him.

"My dad's not home," said Andy.

"I see. Then you should wait until he gets back."

Now the expression on Andy's face grew stubborn. "I broke the window. I'll fix it."

It was difficult to argue with such a pronouncement. Kim took a different approach.

"Tell you what," she said. "I'll let you in, and we'll make some lemonade while we discuss repairs."

His withering glance said it all: lemonade was childish. He fingered his screwdriver, clearly not willing to be put off.

"It's my only offer," she informed him.

He grimaced a bit, but after a few seconds Kim heard the screwdriver thump to the ground.

She unlocked the door for him and led the way back to the kitchen. It was a welcoming room, but it also seemed slightly pathetic to Kim. She'd originally designed it with a family in mind—Stan and her and their someday children. Since then she'd learned that families, particularly the idyllic kind, were not all that easy to come by.

Now she opened the refrigerator and took out a thawing can of concentrated lemonade. "It's better when you start from scratch—squeezing the lemons yourself—but we'll have to make do," she told Andy.

"Sure," he muttered. He hovered near the door, his stance declaring that he had far more important things to do than share lemonade with the neighbor lady.

Kim dumped the lemonade and some water into a pitcher. She set the pitcher on the table and then handed Andy a large wooden spoon.

"Mix," she instructed. He seemed about to protest and Kim could understand why. What self-respecting eleven-year-old boy would rather exchange a screwdriver for a spoon? But at last, with a grudging air, Andy began stirring.

"I don't suppose you're hungry," she said. "I have some hazelnut cookies."

The offer seemed to interest Andy. He glanced up. A few moments later they were seated at the kitchen table with glasses of lemonade and a plate of cookies between them. Andy drummed his fingers on the tabletop, glancing toward the door, but that didn't stop him from going after the cookies. Pretty soon he started on his third one. Kim wondered if she ought to let him fill up like this so close to lunch. What would Michael have to say about it? Was he the kind of father who enforced mealtimes and eating habits, or the kind who sent out for pizza? She suspected the latter, but you could never be sure.

"Have you heard from your mother?" she asked. The minute she said the words, she regretted them. Michael Turner's ex-wife wasn't any of her business.

"What else," Andy said in the cynical tone that was too old for his years. "She calls all the time, like she thinks my dad and I will set the house on fire or something."

"Sometimes it's hard to trust other people," Kim said. "Even when you love them. Especially when you love them. You start to think you have to be around to keep them safe."

As Andy considered this, he deigned to take a sip of lemonade. "Yeah, well, my mom doesn't like my dad much anymore. That's why she doesn't trust *him*."

"Divorce is pretty rotten, I guess," Kim said.

If she expected any confessions of youthful anxiety, she was disappointed. "Are you divorced?" Andy asked matter-of-factly.

It served her right, she supposed, to have the subject turned on her. "No," she said. "My husband... died a short time ago."

"Oh." Andy looked nonplussed for a second or two, but then he went on, "Do you miss him?"

Kim was startled by such a direct question. "Why... yes, I suppose I do." She'd known for quite some time that she no longer loved Stan. Even when she'd been fighting to save her marriage, deep down she'd known it was hopeless. She could never forgive him, never care for him as before. A husband's infidelity could do that—kill your love—but even so, it didn't mean you wanted him dead.

Silence descended on the kitchen. It wasn't an uncomfortable silence, however. It simply seemed that both Kim and Andy knew there wasn't anything else of significance to say at the moment, so why bother with useless chatter?

Between the two of them, they finished the cookies on the plate. Kim brought the package over so they could dispense the last few. She glanced at the familiar Bennett logo on the front of the package and gave a humorless smile. Old habits really did die hard. Unfortunately the family business put out good food—Sophie allowed nothing but the highest quality. It was going to be damn hard to give up hazelnut cookies.

Andy was gazing out the French doors toward the patio. "You have a pool," he said, and for once he almost sounded like a kid.

"Come on," she said. "I'll give you a tour."

They went outside with their lemonade. The pool was still covered; somehow Kim hadn't been able to muster the enthusiasm to have it cleaned and filled this year. The surrounding patio furniture looked forlorn, abandoned.

"I used to go swimming," Andy said, "with my dad." He made it sound as if it was something he'd been obliged to give up.

"Too bad you don't have a pool next door," Kim said.

He shrugged. "I don't care."

She wasn't convinced; she'd heard that spark of enthusiasm in his voice when he'd noticed her pool.

"I used to swim a lot, too," she said. "When I first moved to this house, I could hardly believe it—a pool in my own backyard."

"I guess you're pretty rich."

"Yes, I suppose so." Bennett money, however, had never seemed Kim's own. Even in those early days, when Stan had been so generous, so extravagant, the whole thing had felt like a pretense. She'd enjoyed the unaccustomed luxury—who wouldn't? But it had always seemed as if she and Stan were playing a game. She'd kept waiting for their real lives to start, the real sharing.

"I guess you don't have to work," Andy said.

"I don't have to, but I want to work."

"If I had lots of money, I wouldn't work," said Andy.

"That's what one always thinks. But you get restless. And you figure out that you need to do something that belongs just to you. Not to anybody else—just you." Kim sipped her lemonade, wondering why she was trying to explain herself to an eleven-year-old boy. But Andy was watching her seriously.

"What belongs just to you?" he asked.

It was a very good question. Kim thought about those library books upstairs on her desk, the ones she'd just been reading. They offered such splendid promises: find your dream career, untap your potential, make a contribution. She was starting at the very beginning, trying to figure out what she could do. She did have a work history of sorts. She'd been a waitress/cook/general gofer in her father's restaurant all those years growing up, she'd worked at least a few months for Stan as a secretary, and later on she'd hostessed innumerable parties for Stan's so-called clients and investors. All that had to count for something. But now she needed more. Precisely what, she couldn't say, and that was the troubling part. All she knew was that she had an emptiness inside, a yearning for something she couldn't even name.

Andy was still watching her, expecting an answer.

"Everybody wants to be good at something," she said. "Some people are lucky and know what it is right away. And some of us . . . well, we just get a late start, I suppose." She smiled a little ruefully. "In other words, Andy, I'm trying to figure out exactly what I'm good for. It's exciting and scary at the same time." She hadn't told that to anyone until now. Somehow it wasn't easy to say to another adult. But Andy, eleven years old, seemed to understand exactly what she was talking about. He crossed his arms and gazed at the covered pool.

"I used to know what I wanted to do," he said. "I wanted to be a cop, just like my dad."

Kim thought this over. "Your father's a writer, isn't he?"

A look of dismay crossed Andy's face. "Yeah, sure. That's what I meant."

Kim was puzzled. "There's a big difference between being a writer and a policeman."

Andy scuffed his shoe over the patio tile. He looked oddly guilty. "My dad used to be a cop," he mumbled. "But he's not anymore."

"I see." This unexpected bit of information put Michael Turner in a new light. Kim wasn't sure she liked it. "Your dad must have lots of good firsthand experiences he can put in his mystery novels."

"I guess," Michael's son answered morosely. "It was better when he was a cop."

"Sometimes people need a change." Kim knew about that much.

"Yeah, well, I have to get back to work." Andy gulped the last of his lemonade and started heading away.

"Andy," Kim said, "hold on a second. I don't want you trying to repair that window on your own."

"I can do it," he said obstinately.

"Maybe so, but you'll just have to wait for your dad."

"I'll do it my—"

"Andy," she said firmly. "I don't care if you're a master at repairing windows. The answer is no."

Several emotions seemed to battle across his young face: pride, disgust, impatience, disappointment. Fixing that window seemed to hold great significance for him—a bid of independence from his father, perhaps. Kim wouldn't get involved in the middle; it wasn't her place.

At last Andy gave a shrug, one meant to come across as unconcerned. It didn't quite succeed. He turned to go, then stopped himself, the guilty expression flickering back.

"I wasn't supposed to tell you," he said. "You know... how my dad used to be a cop."

Now Kim was really perplexed and she didn't like the feeling. "Why would it be a secret?"

"Maybe you can just... like, not say I told you."

Kim shook her head. "Andy, this doesn't make any sense."

He began scuffing his shoe over the tile again. When he glanced at her, his face was solemn. "I think my dad wants to forget about being a cop. Except then he'll go to the community center and just look around, like he wants to remember stuff. Like he can't decide whether to forget or remember."

Kim did not feel enlightened. She just felt more puzzled than ever. But Andy clattered his glass down on the patio table, then went dashing off around the side of the house. There wasn't time to ask him anything more.

She stood there beside the pool another moment, speculating about Michael Turner. Ex-cop... writer of mysteries... dangerously attractive...

She thought about the way he'd stood so close to her last night, his cheek next to hers. A different type of yearning coiled through her now, as if all she wanted was to have him near her again. But what did she know about the man? Obviously not very much. She couldn't afford to get too close to him. Certainly she couldn't afford to care about his son.

She walked over to the patio table, picked up the empty glasses and took them to the kitchen. Then a restless energy propelled her back upstairs to the study. She looked at the books scattered on her desk, the pad filling up with her careful notes. She wanted to laugh— searching for answers in books, when she knew that the answers had to come from inside. But maybe she was scared to look inside herself. She'd told Andy she was scared.

She pulled her chair back up to the desk, opened another book and forced her eyes to scan down one page, then another.

Clunk-clunk-CLINK. There it came, and this time Kim knew exactly what the sound meant. Were all children this stubborn? She went downstairs and out the front door. Andy was twisting his screwdriver under the window frame with an air of determination.

"Andy..."

He glanced at her with that defiance of his. "I know what I'm doing—"

A strange shuddering sound came from the window. What happened next occurred so quickly Kim took in only confused images: the jagged pane of glass above Andy coming loose and starting downward, Andy's surprised face—and Kim herself, hurtling toward him, fearing she was going to be too late.

CHAPTER SEVEN

"DAMMIT, I'LL SEE my son." Michael felt the anger as if it were a physical entity, something hard and cold and indestructible lodged inside him. From long experience he'd learned how to handle his anger, how to turn and walk away before things went too far. But this time he couldn't walk away. Some damn doctor had just forbidden him to see his own son. To hell with that!

"Mike," said Donna, grabbing hold of his arm. "Wait! You heard what they said. Andy's going to be fine, just fine. Some cuts, that's all. A few stitches."

Michael ignored his partner. He glanced around the emergency room, prepared to yank open every door in sight. "He needs me with him."

Donna wouldn't let go of his arm. "No—I think that's the last thing he needs. He tries so hard to be grown-up he wouldn't want you to see him cry or anything like that. I think that's why he just asked for her. And it's an understandable mistake, the doctor thinking she's his mother..." Her voice trailed off, but what she'd said got through to him all too well.

His son, although hurt and frightened, didn't want him around. Instead, Andy had asked for Kim, a person he hardly knew. He hadn't asked for his own father.

Michael's anger seemed more distant now, something that would eventually recede if he suppressed it long enough. But that, of course, had always been the hard part—the subduing, the restraint of his own damnable temper. It was his inheritance, that temper, and he despised it. Most of all, he hated the long-ago memories it called forth. He sat down heavily in a waiting-room chair.

And now an image of Kim Bennett came into his mind, almost seeming to mock him. The way she'd looked last night at that so-called dinner party. Proud, beautiful, yet vulnerable, too. Had the vulnerability only been an act? Because it just seemed too much of a coincidence: the first time Andy was alone with Kim, something bad happened. Michael sure as hell didn't want to believe her guilty. But could he risk believing in her innocence?

Donna remained standing beside him. "Mike, I'm so sorry," she said miserably. "I should have been there, watching the house. But I was gone for such a short time..."

"You might as well explain why you left." He spoke automatically. He was thinking about his son, somewhere in this place, trying not to cry while they put in stitches. It could have been so much worse.

"My mother-in-law called," Donna said. "She got me on the car phone. She said she was at an antique sale and she'd found the most wonderful cradle. Only she didn't want to buy it without my approval. She knows that sometimes she has a tendency to butt into my life and take over, and she doesn't want to be like that anymore, particularly with the baby coming. She doesn't want to be one of those pushy mother-in-laws who drives the daughter-in-law crazy..."

Michael wished Donna would get to the point. He'd been working all morning on the Jacobs case—hunting down information on a runaway teenage girl at the request of some worried parents. He'd left Andy at home seemingly engrossed in P. G. Wodehouse—imagine, a son of his reading P. G. Wodehouse. He'd also left Donna in charge of the Bennett case, confident she'd do her job well. It appeared he'd been too confident.

"Mike, she's been different ever since this stupid baby thing," Donna was going on. "My own mother-in-law, swearing she'll change her obnoxious, pushy ways.... I couldn't resist. I told her I'd just run over to the antique store and have a quick look at the cradle. I was sure it'd be all right. We've been watching Kim Bennett for days and nothing ever happens."

"Until now." He rubbed the back of his neck and swore silently. It *couldn't* be a coincidence. The one day his partner fouled up on the job, his son had an accident. And Kim Bennett had been the only one around.

"I got back to the house right after it happened," Donna said. "And I drove Andy here as fast as I could. Kim, too, of course. She had some cuts of her own."

Michael couldn't afford to think about that at the moment. "You can't excuse what you did, Donna. You can't minimize it."

She looked stricken. "I know. If Andy had been really hurt...oh, God, I never would have forgiven myself."

Michael never would have forgiven *him*self, either. And maybe that was the real source of his anger: he hadn't been there this morning when his son was hurt.

A nurse walking by stopped to study Donna in concern. "Are you all right?" she asked.

"Yes, of course I am," Donna answered distractedly. "Why wouldn't I be?"

"Honey, you look like you're six months pregnant," the nurse said. "You're pale and shaky, and you're carrying rather high." The nurse eyed her attentively. "Mighty high."

"Yes... well, it runs in my family—high babies and all. Thanks for your concern... Bye-bye now." Donna watched the nurse go down the hall, then glanced at her rounded belly. "For crying out loud," she muttered, "I forgot I'm still wearing the damn pillow. Six months along—what a joke." She sank into the seat beside Michael's and gave a sigh. "I'm a mess," she said. "A real mess. Ever since this baby thing... I've never botched a job before, but now look at me."

"I need to be able to count on you," Michael said quietly.

"Oh, Mike, it won't happen again. You know I never make the same mistake twice. It's just that—" Donna placed a hand on her stomach and gave another sigh. "I'm pretending to be something I'm not, and it's turning me all around."

"So tell the truth," he said. "It's that simple."

"Somehow it doesn't seem to be." She looked miserable. "You don't understand, Mike. After I saw that beautiful antique cradle, my mother-in-law bought it. I'm in deeper than ever!"

Michael couldn't sympathize with her at the moment. All he could do was think about Andy. He supposed he understood a boy's not wanting to cry in front of his dad. Then again, shouldn't a father and a son be able to share everything? He stood up. This time he'd find Andy, no matter what.

He was halfway down the hall, Donna on his heels, when he saw her. Kim. She'd just emerged from a treatment room. In spite of the bandages on her arm, she seemed quite calm. When she saw him, she walked toward him without hesitation.

"Michael, he's fine. He was more frightened than anything else."

Maybe Kim Bennett was too calm. Michael looked her over as dispassionately as he could. She was lovely even with her hair rumpled and smears of blood on her shirt. Her blood—or perhaps his son's.

"Tell me what happened," he said.

At his tone, a flicker of uncertainty crossed her face. She glanced back toward the treatment room and moved a few steps farther down the hall. Then she turned to face Michael again. The uncertainty was gone, her expression carefully impassive.

"Andy came over today with the idea that he'd fix my broken window. I told him he'd have to wait until you came home. He didn't listen unfortunately. The glass came loose somehow... and when it fell, it shattered all over."

Donna spoke up from behind Michael. "Kim's not telling you the whole story. If she hadn't grabbed Andy and yanked him out of the way, it would've been a whole lot worse."

"Donna, thank God you came along when you did," Kim said. "You got us to the hospital in record time."

Michael listened, and he didn't like what he heard. Suddenly his partner and Kim were on a first-name basis, sounding as if they'd been friends for years.

Donna, astute as always, seemed to pick up on his thoughts.

"Mike," she said, "I told Kim how I'm your research assistant. For your mysteries... Anyway, I'm glad I showed up when I did." Donna gave him an entirely virtuous look.

"I just hope all the excitement wasn't bad for you," Kim said.

Donna patted her rounded stomach. "Don't worry about us. We're fine." She smiled fondly at her "baby."

Michael could see he needed to have a frank discussion with his partner in the very near future. For now, though, he had to concentrate on Kim Bennett. He took her arm—the one that wasn't bandaged—and led her yet another few steps along the hall. Donna had the wisdom to stay behind.

Michael and Kim now had a small measure of privacy. He captured her gaze with his. "I'd like you to tell me all of it," he said in a low voice.

"I just did."

"All of it, Kim. Did you touch that glass before Andy showed up today?"

Her blue eyes darkened. "What are you implying, Michael?"

"I'm just asking for the truth."

She pushed a tangle of hair away from her face, and he saw the way her features tightened. "I don't know what you're asking. If you have anything to say to me, you'd better be very clear and straightforward."

It was always Kim's pride that got to him—the way she conveyed a regal self-reliance no matter what the circumstances. She managed to convey it now, in spite of the bandages and stained shirt.

"All right," Michael said. "I'll be clear. Did you tamper with that window?"

"Tamper..." she echoed in a disbelieving tone. "Do you honestly believe I *booby-trapped* my own house in the hope that I'd injure an eleven-year-old boy? It was an accident, Michael! I knew that broken window was dangerous, and that's why I warned Andy to stay away. If you don't believe me, you can just—"

"Are you going to tell me I can go to hell, the way you did with the Bennetts last night?" Maybe he was trying to goad her. She didn't answer, but he could see she was furious with him—two bright spots of color burned in her cheeks. It was possible that the window had been an accident. On the other hand, was it usual for even a broken pane of glass to come crashing down from its frame?

At last Kim took a deep breath. "I'm sure you want to go see Andy. And I'm sure your assistant will give me a ride home. I think I've had enough for now."

Her words implied that she'd had enough of *him*. More than anything, he wished he could believe in her innocence. Usually by this time on a case, his intuition would've kicked in—he'd be making his own guesses about someone's guilt. More often than not, the evidence proved his hunches correct. But with Kim...his intuition seemed to be getting mixed up with his libido. Even now he had the urge to touch her. He restrained himself with an effort.

"You can probably understand that I'm worried about Andy," he said.

"If that's an apology, save it," she answered, the color still flaming in her cheeks. "If Andy were my son, all I know is that I'd do everything I could to keep him safe and happy. That much I do understand."

Again he didn't have any trouble reading the implications: Kim Bennett wouldn't easily forgive him. But she was wrong about one thing—he wasn't apologizing for what he'd said. When it came to his son, he had to damn well cover all the angles. He had to be aware of every possibility.

Kim Bennett... Even if it turned out she'd murdered her husband, why would she want to hurt a child? After all, when the glass fell, she'd rushed to save Andy. Unless she'd already found out that Michael was investigating her, and this was her way of sending a warning to him.

He gazed into her eyes, searching for malice. But all he saw was that haunted quality he'd already sensed in her, as if there was some memory she wanted very much to escape. He didn't feel reassured, but still he had the urge to reach out to her in some way, perhaps smooth her brow with his fingers.

"Goodbye, Michael," she said with a strange finality. She turned and walked toward Donna, moving with unhurried pride. His gaze followed the slender line of her back until both she and Donna disappeared around the corner.

He stood there another moment, held by lingering thoughts of Kim. Today, as always, she'd flaunted her self-reliance, as if to warn Michael not to come any closer. But there was so much more to Kim Bennett, so much that remained hidden underneath the haughty exterior she put on. Was it treachery—or real vulnerability?

Once again Michael cursed himself for a fool. And then he walked down the hall and entered the treatment room where Kim had been.

His son was alone, seated on the examination table, his back held very straight. He had two bandages on his arm, another bandage on his leg, and stitches on the cut above his left eyebrow. His face was a chalky color, his eyes slightly red-rimmed but betraying no other sign of tears. He frowned at his father.

"Where is she?" he asked. At least his experience hadn't changed the belligerent tone of Andy's voice.

Michael didn't have to ask who "she" was. "Donna's taking her home. I think after all the excitement, she could use a rest." He tried to keep his own tone casual, but he didn't think he did too well.

"I broke the window," Andy said defensively, "so I was fixing it."

"It was supposed to be *our* job, son."

"You kept saying we were going to do it, but we never did."

It had been only a few days since Andy's ball had first crashed through Kim Bennett's window. Michael had purposefully delayed the repair job, waiting to do it under circumstances that might help him learn more about the suspect widow. He hadn't factored in the possibility that his son would be overeager to do the work himself.

Kim probably wouldn't have expected Andy to do the work on his own, either. Had she meant that glass to come shattering down on Michael, instead? Or *had* it just been an accident all the way around?

"Andy," Michael said carefully, "I appreciate your...sense of responsibility. But you shouldn't have been anywhere near that window. You shouldn't have gone next door at all."

"Yeah, right," Andy muttered. "I'm supposed to stay locked up in that stupid house all summer, but you get to be a spy."

"Private—"

"I know. Private investigator." Andy exaggerated each syllable just enough to be annoying.

"I don't want you going next door on your own anymore," Michael said.

"I can do whatever the hell I want," Andy mumbled. He darted a glance at Michael to gauge his reaction. But Michael knew that drawing his own battle lines right now wasn't the answer.

"We'll talk about it later," he said. "For now, what do you say we get out of this place?"

"No. I've been having such a great time here I thought I'd move in."

Andy's sarcasm could still take Michael by surprise. Sometimes he liked having a son with a ready wit. Other times all he could see was the wariness behind the caustic remarks. And the same question faced him: why should an eleven-year-old boy be wary around his dad?

Even more, why should an eleven-year-old boy prefer the neighbor lady to his own father?

EARLY THE NEXT MORNING, Michael arrived at the wishing shrine. It consisted of a simple wall, the exposed adobe bricks so old they had long since started to crumble and betray the signs of time. In front of the wall was a mass of candles, some displayed in elaborate candelabra, others resting in modest clay holders. A few of them were lit, flickering in the early-morning breeze, but the others had guttered out, leaving only melted wax behind. Michael knew the legend—if you could keep a candle burning here throughout the night, your secret wish would be granted. Too bad he had passed the stage of believing wishes could come true.

He paced back and forth in front of the shrine. An elderly woman, wrapped in a muffler in spite of the mild Tucson air, bent over one of the candles, cupping the flame with her hands as if to keep it from being extinguished. She remained like that, head bowed. Michael wondered what her prayer was—a plea for help with a wayward son, a difficult husband? Or perhaps she prayed for herself, harboring some youthful longing in spite of her years. After a moment, though, she straightened and walked slowly away, leaving her candle to its own fate.

Michael went on pacing. He knew this area of town well. Once pleasantly shabby and isolated, it was now being encroached upon by fashionable craft and artisan shops. At least it was too early in the day for the tourists to descend. Michael thought over the cryptic message he'd received from a friend on the police force. It seemed that someone had wanted to meet him here— wouldn't give a name or any other information. Michael had been putting out feelers on the Bennett case; maybe one of them was about to give him some results. He just wanted to get on with it. He'd now been waiting here for almost half an hour, and his informant still hadn't shown.

As always, Michael was subtly aware of his surroundings. Without overtly glancing in any particular direction, he knew that two kids were loitering on the corner across the street, and that on the opposite corner a middle-aged man was unlocking the doors of the produce market. Nothing unusual, nothing out of the ordinary, but Michael felt edgy nonetheless. Maybe it was because he was still worried about Andy's accident yesterday—and still wondering about the lovely widow Bennett. Michael had left Andy safe in Donna's care—his partner, true to her word, wasn't likely to make the same mistake twice. But that didn't change the fact that Andy seemed to have developed a liking for Kim Bennett. Somehow it had to be kept under control.

Yet what about Michael's own feelings for Kim? The woman wouldn't leave his thoughts—although, more often than not, the memory of Kim involved her being displeased with him. It seemed neither one of them trusted the other. Why the hell didn't that stop Michael from wanting to take her in his arms?

A man of sixty or so had appeared on the opposite side of the street. He stared at Michael, then crossed to the shrine with an oddly hesitant gait. There was something familiar about him, something in the way he held his head and shoulders.

Recognition came to Michael like a punch in the gut. It had been all of twenty years, but still the old emotions washed over him. Anger, bewilderment, sadness—but, most of all, the anger.

"Mike." The man stopped in front of him. He had changed a great deal, which perhaps explained why Michael hadn't recognized him right away. The once-black hair was now peppered with gray and had thinned. The mouth had set into what seemed a permanently resentful line, the dark brown eyes pouched in wrinkles. But what surprised Michael the most was the man's size. He no longer seemed powerfully large. He'd shrunken, grown small, as if some vital quality inside him had collapsed. Or perhaps it was simply that

Michael himself had matured. He was a man himself now, no longer a fifteen-year-old boy.

He stood very still, giving himself time to absorb the shock of this moment. It was something completely unexpected, but he could deal with it. That had become his forte, he thought ironically. Dealing with the unexpected.

"Mike," the man repeated, as if testing an unfamiliar word on his tongue.

Michael didn't answer. He merely looked his father over one more time. It appeared that Franklin Turner was still barely hovering on the edge of respectability. He wore a well-tailored suit, but the material had begun to sag a little. The expensive shirt, the silk tie, the Italian shoes, all had seen just a bit too much wear. That was Frank Turner, all right, a man who started out by insisting on the very best but then couldn't follow through on his ambitions. Maybe he really hadn't changed so much.

"Hey," Frank said, giving a smile that didn't quite reach his eyes. "This isn't easy for me, you know. I've been trying to work up the courage for years."

"You should've saved yourself the trouble," Michael remarked, allowing no emotion in his voice.

"I guess I deserve that." The words sounded rehearsed. "Believe me," Frank went on, "a thousand times I've regretted it. Walking out on you and your mom..."

"The walking out was the good part," Michael said. It seemed peculiar to him that suddenly he no longer felt anything. Not sadness, not pity, not even the anger. Nothing.

Frank tucked his hands into his pockets, his stance almost capturing the debonair pose of a gentleman, something that Michael remembered from long ago.

"You were always fair-minded, Mike. I hope you still are. Because everyone deserves a second chance." The way he spoke the phrase, it was a platitude, nothing more.

"I'm only curious about one thing," Michael said. "How you found me."

"I've kept track of you off and on. I knew you'd been with the police. I was proud of you for that. So when I worked up the nerve...your buddies helped me out." He made it sound as if Michael's "buddies" had become his own.

"What do you want?" Michael asked in a level voice.

Frank's features seemed to harden, but his own voice remained friendly. "I already told you, son. I want a second chance. I figure you owe me that much."

"Owe? I owe you nothing," Michael said. "We've seen each other. That's enough."

"Mike." Now his father lifted his hands in an obvious plea for understanding. That, too, seemed rehearsed. "We've wasted so much time, you and I. But now I have a grandson. I want to get to know him."

Michael felt a tensing in every fiber of his body. It was a sensation he'd experienced on a few other occasions, when he'd known he was in physical danger and his life depended on his own good judgment. The danger now was more covert, but no less real.

"That's not an option," he said.

Impatience showed in Frank's expression. "I have a right to know my grandson."

It had always been like that, Frank seeing the world only in terms of his own needs and wants. He talked as if his claim to Andy was more important than Michael's.

"You gave up your rights a long time ago," Michael said. "And you'll stay away from my son."

Frank shook his head as if deep in thought. "Afraid it's too late for that, Mike. I've already seen him. Already talked to him. And you know what? I think the kid really likes me. Better than you ever did, anyway."

The urge swept over Michael then. He pictured all the hurting his father had caused, all the pain. It took every ounce of his willpower not to raise his fist. Even so, his fingers curled together, as if his own reflexes would betray him.

He knew that his father saw and understood. Frank smiled almost wistfully. "What's that old saying, Mike? The apple never falls very far from the tree."

With an effort, Michael uncurled his fingers. "Where?" he asked harshly. "Where did you see him?"

A shrug this time, exaggerated in its carelessness. "Mike, I *am* his grandfather."

More memories flooded over Michael, unwelcome in their intensity. He remembered what it had been like as a kid trying to bargain with his father in some obscure power play, feeling overmatched, outwitted. Today, seeing the man after twenty years, he no longer felt unequal. But Andy...*he* was still a child.

"You'll stay away," Michael repeated.

A strange expression passed across his father's face, gone too quickly to be defined. Surely it couldn't be regret. "Do you really hate me that much?" he asked. "Was I such a lousy dad?"

It was amazing he could even ask the question. But Michael had only one thing to say to his father.

"Just stay the hell away."

CHAPTER EIGHT

EVEN AFTER EIGHT YEARS, it could still astonish Kim—
the power of money to make thinks happen quickly,
efficiently, expertly. It hadn't taken much waving of the
Bennett credentials for the maintenance company to
send their people on the double: already Kim's backyard pool had been uncovered, cleaned, filled, and
treated. The water shimmered invitingly in the sunlight. Too bad young Andy wasn't here.

She stood at the edge of the pool, battling a peculiar
sense of letdown. After that encounter with Michael
Turner at the hospital yesterday, she wasn't on the most
cordial terms with him. Certainly she couldn't go next
door and invite his son to come take a swim. So how
did she explain her impulse to see water in the pool?

How did she explain *any* of her inexplicable impulses these past few days? Inviting Michael to that
wretched gathering of Bennetts—that had been her
first mistake. Since then, everything had rushed ahead
much too quickly—the uncertain way he made her feel,
the restless expectancy he inspired in her. Even after the
way his accusations had wounded her yesterday, her
gaze strayed next door. What was he doing right now?
What was he thinking? And why on earth did she care?

At last she forced her attention away from Michael's house. Draping her towel over the patio lounge,
she sank down on it. She was wearing a bathing suit

that hadn't seen the light of day for quite some time—
a simple black maillot. For all its simplicity, though, it
was cut in daring, provocative lines. Kim tugged at it,
feeling out of sorts. Too many of her clothes were like
this: couture items, fashioned to make a statement
rather than to provide comfort. She had no one but
herself to blame. During the first years of her marriage, she'd luxuriated in buying new clothes, most of
them gorgeous and impractical. Later, spending Bennett money had lost its charm, but the relics of her
shopping sprees remained.

Now she settled back and opened the magazine she
had brought downstairs with her, but found it difficult
to concentrate. Her eyes kept straying toward the house
next door. How was young Andy doing after that
dreadful accident with the window? Michael Turner, of
course, had blamed her. She'd already had the window repaired—*professionally*—but Michael's accusations still plagued her.

"Damn him," she said out loud. It didn't help. The
hatefulness of his words coursed through her. How
could he think she would purposely harm Andy? He
could take those accusations and just—

She stopped herself there. If she had any sense at all,
she wouldn't waste another moment's thought on Michael Turner. She had better things to do—such as figure out what she was going to do with her life. She
snapped open her magazine again and forced her gaze
down the page.

She succeeded admirably for some twenty minutes,
turning one page after another. But then the image of
Michael Turner intruded into her mind all over again—
the way he'd stood there arrogantly in that hospital

corridor, asking her flat out if she'd tampered with her own window.

She'd been so disgusted with him afterward she'd immediately had a repairman come out to the house to fix the window. But obliterating signs of the accident hadn't made her feel any more favorably inclined toward Michael. His accusation had stayed with her, rankling deep inside.

"Damn him!" she repeated, more emphatically this time.

"Speaking to me?" came Michael Turner's voice from behind her. She started, and the magazine slid from her fingers, tumbling to the ground. She reached to pick it up, but Michael got there first. He retrieved it, glancing at the title.

"*Career Resources,*" he said. "A journal, no less. That's impressive leisure reading, Ms. Bennett."

She tried struggling to a more dignified position. Unfortunately lounge chairs were inherently undignified, which left her at something of a loss—legs stretched out, body reclining in spite of her best efforts. Michael's gaze traveled over her appreciatively, and suddenly she flushed from more than the summer heat. She stared back at him in silent challenge. That proved to be a mistake, however. Michael Turner looked good today. Very good. Still, a certain grimness never left his features; it was there today, in spite of the light tone he'd used. Everything about Michael warned that he was prohibited territory, no trespassing allowed. But trespassing held an undeniable allure.

She caught the wayward direction of her thoughts. Only a few seconds ago she had been cursing the man—a much better choice, as far as she was concerned. But now Michael was gazing at her bandaged arm.

"It's worse than it looks," she said shortly. He didn't seem to be paying any attention to her words. Instead, he sat down on the patio chair next to hers and touched her arm in the most gentle way imaginable. When she looked into his eyes, however, all she saw was the hardness there—no gentleness at all.

She held out her hand for the return of her magazine. Michael seemed to take this as an invitation to flip through the pages.

"Emerging fields...top twenty employers...on-the-job training. Looks like they've covered just about everything."

"Mr. Turner," she said, "it's not really any of your business, is it?"

"I'm an expert at career change," he answered. "If you want any advice, I'd be more than happy to comply."

"How could I forget?" she said acidly. "You're a policeman turned mystery novelist. That's definitely quite a jump."

His expression immediately became reticent. "It seems Andy's pretty talkative with you."

"Not today—I haven't seen him. I'm dangerous, remember?"

"Kim—"

"I suppose it does make a perverse sort of sense. You used to be a policeman, which means you dealt with criminals all the time. So maybe you think everyone is a criminal. Fine. I understand. Now you can leave."

He looked somber as he continued glancing through her magazine. "You're right. When you're a cop, you start to view the world a certain way. You realize that too many people can't be trusted. It's easy to end up suspecting everyone's motives.''

"Is this an apology?" she asked. "Because, Michael, if it is, it's quite a poor one and I don't accept it.''

"You have a habit of doing that," he murmured. "Not accepting apologies."

She made the mistake of gazing at him again. His eyes were very dark, and there was something enigmatic in them that sent a shiver through Kim. Looking into those eyes was like sensing a storm about to break—without knowing when or how.

She leaned forward and retrieved her magazine. She set it open in her lap, but that didn't make her feel any less exposed. "How's Andy doing?" she asked reluctantly.

"He's fine. Kids are pretty resilient."

"So I've heard." She stared unseeingly at the page before her. "Well, I'm sure you want to get back to him.''

"He's not home. He went off with Donna and her mother-in-law. It's an expedition to... outfit the nursery.'' A funny expression crossed Michael's face, something between amusement and perplexity.

Kim had liked what she'd seen of Michael's assistant. Granted, she hadn't met the woman under conventional circumstances. It had all been a blur—grabbing Andy as that glass shattered, both of them bleeding, Andy doing his very best not to show how scared he was, Donna showing up and driving them to the emergency room. She'd been so competent and down-to-earth about everything, possessing a sense of humor, as well. No doubt she'd make a very good mother.

"When's the baby due?" Kim asked.

Michael rubbed his jaw. "Hard to say."

Kim wondered why she was even bothering to have this conversation. All she wanted was for him to leave her in peace.

"Goodbye, Michael," she said pointedly. "I know you're very busy, being a writer and all. I'm sure you want to get back to your novel."

He rested his elbows on his knees as if settling in for a while. "I'm still having problems," he said. "With my heroine."

Kim rattled the pages of her magazine. "Really. How interesting. Too bad you can't stay and tell me all about it."

"She won't let me know what's going on inside," he said almost grudgingly. "I keep trying to imagine what she's thinking or feeling, and I don't get through."

Kim shut her magazine. "I'll tell you what your problem is, Michael. You say you want to get to know her, your heroine, but I don't really think you do. Every time you talk about her, you make assumptions...accusations. No wonder she remains aloof."

He frowned a little. "She's difficult, that's all. She wants me to believe she's the genuine article, but then she does everything she can to hide her real self. She puts up all kinds of barriers. I need her to be more...forthright."

"Forthright," Kim echoed in disbelief. "What do you expect people to give you, Michael? Signed affidavits that they're telling the truth? Being a policeman really *did* affect you."

Michael looked dissatisfied. "I've already admitted I might need to be less...jaundiced about human nature. But I still need something to go on, something that will allow me to decide who's worth trusting.''

''So we're back to your heroine,'' Kim said mockingly. She couldn't sit still any longer, reclined in this ridiculous position. Swinging her feet down from the lounge chair, she stood. But this was hardly any better, parading before Michael in her bathing suit. She grabbed her towel and wrapped it around her waist. That made her feel at least a little more protected.

''Michael,'' she said, ''I'll give you a heroine. Someone who made a mistake, who rushed into a bad situation because *she* was looking for someone to trust . . . someone to love.'' Kim knew it was ridiculous to go on, but couldn't seem to stop. ''She was naive. She thought if you just opened your heart to someone, you'd be safe. She found out pretty soon she'd never be safe, not with him, and even then she tried to make it work. To the very end, she tried.'' Kim took a shaky breath. ''I guess you could say she was disappointed,'' she went on, as flippantly as possible. ''But she learned. And she damn well won't be disappointed again.''

Michael rose to stand beside her. ''It sounds like she has exactly the same problem I do. She doesn't trust very easily.''

''Not anymore. You see, Michael, maybe you're the one on probation, not the other way around.''

He studied her gravely. ''Maybe I am at that.''

Surely there was nothing more to say. Kim turned from him, but then she felt his hand on her arm, his touch very gentle again.

''Does it hurt?'' he asked.

She'd almost forgotten about her injury. ''No, it's just a few cuts. I keep telling you, it was the scare more than anything else...." She realized he was standing close to her, almost as close as that night on the veranda. The summer sunshine spilled down on them; the clear water sparkled in the pool. Michael bent his head and slowly brushed his cheek against hers—just like that night, too. She couldn't seem to move. She just stood there, aching with need, knowing this time she would not retreat from him. She would give him no sign of her desire, her longing, but she would wait for his kiss.

For one more tremulous moment he stood beside her, his cheek next to hers. But then he stepped back. When he looked at her, his eyes were even darker than before.

"I'm sorry," he said in a low voice. She didn't know what he meant. Was he sorry for accusing her—or for touching her? Then Michael left her to stand alone by the pool, that aching need still deep inside her.

IT WAS LATE that afternoon when Kim headed home from her exercise class. A brisk hour of aerobics had done nothing to quell the restlessness inside her, and she allowed her foot to press down on the gas pedal. She was driving too fast, but she didn't care. She couldn't shake her conviction that *everything* was moving too fast since she'd met Michael Turner. Michael, damn him, who hadn't taken her in his arms—who hadn't kissed her today.

The worst of it was that Michael knew she wanted him. How could he *not* know? She'd given him every sign. This morning, standing there by her pool, she'd waited, trembling for his touch. Why couldn't she stop herself? Why did he have this effect on her?

Kim glanced in her rearview mirror and noticed the gray sedan a short distance behind her. It was a nondescript vehicle; nothing about it stood out as distinctive or unique. For several blocks now, this gray sedan had taken the exact same route she had chosen. Coincidence?

Kim forced her gaze straight ahead, telling her imagination not to get carried away. Lots and lots of cars traveled these same routes, over and over. There was nothing unusual about that.

She took a right, and then a few moments later signaled left. The gray sedan remained a few cars behind, but also took a right and a left. Kim battled her uneasiness. Still only coincidence, she tried to tell herself. Why would anyone be following her?

She turned on Florence Avenue. The sedan, now only one car behind her, also turned on Florence.

Kim had been a good driver ever since her days as a thirteen-year-old, when her father had taken her out on dirt roads and taught her how to maneuver a car. Starting so early, driving had become second nature to her. At this moment she could only be grateful for a skill she usually took for granted. Maybe her imagination had grown overactive, but she needed to find out for sure. Veering right, she ducked down a side street.

Halfway down the block, she saw the sedan in her rearview mirror.

She went left, then left again. The sedan, always a car or two behind, shadowed her every move. There could no longer be any doubt—it *was* following her. But why? And who?

This gray shadow had tinted windows, which made it impossible to see the driver. Kim tried to think if she'd ever seen the car before. She couldn't place it; there were too many nondescript cars in the world. It seemed precisely the type of vehicle you'd choose if you wanted to tail someone discreetly.

Kim gripped her steering wheel. She was on a busy street now, no need to panic. Whoever was driving that car couldn't do anything to her. But even so, she felt a kick of adrenaline through her body, almost a sickening sensation.

She eased up a little on the gas. *Think,* she commanded herself. The important thing was to stay on well-traveled streets. She headed onto Paseo del Sur. The sedan cut around another car, placing itself right behind her. Maybe the driver no longer cared about being discreet. The damn car was closing in on her bumper.

Kim signaled right, then abruptly sped into the left lane. Cars honked behind her as she wheeled onto Candelaria. The sedan was getting reckless. It came through the intersection behind her on the red. More cars blared their horns.

This can't be happening. Kim didn't know if she spoke the words out loud or merely thought them. By now she was operating only on that sickening rush of adrenaline. She ducked down one street, then another, weaving through traffic. Sometimes the sedan dropped back, sometimes it was right behind her, as if playing a game of cat-and-mouse. She punched the gas, taking yet another corner, going so fast she swung recklessly wide. And suddenly she had more to worry about than the sedan behind her. She was headed for a blue

Jeep straight in her path. Her foot slammed on the brake, and she heard the sound of her own voice yelling.

AT FIRST MICHAEL THOUGHT Kim Bennett was going to hit him—her Jaguar catapulting around that corner, tires screeching. He barely had time to yank on the steering wheel before she came to a shuddering halt, just inches from his bumper.

He swung out of the Jeep and went to her car, pulling open the door. "Lord, Kim," he said, his voice strained, "are you all right?"

She didn't speak. She just nodded, sitting there and clinging to the wheel. Her face was very white. He took one of her hands, feeling how cold it was. When he tried to draw her from the car, she resisted.

"No," she said automatically. "I'm blocking traffic. I...have to get out of the way."

He couldn't deny that cars were bunching up to either side, the driver of a truck impatiently poking his head out his window. "Just pull over to the curb," Michael told her. "And wait for me. Don't go anywhere, do you understand?"

She gave him an irritated glance. "I may be in shock, Michael, but I haven't lost my brain."

Her caustic tone reassured him. He closed her door and went back to the Jeep. A minute later they were both parked at the curb. Kim got out of her car and leaned against it. He could see she was trembling, and instinctively he reached to put his arm around her. His protectiveness had taken over again, but she didn't seem to want it. She stiffened, pulling away from him.

"Don't. Just...don't."

"It's all over," he said. "It was simply a near miss. But the way you came around that corner... you did have me worried there."

She stared at him. "Someone was following me," she said, each word carefully distinct. "I was trying to get away."

Michael's concern for Kim always warred with distrust, and he never knew which was going to win out. "I didn't see anyone," he said almost to himself.

Immediately her expression grew wary. "Why would you have seen anyone? You weren't *there*. I don't even know what you're doing here now. It doesn't make any sense." Color was coming back into her face, no doubt a result of her indignation with him.

That had been a blunder, what he'd just said. Michael wasn't used to making mistakes when it came to work. But with Kim, nothing he felt was usual.

"Michael," she said, gesturing at the warehouses and loading docks along the street. "What business could you possibly have here?"

He didn't answer. He'd been tailing her today, doing his shift. She'd gone to her twice-weekly exercise class—the dance aerobics thing. That was according to schedule. Afterward she'd taken the same meandering route as always. Michael, unfortunately, had lost her on the corner of Stinson and Lomita; that was when an ambulance had came wailing through the intersection. Michael's long tenure with the police had worked against him then—he always yielded for emergency vehicles, above and beyond the call of duty, knowing that even a few seconds could mean the difference between someone's life and death. So he'd sat there at the intersection even though the light was green, cursing the vehicles that didn't yield.

He'd figured it wouldn't take him long to catch up to Kim, even though he'd lost sight of her in all the traffic. She always headed to the same area of town after her exercise class. And so, once the ambulance passed, he'd taken a shortcut to that area—yes, an industrial district of warehouses and loading docks. Surprisingly, though, he hadn't been able to find Kim along her customary route. He'd looked for her, expanding his search in a rough grid to cover every possible street. And then she'd come wheeling around the corner, headed straight toward him.

Now she continued to watch him suspiciously. "What *are* you doing here, Michael?"

"Hmm . . . just tell me what happened."

She slumped back against the Jaguar, rubbing her temples. "Maybe I really am going crazy," she muttered. "But there was a gray sedan, and it was following me."

"When did you first notice it?" he asked.

"Why does that matter?"

"It matters," he said brusquely.

"I don't know . . . I suppose about ten minutes ago, when I was headed up Granger. Michael, what's going on?"

"I wish I knew." The way he figured it, Kim would have been on Granger only a short time after he'd lost her. Pretty convenient—one tail loses her, another picks her up. Except that no one else was supposed to be tailing Kim Bennett.

Michael didn't like the feel of this. He considered the possibilities. Had the gray car been waiting for its moment, moving in as soon as Michael's Jeep was temporarily out of the picture? Or was Kim Bennett spinning some story for her own purposes? Had she realized Michael was tailing her and decided to lead him on a chase?

"Dammit," she said. "Tell me what you're doing here."

That sounded like genuine outrage. Michael considered his answer.

"I'm doing research," he said at last.

"I thought Donna was your research assistant," she came back.

"As you can tell, lately Donna has reason to be a little occupied with . . . other things." Michael listened to himself, at how readily the lies came. Well, technically they weren't lies, but they sure as hell weren't the whole story, either. Subterfuge again.

Kim still looked doubtful. "If Donna's smart, she'll have her baby and then get herself a new job—working for someone else." With that, she walked around to the driver's side of the Jag and pulled open the door.

"Where are you going?" Michael said.

"Away from here."

He understood her tone—she wanted to get away from *him*. He was good at picking up on this type of clue.

"If someone really was following you," he said, "we have to find out why."

She gave a bleak-sounding laugh. "Michael, listen to yourself. You say *if* someone was following me. Once again, you don't really believe me." She slid into the driver's seat. "So I think I'll just keep safe on my own."

Michael came around to her side, preventing her from closing the car door. "Kim," he said, "if someone *was* following you, we need to find out what's going on."

She gazed at him. "Why?" she asked scornfully. "Why all the interest, Michael?"

If he were at liberty to tell her, he had one good reason—it was his job. But there was the other reason, too, the one that drew him more and more. It had to do with that shadow in Kim Bennett's eyes. What had she known, what had she seen, to leave behind that trace of pain?

"If you go off by yourself," he said, "I'll just have to follow you."

"Be my guest," she said acidly. "It seems to be a popular activity today."

Whether or not she knew it, she was right. Michael stepped back as she slammed her door and started the engine. But then, almost before she'd pulled away from the curb, he was in his Jeep—once again tailing her.

CHAPTER NINE

THE ART OF PURSUING a vehicle had its nuances. As a cop, Michael had perfected the siren-blaring type of chase, where you didn't make any secret of the fact that you were after someone. As a private investigator, he was obliged to excel at the more subtle form of pursuit. The sneaky kind. You couldn't get too close—it was always best to leave a few other cars as shields between you and the subject. At the same time, you couldn't lag too far behind. You couldn't be too obvious about anything; in fact, you couldn't be too obvious about not being obvious. More sophistication was required all around, but Michael missed the blare of a siren, that unequivocal announcement of your presence.

Today, however, he was in a peculiar situation as he followed the lovely widow Bennett. She knew he was behind her—no sirens needed. No subtlety needed, either. Michael stayed right on her bumper, just short of tailgating.

He knew where she was going, too. After her exercise class, she always headed this way before she went home, always ending up on one particular street. That was no doubt why he had been lucky enough to nearly run into Kim—he had her schedule down pat. Now, just as he expected, she turned onto a block of run-down commercial buildings, many with boarded windows and faded signs over padlocked doors. It was like a small ghost town set in the middle of the city. As usual, Kim stopped in front of one particular building, a looming brick warehouse. As Michael parked behind her, he scanned the street. It was deserted except for the two of them. He didn't like her coming here so often on her own. If someone really had been following her, isolation was the last thing she ought to be seeking.

If. There was that word, echoing in his head. *If* she was telling the truth, *if* she could be trusted.

She could very well wonder the same about him.

Michael swung out of his car and followed her to the door of the warehouse. She was making an obvious effort to ignore him as she searched through her key ring, then found the one to insert in the lock.

"Not exactly the Waldorf, is it," Michael said.

Kim pushed open the scarred wooden door. "If you're going to come along," she said, "keep the skepticism to yourself."

Technically it wasn't an invitation, but she didn't shut the door in his face, either. Sunlight filtered through the dirty windows, revealing a heap of carpet remnants and litter of the past. Michael bent down and picked up a yellowed piece of paper from the floor. It was an invoice dated some thirty years ago listing a consignment of furniture. Armchairs, a rocker, a settee—prosaic stuff. But why was Kim hanging around here?

She'd wandered on ahead, seemingly lost in thought. He found himself tailing her again, keeping his distance. It appeared that she'd almost forgotten his presence, but then she turned toward him.

"What do you feel?" she asked, her tone abrupt.

It was a hell of a question. He felt a lot of things—concern for Kim, awareness of her beauty even in these decrepit surroundings, always his doubts about her.

"Just tell me," she said. "How does this place make you feel?"

He glanced around. "I feel like . . . I'm in a warehouse."

"Very amusing," she said.

He hadn't meant to make a joke. It was the truth, but he was willing to play along with whatever she had in mind.

"Okay," he said. "I gather some furniture company used to operate here. Possibly they went out of business or maybe just moved on. That's the kind of place this is. It tells you that you should be moving on."

Even in the dim light, he could see a flicker of disappointment cross her face. He had the sensation he'd failed a test of hers somehow.

"It says something entirely different to me." Her voice was soft. "It says there are all kinds of possibilities here."

"Such as?"

She made an impatient gesture. "That's what I'm trying to figure out." She continued walking ahead of Michael. One thing about warehouses—they were damn big. Lots of space, lots of emptiness. He didn't have much to focus on except for Kim. She was wearing an oversize T-shirt and a leotard that revealed the slim, graceful shape of her legs. The T-shirt moved against her hips as she walked. Michael swore to himself and tried to look at all the emptiness, instead. His gaze came right back to Kim's T-shirt.

"As long as we're here," he said, "want to enlighten me? It can't hurt."

She went over to a wall and ran her fingers along the brick. "You're awfully curious, Michael. About everything."

"Occupational hazard," he said.

She gave him an astute glance. "Is that the ex-policeman talking or the writer?"

He paused. "The ex-cop."

Kim surprised him. She sat down on the littered floor as if perfectly at home, resting her back against the wall. "What kind of policeman were you, Michael?"

He didn't like the turn of the conversation, but he sat down next to her, anyway. "Homicide detective," he said.

He saw the flash of unease in her expression. "And you left it to become a writer."

"I left it," he acknowledged.

She brought her knees up and wrapped her arms around them. "It sounds so ominous. Just the word itself—homicide."

"Murder's another word," he said. He could have imagined it, but he thought he saw her arms tighten. Was he trying to goad her? It didn't feel good, whatever he was doing. Maybe that was because a part of him still wanted to comfort her, without knowing why or even if she needed comfort.

"I wish I could be as cynical as you," she murmured. "Believing the worst about people. I suppose that's a relief in a way. You can stop hoping that anyone will live up to your expectations."

It was disconcerting to have himself described that way. "I still have hopes for a few people," he said.

"I wonder who." She didn't sound convinced.

"My son. And Donna isn't the type who would let anyone down on purpose."

"Two people—that's it?" Kim asked. "You'll throw the rest of us out?"

"It's not that simple," he said. "Being a police detective, I learned that the best thing to do is reserve judgment. You don't make a decision about someone one way or the other until you can be certain."

"Reserving judgment," she said disdainfully. "That's an out, if I ever heard one."

"Don't you do the same thing, Kim?"

She gazed at him. A hazy patch of sunlight reached her from one of the high windows. She'd smoothed her hair back with a sweatband, which only emphasized the loveliness of her face—the dark fan of her eyelashes, the clear outline of every feature, the scattering of freckles across her nose. It was always the freckles that got to him.

"No," she said, "I try to be cynical, but deep down I know I'm not. That's what scares me." She spoke reluctantly, as if not wanting to make the admission. Then she stood in a fluid motion, moving away from him. "Anyway," she went on in a lighter tone, "you're trying to figure out what I see in this place."

He remained seated. "For all I know, this is just one of your many holdings."

"You have me confused with the other Bennetts," she said, a trifle sharply. "I don't even own this building."

"Funny," he remarked. "You have the key."

Kim shrugged. "When I told the Realtor I was interested in the place, she lent me a key so I could come here whenever I wanted. I can tell she'd like to get it off her hands."

"I don't suppose too many people are interested in buying old warehouses—in a part of town that doesn't have a hope of becoming gentrified."

He could tell that he'd annoyed her again; he seemed to be good at that. She walked to another wall, pressing her hand against the brick. "I haven't made up my mind yet," she said. "It's just that...I went down this street by accident one day. I was on my way somewhere else, and I took a wrong turn. And here it was, just waiting. What could I do?"

He wondered what it was she saw here. To him, the place was still just an old warehouse. Nothing special, nothing out of the ordinary. Even the stuffy air had a discarded feel to it, as if it had been overused and then abandoned.

"Kim," he said, "warehouses are for storing things. If you did buy it, what would you store?"

It was a practical question—and perhaps that was why it seemed to annoy her. She drew her eyebrows together. "I don't know. That's what's so frustrating. You see a place, and you have to keep coming back to it—and you don't even know why. I know how ridiculous it seems."

"No. It's intriguing." For just a minute or two, he'd like to see the place with her eyes. Maybe he'd discover something that had escaped him thus far. A lot of the time, he felt like that with Kim—trying to discover something elusive, something that hovered just on the edge of his perceptions.

She was walking away. He stood and caught up with her.

"Kim, I don't like the idea of you coming here the way you do...alone. Let's say someone *is* following you. He—or she—will get to know your patterns. That's always dangerous."

"So now you believe me?" she said derisively.

"Maybe even *you* don't know what to believe. Can you tell me if you've sensed it before—someone following you?" He knew Donna would laugh if she heard him ask that one. Too bad he wasn't in a joking mood.

"Of course not," Kim said. "I'm not paranoid."

Michael supposed he ought to congratulate Donna and himself for doing their jobs well. But he wasn't in a congratulatory mood, either.

"Besides," Kim went on, "why would anyone want to follow me?" She sounded as if she was arguing with herself. "It could have been just some random creep having his fun for the day."

"I'm not a big believer in random," he said.

She nudged a crumpled paper bag out of her path. "Are you trying to frighten me, Michael?" Her voice was tight.

"If that's what it takes. I don't want you coming here anymore."

She swiveled around to face him. "You're my damn next-door neighbor, not my...my guardian. And it's still just a little too convenient, how you happened to be doing your research in this part of town. Exactly what research, Michael? I'd like to know." Those two spots of color burned in her cheeks, the ones that told him she was getting furious.

He was better than he liked at coming up with answers to disguise his work—half-truths, half-lies, whatever you wanted to call them. He knew he should give Kim a few of those now. He might even convince her if he tried hard enough. But he couldn't do it. He couldn't spin the half-answers. Instead, he followed the impulse that had been building in him since he'd first seen her. He took Kim into his arms and he kissed her.

Her mouth was soft under his, as he'd imagined it would be. But now it was up to her what she would do. He waited for her to retreat from him, feeling already the sense of loss that would bring.

But she didn't retreat. She stood with her face lifted to him, and she was warm and sensuous and giving, yes, everything he'd imagined. . . .

Neither one of them stepped away this time. They kissed each other as if both had long been denied something precious, something elemental, and would only find it in this moment. But it was a beginning, not a culmination, tantalizing without fulfilling. Michael wanted more from Kim, and he knew he could not— should not—have it.

When they stopped it was only for breath, but that was enough to break the tenuous spell between them. Kim remained in his arms, but she bent her head so he couldn't kiss her again. He felt the trembling of her body.

"No," she whispered. "No, Michael."

And, with her denial, came the sense of loss.

IT STAYED with Michael, that sense of loss. He hadn't slept much during the night after his visit to the warehouse. Instead, he'd gone to his bedroom window and gazed at the house next door. He'd seen a light shining from Kim's window. It seemed she hadn't been able to sleep, either.

Now it was morning, and Michael had to force himself to concentrate on the Jacobs case, the one involving a runaway teenage girl. He sat in Luanne Jacobs's living room. The woman had clearly prepared herself for today, dressing up and wearing high heels as if that would bolster her for this ordeal. She'd recently been to the beauty parlor.

From what Michael had seen so far of the woman, new hairstyles and dressing up weren't everyday occurrences. Maybe she thought that if she transformed her outer appearance somehow, the rest of her life would change, too, and her daughter would come home.

She sat next to Michael on the sofa, a photograph album spread open on her lap, and pointed at one of the photos. "That's Melissa at four. It was her birthday party. We had a cake specially made in the shape of a dinosaur—a stegosaurus. Melissa liked dinosaurs long before they were popular. It wasn't just part of some craze for her." She spoke with the pride of all parents—my child is the best, the smartest, unique. But underneath her words was the more anguished, unspoken side of parenthood: I loved her, I celebrated every birthday with care and rejoicing... What went wrong?

Michael examined the photograph. Melissa Jacobs looked as any four-year-old should, happy and shy at once, posing beside her stegosaurus cake. The picture didn't tell him anything he could use to find her now as a runaway teenager. Nonetheless, he let her mother go on turning the pages of the album. He knew how to be patient in such cases. There might be some small detail he would garner today, something that would provide a clue.

"She's ten here," said Luanne. "See the ribbon—she'd just won a math contest at school. She's always been good at math. She wanted to take calculus in high school, can you believe it?''

And so Melissa's young life unfolded before Michael. He saw pictures of her with her dog and cat—Melissa loved animals; pictures of her on her bike—Melissa always had been fearless; pictures of her going off to camp—Melissa knew how to make all types of friends.

''This camp,'' Michael said, ''is it a place she enjoyed?''

''Oh, of course,'' said Luanne Jacobs. ''We wouldn't have sent her there otherwise. Every summer for one month, from the time she was eleven until she turned fourteen. She adored camp.''

''Why did she stop going at fourteen?''

Luanne stared at him. ''She was too old by then of course. She'd outgrown it. She said so herself, and we've always allowed Melissa to make as many decisions as possible. We've always trusted her judgment. She's more mature than most girls her age.''

Michael heard the brittleness in her voice, the uncertainty creeping in despite her confident words. Deep down, Luanne Jacobs was probably very worried about her daughter's judgment and maturity.

Michael realized this case was going to be more complex than he'd envisioned. But it was always like that. People contradicted themselves, stumbling over their own memories, their own hopes and fears. The challenge was to find the truth—or at least a close approximation of it—buried there somewhere in all the emotions.

Michael noted something else having to do with the photographs in this album. The camera was always focused on Melissa, rarely capturing either of the parents. Michael wondered how Melissa had fared, being the center of so much fond attention.

He listened to Luanne Jacobs talk a while longer about Melissa's accomplishments and talents. When he tried to press for hints of any problems at school or home, he met with firm resistance.

"Oh, no, Mr. Turner, Melissa was very well adjusted. She was happy. She gave no sign of anything wrong. I'm sure she would have told us if anything was troubling her." But underneath the words was still that unspoken anguish. What went wrong? Why did she leave us?

According to Luanne and Derrell Jacobs, their sixteen-year-old daughter had simply disappeared three weeks ago without warning. She'd packed a suitcase, taking with her a favorite stuffed animal from childhood. This was a sign that she had left voluntarily rather than meeting with foul play; certainly nothing had shown up at the local hospitals or morgue. None of Melissa's friends seemed to know where she was—at least, if they did, they weren't willing to talk about it.

Michael didn't have a whole lot to go on, but today's meeting with Luanne Jacobs was turning out to be informative, after all; what she didn't say told him a whole lot more than what she did. His instincts were starting to kick into gear, and he had a couple of theories to follow up on young Melissa.

"Mr. Turner—" Luanne Jacobs closed the photo album "—all Derrell and I want is to find Melissa. I can assure you we will have no recriminations for her, no questions. We just want her back with us, safe and happy."

It occurred to Michael that Luanne and Derrell Jacobs *ought* to have questions for their daughter. Maybe sometimes recriminations weren't such bad things—they could get problems out into the open. But Luanne sat there with a mixture of forlornness and hope on her face. She'd invested her entire life in her daughter, that much was evident, and Michael couldn't help feeling sorry for her. Being a parent was difficult under any circumstances, and Luanne was struggling with one of the worst. Michael thought about how he'd feel if Andy disappeared. That scare with the window had been bad enough.

"Mrs. Jacobs," he said, "I'll continue doing everything I can to locate your daughter."

Her expression brightened for just a moment. "Mr. Turner, if you find her—*when* you find her—just tell her that . . . we love her."

Those words seemed to echo behind Michael as he left the Jacobs house. He wondered if it was possible to love a child too much? It wasn't a question he knew how to answer.

He went to his Jeep and climbed in, but for a moment or two he didn't start the engine. He just sat there, gazing out through the windshield. His mind drifted to Kim. Of course, it had been drifting that direction a lot since he'd kissed her.

He couldn't think of too many mistakes worse than taking a suspect in his arms, but that wasn't what bothered him. It was the way Kim made him feel—as if he needed to protect her, watch out for her. Yet it was even more than that. She made him feel as if he needed *her*.

Michael wasn't used to needing, and he didn't like the sensation. But that didn't seem to stop him from thinking about Kim. He wondered how she would act if she was in Luanne Jacobs's place. Judging from the no-nonsense way she treated Andy, Kim would be strict but fair with any child of her own. She wouldn't be the type to indulge a kid too much. She'd probably know how to love just the right amount.

Michael wondered what the hell he was thinking and why. He knew as well as anyone that love couldn't be neatly measured. But now he'd worked himself around to reflecting on his marriage. Somehow he and Jill had gotten the balance wrong. Eventually Michael had become aware of a shift in their small family. It had become apparent to him that Jill put motherhood before being a wife. Andy came first, Michael a distant second.

He supposed it was as much his fault as hers. Over the years he'd become absorbed in his job, Jill in her studies. Certainly they'd stopped being absorbed in each other. Maybe it was just natural that Jill had obtained more satisfaction from being a mother than anything else. Still... the balance had been wrong. It had been one of the main reasons for their divorce.

Kim Bennett, of course, hadn't had a chance to try the balance one way or the other. She didn't have any children, and her husband was dead—possibly murdered.

He kept forgetting to add the last little part: the husband had very possibly been murdered by Kim herself. No matter what had happened in the warehouse yesterday, she was still a suspect.

Michael revved the Jeep's engine. He was getting the balance in his own life wrong, too, and he knew it. He had to stop thinking about Kim Bennett the way he did, remembering the taste and the feel of her....

He wheeled from the curb, turned the corner and merged into traffic. It didn't take him long to travel the six miles or so to the community center. Parking again, he swung out of the Jeep and went into the gym to find his son.

Andy was playing a game of one-on-one with his friend Doug. Or maybe that was *ex*-friend, Michael reminded himself.

Michael stood and watched the game. Andy was doing well, handling the ball aggressively. Even though he was shorter than Doug, he was quicker, more adept. From the top of the key, he turned, aimed the ball and sent it in for a score. *Way to go!*—Michael sent the message silently to his son.

But then Andy turned and saw Michael. He made no acknowledgment of his father, no wave or hello. He just kept playing, except now he wasn't doing nearly as well. He fumbled the ball, losing it to the other boy. And when he got a chance to shoot, the ball went veering wide, not even making it to the backboard.

It didn't matter to Michael if his son made a basket or not. What disturbed him was that his presence could so obviously unsettle Andy. Why was it like this, the two of them never in sync, never easy with each other?

The game frittered to a halt, and Andy came toward Michael, dragging both his feet and his duffel bag.

"Hi," Michael said, forcing cheerfulness. Andy didn't answer, just hiked the strap of his bag over his shoulder. He headed for the door, but Michael stopped him. "Let's go sit on the bleachers."

Andy looked suspicious. "Why?"

"No good reason. Just thought we'd hang out a little, that's all."

"Yeah, right," Andy muttered. "You're real good at hanging out, Dad."

Michael felt the familiar irritation at his son's sarcasm. He'd already given Andy lectures about it, but they never seemed to do any good. He knew that Andy was trying to provoke him, testing to see how far he could go. The trick, of course, was to stay in control, not be provoked. Michael felt an unwilling sympathy for Luanne Jacobs. Had she been like this with her daughter? But what other choice was there? You couldn't lose your temper with a child. You could reason, explain and, yes, lecture. But anger—you could never let that spill over onto your child.

Michael went to the bleachers and sat down. After a second or two of defiant hesitation, Andy scuffed his way across the gym floor and plunked himself down at a distance from Michael. He leaned forward, resting his elbows on his knees; it was an effective way to keep his back toward his father.

"Andy," Michael said, "you remember what I said, don't you? About not talking to anyone...unusual."

"Right, right," Andy said in a world-weary voice. "Don't talk to strangers and all that crap."

"Andy—"

"All that stuff."

Michael thought it over. It seemed more than likely that his father had been bluffing—Frank hadn't actually tried to speak to Andy yet. But what about the future? That was Michael's main concern.

He tried again. "I'm serious about this, and I also expect you to level with me. If you should meet someone new, someone older, and they try to talk to you—"

Now Andy twisted around and glared at Michael. "I got it, Dad, okay? I'm not supposed to talk to the lady next door. I'm not supposed to talk to anybody else, either. Hell—heck. Just lock me in that stupid house.''

Michael felt it again, the reluctant sympathy for Luanne Jacobs. You tried to keep your kid safe and maybe sometimes you went overboard. But Michael couldn't change that. Given the circumstances, there were only a few places he felt comfortable leaving Andy. This was one of them—the community-center staff always watched out for the kids here.

''Andy,'' Michael said, ''you could give me a break now and then. I'm not the enemy.''

But Andy had already twisted forward again, his skinny shoulders hunched against anything else his father might say.

CHAPTER TEN

IT HAD BEEN another restless night for Kim. Yawning wearily, she buried her head in the pillow, but the early-morning light prevented her from dozing. She turned over, pushing back the rumpled sheet and blanket. She hadn't slept well since the other day, when that car had followed her. When Michael Turner had kissed her.

She closed her eyes, the sensations Michael had evoked in her as fresh as if he had only just now lifted his lips from hers. Longing...need...wanting...

"Damn him," she said out loud. It didn't do any good. What really bothered her was not knowing *why* sleep eluded her. Was it because of that gray sedan? Or because she couldn't stop thinking about Michael?

Sweeping back the sheet once and for all, she climbed out of bed and slid into her robe. Cinching the belt at her waist, she went to the window and gazed out. Even this early, she could tell it was going to be another scorching day. The sky had a pale look, the colors of sunrise already burned off. Against her will, her gaze strayed next door.

She hadn't seen Michael since the day at the warehouse, but in an odd way his presence seemed to linger with her. Maybe it was because she felt safer, just knowing he was next door.

Still, there was something about him that disturbed her; she'd sensed it from the first time she'd met him.

It was a sort of watchfulness, an attitude of being constantly on guard. But against what? Even when he'd kissed her, she'd felt it—as if he couldn't lose himself entirely in the moment, as if he always had to be ready for something. Even with his lips warm and demanding on hers, he'd withheld some essential part of himself.

It had only been a kiss. Why was she reading so much into it? Why was she remembering—and remembering again?

"Fool," she whispered to herself. Retreating hastily from the window, she went downstairs to the kitchen. Once the coffeepot was percolating, she felt a little more collected. She had things to do today. She'd be busy. Surely she could keep her mind occupied with something besides Michael Turner.

But then she glanced around at her homey kitchen and remembered what it had been like to have Michael's son here, drinking lemonade and eating cookies. It had been . . . cozy. Familiar somehow, as if she'd slipped naturally into a role she was meant for. Not that Michael would agree with her.

Damn the man! Now she was suddenly angry at him. It was very clear he wasn't letting Andy near her, as if he truly believed her capable of harming the boy. He always appeared to be searching for some dark, secret guilt in her. But *he* was the one who seemed to have something to hide. Why *had* he been so conveniently nearby the day she'd gone to the warehouse?

She was about to sit down with her cup of coffee when the doorbell rang. Who could be here this early? Kim knew she must look a sight—hair uncombed, eyes bleary. Grumbling to herself, she went down the hall to the front door and looked through the peephole.

She had to restrain a groan. Her brother-in-law Thad Bennett was standing on her front porch. Behind him hovered his dutiful wife, Norie. What on earth could they want?

Kim was tempted simply to ignore them and go back to her coffee. But she knew her in-laws too well; they were persistent. She unlocked the door.

Thad crossed her threshold with that ponderous air of his, as if he was about to start discoursing on some arcane subject.

"Good morning, Kim," he said, always one to observe proper etiquette.

"Good morning, Thad."

Norie trailed after him, wearing a penitent expression. "I'm sorry, Kim. I told Thad we should call first. I just knew we were going to wake you up."

"I was already awake."

"Yes, but I can tell we've caught you in the middle of something. You're not even dressed. I mean—" Norie stopped, and now she looked chagrined. She had a habit of looking that way, just as she had a habit of saying the wrong thing.

"It's all right," Kim said. "I'm up, and I'm about to have coffee. You can join me." She began leading the way back to the kitchen.

Thad didn't seem happy about this. "The living room might be a more appropriate setting," he said.

"Thad's afraid he might get trapped in a coffee klatch," Norie said distinctly. Kim always felt a renewed interest in her sister-in-law when she did that— dropped the meek-wife routine for a second or two. Thad, however, didn't seem to notice his spouse's gibe. Maybe that was on purpose.

"I suppose anywhere will do," he said as if granting his permission.

A moment later Kim poured two more cups, placed them on the kitchen table and then sat. Norie, unfortunately, went right back to being the solicitous wife. She put milk and sugar in Thad's coffee, stirred, and arranged the spoon at a precise angle on his saucer. Her husband didn't acknowledge this with so much as a nod.

"Kim," he began, his tone important, "Norie and I feel that the family owes you an apology."

This was a surprise, because the Bennett men were not fond of apologies. Kim stirred her own coffee and tasted it. She'd made it extra strong.

"We believe you were treated unfairly at dinner the other night," Thad went on. "The subject was presented to you with very little ... finesse. If I had been informed, I might have been able to circumvent that."

Kim realized he wouldn't come any closer than this to criticizing his mother. "You might as well get to the point," she said.

He looked displeased. "This *is* the point. We're apologizing."

"I hardly think so," Kim said.

"But it's the truth," Norie rushed in. "I convinced Thad that we couldn't let you believe the worst—that *we* had anything to do with it."

"Coming here this morning was my idea," said her husband.

"For goodness' sake," said Norie, "you weren't even willing to rearrange your schedule. I practically had to drag you here."

Kim remembered what Michael Turner had observed about her—that she wasn't very good at accepting apologies. He was probably right about that, but she wasn't going to change anytime soon.

"Let's just get it over with," she said. "What you really came to say."

Thad pushed his untouched cup aside. "Very well. No matter how poorly the subject was addressed, the truth remains, Kim. You have never expressed any interest in Bennett Industries. It simply makes no sense for you to hold on to those shares."

"Thad!" Norie exclaimed. "You never said we were going to discuss this. Kim, I swear to you, all I wanted to do was offer a sort of... a sort of olive branch."

"We must discuss it," said Thad.

Kim stood, walked over to the sink and rinsed her cup. "I already gave my answer. I'm keeping my shares."

"But why?" Thad sounded as if he actually wanted to know.

Kim stayed at the sink and took her time answering. "It seems so important to all of you, my giving up my hold on Bennett Industries. It's funny, but I think it's more than just wanting to get rid of me. I'd like to figure out what else is going on."

Thad made a production of standing and pushing his chair back toward the table, all his movements deliberate. "This is absurd," he said. "I thought we could resolve this. Apparently I was wrong."

"Apparently," Kim agreed.

"I knew it was a mistake to come here," he muttered. "We're leaving, Norie."

"You run along," said his wife. "I think I'll just stay with Kim for... a chat."

Thad stared at her. "That's not a good idea."

She stared back. "I think it is."

Kim had her own opinion. "You'll both have to leave. I have a lot to do this morning and I want to get started."

"Kim," Norie said urgently, "I really would like to stay and . . . chat." She seemed to be trying to communicate with her eyes. She wasn't doing a very good job of it—all she managed was to end up squinting a little.

"All right," Kim said, giving in. "You can stay—for a little while."

Thad treated his wife to another quelling stare and left. Norie waited until she heard the front door slam shut, and then she was instantly transformed. She kicked off her shoes and curled her legs up on the chair.

"I thought I'd never be rid of him," she said. "Thad at seven o'clock in the morning is a bit much to take. Thank goodness he spends so much time at the office." Her remarks were nothing unusual; for years she'd been carping about Thad behind his back.

Kim wished briefly for solitude, but she realized that Norie had something of her own to say. Might as well get it over with. She sat down at the table again. "What *do* you want, Norie?" she asked. "I really am busy."

"You make it sound as if your schedule's worse than his. I did think we could just have a chat, Kim. You know, like sisters-in-law. We're still relatives, you know. A tie like that doesn't fall apart just because . . . well, just because." Norie got her flustered look.

"What do you want, Norie?" Kim repeated with a patience she didn't feel.

Now a wistful expression crossed Norie's face. "Maybe I want us to be friends. It's what I've always wanted. Is that so hard to believe?"

"Yes, it is," Kim said evenly. "You're too worried about your own position in the family. You're afraid they'll start to exclude you, the way they do me."

"You might as well accuse me of being a coward," Norie said.

"I'm not accusing you of anything."

Norie wrapped both hands around her coffee cup. "I'm not going to pretend with you. We both know what the Bennetts are like. They never want anyone else in the inner circle." She sighed. "If it wasn't for the children, Sophie would have frozen me out a long time ago. But I did the right thing according to her—I produced three new Bennetts right on schedule. Because of that, she'll forgive me a great deal. Mainly, she'll forgive me for not being a Bennett."

Kim felt a coldness inside. "You're not telling me anything I don't know," she said.

Norie reverted to penitence. "Oh, Kim—I'm sorry. I know how much you and Stan wanted children. I didn't mean . . . It was just bad luck, that's all."

Norie didn't have it exactly right, but Kim wasn't about to waste the effort correcting her. And she wouldn't think about Stan, wouldn't relive yet again the humiliation of her marriage. "You stayed behind for a reason," she said. "What is it?"

Norie sat back, a faraway expression taking over her face. Kim had seen this look before. Norie often seemed like an actress running scenarios through her mind, deciding which one to dramatize.

"Dear me," Norie murmured at last, glancing around. "It's eerie, in a way. All the memories. I can almost picture Stan over there by the pantry, angry with you that time you made mashed potatoes."

Kim raised her eyebrows a little. "I'm curious. Why did you choose that particular incident?"

Norie looked displeased, as if her concentration had been disturbed. "It was a random thought..."

"Why not choose a time when Stan was happy with me? Or don't you think there were any?" Kim realized she'd spoken too sharply.

"I know you and Stan had your problems. But I wasn't trying to make an issue of it, believe me."

The coldness settled deeper and deeper inside Kim. Despite everything, she *did* remember—the way she'd been so certain of Stan in the beginning, so sure he loved her. And then, gradually, the disillusionment, the realization of Stan's weaknesses. The knowledge that he was so dominated by his family no act of rebellion could truly free him. It had turned out he had no love to spare for Kim, after all.

"What does any of it really matter?" she said now. "It's over."

Norie looked downright peeved. "You're missing the point. And I did have one, you know." She took a deep breath, the kind she'd no doubt learned in her yoga class. Norie was always trying different methods of relaxation and never seeming to get a handle on any of them. "The point being... this house must be full of memories for you. It's been so difficult, Stan's death and all, and the family hasn't given you the support you need. But I'm not like the others."

This was typical Norie. Half the time she tried to meld into the Bennetts, the other half she tried to assert her independence.

"I'm doing just fine," said Kim. "I'm getting on with my life."

Norie arranged an expression of sympathy on her face. "I'd like to help with that if I could. There must be something I can do. Why, you haven't even started to go through Stan's things yet, have you?"

Unfortunately Norie was right about that. Kim hadn't been able to bring herself to sort through Stan's clothes and effects. But it wasn't because she cherished her memories. It was because she wanted to forget them.

"I'll get around to it soon enough," Kim said.

Norie smiled consolingly. "I'll help you. After all, you shouldn't have to do it alone. I'll be there for you."

"That won't be necessary."

"For once," Norie said in a reproachful tone, "I wish someone in this family would admit to *needing* somebody else. I didn't think you'd become so much like them, Kim."

This was truly masterful. Norie apparently knew the one thing that could get to Kim—any suggestion that after eight years among the Bennetts, she'd acquired their characteristics. But Kim didn't let the remark sway her too much.

"I suppose I could start packing up Stan's clothes. On my own," she added.

Norie looked disappointed. "All I want is to feel useful. Why won't you let me? And think about it. You and I—we could stand against the rest of them for once."

"Siding with me..." Kim mused. "That won't give you any advantage where the family's concerned. What gives?"

"I only want to help," Norie protested. "Really, Kim. You do sound just like them—trying to see what the angle is."

Perhaps there was some truth to that; living among the Bennetts could make you cynical regardless of your best intentions. But the fact remained—Norie was always searching for a power base within the family. Now, for some reason, she wanted to include Kim in her struggle—and Kim didn't like it.

PEACE AND A FRESH CUP of coffee at last. Kim had made herself presentable in jeans, a sleeveless blouse and sandals—summer wear. She'd settled at the kitchen table again, after finally managing to shoo her sister-in-law out the door. To watch Norie speed away in that little sports car, anyone would have assumed she was an adventurous blond bombshell, not an insecure Bennett wife.

But she was gone—that was the important thing. Kim sipped her second cup, deciding it tasted much better than the first. Entirely against her will, her gaze strayed to the window, the one that looked out toward the house next door. Wrenching her thoughts away from Michael, she tried to concentrate on her plans for the day, but suddenly she wasn't in a hurry to get started on them. A trip to the grocery store, another to the library, and of course she'd made an appointment to talk to an admissions counselor at the university.

She grimaced. The sorry truth was that she'd never attended a day of college. After high school, she'd stayed on at her father's restaurant to work full-time, and after her mother's death, she'd packed up and fled to Tucson, taking the first job she could find. It had been something of a coup, landing the position as Stan Bennett's secretary when she'd never worked in an office before. Not that she was kidding herself. The attraction between her and Stan had been immediate, and she knew he'd given her the job because of that, not her qualifications. Nonetheless, it all added up to the fact that Kim had never been to college. She didn't know if it was the answer for her now—the solution to her yearning for something meaningful in her life. She'd just have to go talk to that admissions counselor, see if it gave her any inspiration.

Inspiration—that was what she lacked. She envied all those people who seemed to know exactly what they wanted to do with their lives. Wasn't it a bit embarrassing to have reached the age of twenty-nine and not know where you were headed? She had to find the answer, and soon.

The doorbell rang again, two times in quick succession.

"What now?" Kim muttered grouchily. She went down the hall and peered through the peephole. A woman stood on her porch—Donna, Michael Turner's research assistant. Donna looked determined and rang the bell yet a third time.

It occurred to Kim that peepholes gave you a singular advantage. You could just stand there and scowl at whoever was trying to disturb your morning's reflection. She had nothing against Donna personally, but she welcomed no more intrusions.

The woman rang the bell again, obviously not one to give up easily. Kim swung the door open.

Donna didn't waste any time on greetings. "Is Andy over here with you?"

"No, he's not."

"Damn. I can't believe he got away from me. He has a new game—Ditch Aunt Donna. He was supposed to be fixing himself breakfast. By the time I figured out he'd rigged the toaster to trigger the smoke alarm, he'd made it out the door. I thought for sure he was over here with you. Are you absolutely certain he didn't sneak in somehow?''

Donna, obviously the take-charge type, didn't even wait for Kim to answer. She wedged her way into the door and began looking about. She was a bit over-whelming, like a steamroller in high gear. But Kim assessed the situation quickly.

''Let's check the backyard just in case. I've wondered if my swimming pool might not prove too much a temptation.''

She hadn't even finished speaking before Donna headed down the hall. Kim found herself obliged to bring up the rear. When they reached the back patio, no curly-headed eleven-year-old boy could be seen lurking in the bushes or splashing in the pool.

''Are you sure,'' Donna said, ''he's not in your house?''

It sounded almost like an accusation. ''Of course I'm sure.'' Kim stared at the other woman. Something was different about Donna today, something she couldn't quite put a finger on. New hairdo? No. Still shoulder length, pulled back with a barrette. Donna wore shorts, with a longish vest over her shirt—nothing unusual about that. But now it struck Kim. The woman's stomach was perfectly flat.

Donna followed the direction of Kim's gaze and clapped her hand over her stomach.

''Oh, damn!'' she exclaimed. ''I forgot the baby!''

Was the woman insane? But already she was heading back along the path toward the front of the house. No explanation, no ''thank you very much,'' no ''good-bye.''

Kim stood where she was for a moment, thinking about the schedule she'd arranged for herself. The grocery, the library, the university...

Suddenly she just couldn't picture walking through all the mundane details of it. Acting sheerly on impulse, she hurried after Donna. "Wait!" she called.

Donna either didn't hear or didn't choose to hear. She was already halfway down the block, moving at a good clip—on the lookout for Andy, no doubt. Kim had to jog to catch up to her.

"Wait!" she repeated breathlessly. "I know all the places where the neighborhood kids like to hang out."

Donna barely spared her a glance. "I'll handle it," she said.

Kim maintained a good pace right beside her. "You know," she said, "it's a little strange. When someone's pregnant one day, and the next... well, you get the idea."

Donna didn't slow even a fraction. "I suppose it does seem a bit odd."

"Just a bit," Kim said ironically.

"Oh, hell," Donna muttered. "Any woman married to *my* husband ought to have her head examined."

Kim didn't say anything more. She had a feeling that Donna, in spite of her brusqueness, needed to unburden herself. And at last Donna glanced over at her with a look of exasperation.

"All right, this is what Brad did. Out of the blue, he announced to his mother I was pregnant. My dear old mother-in-law was overjoyed—and I was subsequently in a monumental fix. Because of course I *wasn't* pregnant."

Kim thought it over. "Why didn't you just tell her the truth?"

Now Donna looked annoyed. "Easy for you to say."

"I know all about mothers-in-law," Kim answered. "My own fully expected me to reproduce within a year of marriage. When I didn't oblige her, well . . ."

Donna kept right on striding along. It was amazing how fast she could move. As a conversationalist, however, she left something to be desired.

"We should cut across here," Kim said. "There's a park nearby where the kids like to congregate."

"I'll handle it," Donna repeated, but she did take the route toward the park. She was silent for about half a block, and then she gave Kim a defensive glance.

"It's really not that simple," she said. "Brad's mother couldn't have any more children after he was born, so she's always put her hopes in grandkids. Brad's stupidity was brought on by good intentions at least. That's the kicker—he really wants his mom to be happy. And now . . . well, how do you tell an aging woman that her fondest dream isn't about to be realized, after all?"

Kim found she didn't have an answer readily available. And it took all her breath to keep up with Donna. This was better than her aerobics workout.

"Did *you* want children?" Donna asked abruptly.

"What?" Kim was obliged to jog again for a moment or two.

"When your mother-in-law put the pressure on you. Did you want children?"

First the woman tried to brush her off and now she wanted to have a heart-to-heart. But being out of breath made Kim get right to the point.

"Yes," she said. "Very much."

"Never a doubt?"

"Not about that. I wanted children more than anything." She'd never admitted it like this before, never said the words so plainly. It gave her an unexpected sense of relief. But she couldn't explain the rest of it. She couldn't tell Donna *why* she'd never had children: her husband's inability—or sheer unwillingness—to make love to her. Which had it really been?

Donna slowed down at last, a glum expression on her face. "I envy you that certainty about wanting a child. Because I can't make up my mind at all. This whole thing would be so much easier if I knew, one way or another. Sometimes I think it would be great to have children. And other times . . . frankly, it scares the hell out of me. Brad and I have a pretty good thing going in spite of the amazing things that pop out of his mouth when he's around his mother. How do I know children won't ruin that?"

Again Kim didn't have an answer. "My marriage was . . . pretty rotten," she said, surprised she was telling this to Donna. "Maybe part of me thought having children would salvage things. But it was more than that. I just had a conviction I was meant to be a mother. I wish I felt the same way about a career. That's where I can't seem to find any certainty."

"We're exactly the opposite," Donna said. "Because I always knew what I wanted in a career. Even from the time I was a little girl, I knew."

"You wanted to be a research assistant?" Kim asked in puzzlement. "Most children aren't quite that specific."

Donna got a strange expression on her face. "Yes, well, I was a precocious little tyke, wasn't I? But I really can't shoot the breeze with you, Kim. Have to find

Andy and all.'' Donna shifted up to high speed. Kim kept up with her, more put out than ever. What *was* the woman's problem?

"All right, I give up," Kim said to Donna's back. "When you were a little girl, what was it you *really* wanted to be?"

This time Donna actually waited for her to catch up. "Look," she said, "I wanted to be a cop, okay? A detective. Because my dad was a detective, and his dad before him."

Kim mulled this one over. "Hmm, what a coincidence. Michael used to be a police detective."

"I was with the police, too," said Donna. "For ten years. Three of those years I was Michael's partner. It turned out that eventually both of us needed a change—so here we are."

"Michael's a writer now and you're his assistant?"

"Yes," Donna said irritably.

Kim couldn't really see Donna as anyone's assistant. She appeared more the type to tell *other* people what to do.

Nothing about this seemed quite right.

CHAPTER ELEVEN

A FEW MOMENTS LATER, Kim and Donna reached the neighborhood park. With its lush grass and shade trees, it was a denial of Tucson's desert setting. If you didn't know better, you'd almost think you were in New England. Such was the power of wealth; it defied even geography.

A couple of young children played on the swing sets, but the older kids were showing off on their bikes down at the far end of the park. Heading that way, Kim barely managed to keep up with Donna. How on earth did the woman move so fast? She wasn't particularly tall, didn't have long legs. She just seemed propelled along by that irrepressible energy of hers.

Andy sat astride his bike, watching the other kids but keeping something of a distance from them.

"Boy, is he in trouble," Donna said.

Kim plunked herself down on a bench. "Just wait for him here," she advised. "Let him see you and then wonder whether or not you're going to come after him. It's much more effective than the usual berating."

"A dose of psychology?" Donna asked.

"You could call it that."

Donna considered the plan and then sat down beside Kim. "You sound like you know what you're doing."

"Trust me."

They waited. It didn't take long for Andy to spot them. For a second or two it seemed as if he'd go wheeling off, but then he hesitated. He pretended he hadn't seen them, after all. Five minutes passed, perhaps more. At last the suspense seemed too much for the boy. He rode slowly toward Kim and Donna, stopping some yards away.

"Hello, Andy," Kim said.

He frowned. His dark curly hair was rumpled so that he looked just like his dad. Kim felt that poignant longing inside and tried to fight it. She saw the bandages still on Andy's leg and arm, the stitches standing out above his eyebrow. A hint of a shiver went through her in spite of the heat. Could Michael be right? That the glass crashing down *hadn't* been an accident? That someone had tampered with it?

"Dammit, Andy," Donna said as if she could no longer contain herself. "You're supposed to stay with me when your father's not around. What the hell were you thinking?"

His frown deepened. "If I can't talk like that, you can't, either."

"The *hell* I can't."

"I don't like being stuck in the house all day," Andy said.

"So you want to go to the park, we'll go together," Donna returned. "That's the way it has to be."

"I can take care of myself."

Kim understood the problem. As an eleven-year-old, it would be humiliating to have "Aunt Donna" escorting you everywhere you went. "We're going to sit here a while longer," Kim said. "Just don't go out of sight."

Andy stared at her, seeming to take her measure. She gazed back. And she sensed it again—some unspoken affinity between them, as if they knew and understood each other's thoughts.

Andy gave no outward sign, though. His gaze slid from hers and he pedaled away, going once again to hover a little beyond the other kids.

"What I really want to do is rake him over the coals," Donna said.

"Plenty of time for that later," Kim told her. "At least this way he gets to keep up the front that he has some independence." She paused for a moment. "I wonder what your instructions were," she went on. "You're too... tough to be a baby-sitter. Did Michael tell you to keep Andy away from me?"

Donna gave Kim a measured glance.

"No one's that overprotective without a reason," Kim continued, battling her disappointment. She already knew that Michael didn't trust her. Why did she expect that to change?

Donna slumped back against the bench. "Look," she said, "Mike's not a bad guy. He's just had some lousy luck in the past. Things he's had to take care of on his own because nobody else could. Things *no one* should have to handle alone."

"Try being just a little more oblique," Kim said caustically.

"I wish I could tell you more," Donna replied. "But it's not up to me."

Kim asked herself why she was sitting on this bench having this frustrating conversation. "I'm wondering," she said, "exactly what kind of research you do for Michael."

"Oh, you know how writers are," Donna said airily. "They always want you to check this or that."

"Really."

Donna gazed at her. "What's the story, Kim? I mean, you seem to be digging for something. But Mike and I work well together, always have—at least, until lately." Donna put a hand on her stomach. "Ever since my little 'pregnancy,' I'll admit things haven't gone quite as well."

"I'm not obtuse," Kim said. "I realize you just deflected the conversation—very neatly. It almost worked."

Donna showed her irritation again; she certainly was prickly. "Look, I can't talk to you about Mike. It's not my place."

Kim wondered how she'd gotten herself into this. Somehow Donna made her feel as if she was prying for details of Michael Turner's personal life.

"I don't want to know about Michael." As soon as she said it, she knew it was a lie. She forced herself to go on. "All I'm saying is that something doesn't seem exactly right."

"I shouldn't even be telling you *this* much," Donna said as if Kim hadn't spoken. "Mike's just gone through a difficult divorce. I have nothing against Jill, believe me, but she really was a pain about the whole thing. She fought with him on every little detail. The custody arrangement was the worst. You know, it's a miracle he even got Andy for the summer."

Kim looked across the park to where Michael's son remained on the very edge of the group. She knew what it felt like to be on the outside, pretending you didn't want to belong but deep down wishing you could.

"I can tell Michael's a good father," she said. "Overprotective, yes, but still a good father."

"Can't argue with that," Donna said, resting her arm against the top of the bench. "Mike's the best. I wouldn't want anyone else as my partner."

"So you were both homicide detectives," Kim said thoughtfully.

"Yes, but we knew each other from way back, when we were both still in uniform. Mike went up through the ranks a whole lot faster than I did. It was really something to see. He just had a drive about him, so relentless, so *complete.*" Donna gave a reminiscent smile. "Have you ever been around a man who believes totally in the work he's doing? Who sees the meaning and just goes after it? That was Mike—some time ago."

Meaning. It was what Kim sought in her own life. She didn't seem very good at finding it yet—that was the problem. But the way Donna described it, she made it sound as if Michael had been almost too dedicated to his job.

Kim thought about other men she'd known. Her father, struggling along with that small restaurant. He'd kept at it only because it was something he knew, something he could depend on in all the erratic ups and downs of his marriage. And then there was Stan of course, trying to declare his independence from the Bennett family by setting up his own investment firm. He'd tried putting together vague, grandiose deals that never quite came through. Sophie had continually bailed him out of one fix after another; so much for his independence.

Michael sounded very different than either Kim's father or husband. She moved restlessly on the park bench. "You say he used to be relentless. What changed?"

Donna settled herself more comfortably; in spite of her protests, apparently she liked talking about Michael. "Think about it," she said. "When you care that much about what you do, the danger is that you'll burn out. I could really see it when I became Mike's partner. I kept telling him he needed to ease up a little—have a life outside his job. He didn't listen of course. But then we worked on this one case..." The timber of Donna's voice changed, almost imperceptibly. "I can't go into details, but let's just say it wasn't a good experience. Through no fault of mine or Mike's, someone got hurt. And what happened after that with Mike, I don't blame him—" She stopped abruptly, straightening. "Oh, hell. I shouldn't be telling you any of this."

Kim didn't buy it. Donna wasn't the type of person to let anything slip inadvertently. Whatever she'd said about Michael had been said on purpose.

That she had captured Kim's attention, there was no doubt. Now, more than ever, Kim couldn't stop thinking about Michael. Donna had described a man of integrity, but also one of dark undercurrents. It was all very puzzling and, yes, disturbing.

Kim found herself shivering. She got up from the bench. "You're right. You shouldn't be telling me about him."

"I guess I just wanted you to know that he's all right. Not someone you have to worry about." Donna seemed very earnest, and that in itself put Kim on her guard.

"I'm sure you can handle Andy on your own now," she said.

"This time he's not getting out of my sight," Donna answered firmly.

"Goodbye, then." Kim gave one more look in Andy's direction. Still on the outside... She started to walk away.

"Hey, Kim—thanks."

Kim glanced back. "What for?" she asked dryly.

Donna shrugged. "I don't know. Maybe for listening to me complain about my mother-in-law and my husband's big mouth."

Kim wasn't convinced by the other woman at all. There was too much unspoken here, too much Kim didn't understand.

Donna stood now, as if she, too, had grown restless. And that was when Kim saw it, just a glimpse as Donna's vest rumpled away from her shirt—the dark sleek metal of a gun tucked into a holster.

"THAT HAS GOT TO BE the ugliest bush I've ever seen," Donna said.

Michael tried to ignore her. He dug the shovel into the ground, clearing away more rocky dirt. The bush lay on its side next to him, roots swathed in damp burlap, tufts of evergreen sprouting from its branches. The thing reminded him of a gnarled corpse with a bad haircut.

"Sophie Bennett is going to have your head for planting it in her backyard," Donna said. "I don't think there's anything in our contract that says we can desecrate her property."

"Her son trimmed the damn thing. Seems it ought to come back to her." Michael didn't appreciate the chain of his thoughts. Thinking about Stan Bennett and Sophie Bennett led his mind straight to Kim.

Lovely, alluring, solitary Kim, who may or may not have killed her husband. Why couldn't Michael's instincts give him the answer? Maybe because they were more mixed up than ever with his attraction to Kim.

He regarded the bush sourly. He also regarded Donna sourly. She wasn't high on his list of favorite people right now.

Donna, from long practice, seemed able to read his gaze accurately. "I didn't have any choice, Mike," she said. "When are you going to understand that? I had to divert her attention. She's suspicious about us."

"And you made her less suspicious," Michael said.

Donna took a long swallow of her Coke. "Damn, but it's hot. Think I could convince Brad to move to Antarctica?"

Michael only looked at her. And at last she let out an explosive sigh. "I didn't tell her anything incriminating. I just dropped a few hints about Jill and about police work—enough to get her thinking. Believe me, that wasn't difficult. She likes talking about you."

"Maybe you could explain your logic to me," he said grimly. "I didn't seem to get it the first time."

Donna lowered herself carefully into a lawn chair, balancing the Coke on her rounded stomach. That pillow in her pants effected an amazing transformation. It made her move slowly, heavily, as if now she could take all the time in the world to get things done.

"It's perfectly logical," she said. "Kim Bennett was starting to wonder what type of research I do for you, and I wanted to give her something else to think about."

"You're forgetting something. It was your bright idea to call yourself my research assistant."

Donna gave an elaborate shrug. "You have to admit that was quick thinking. The day of the accident I pretty much had to come up with something on the spur of the moment. And I like the sound of it. Doing research could be just my type of thing."

Michael returned to his shoveling. He wished Donna would lose that pillow. Ever since this crazy pregnancy scheme, she hadn't been herself—she'd been messing up. In their line of work, they couldn't afford to mess up.

Which brought him right back to Kim. He didn't like her knowing about his failed marriage. Jill's resentment of his work, her jealousy almost, all the little ways she'd tried to get back at him, the confidences she'd turned against him when she saw her chance.

Michael didn't want Kim Bennett knowing about any of that, but he wasn't happy about the deceptions, either.

"Too many lies," he said.

Donna peered at him over her Coke. "What are you talking about?"

"Exactly that—too many lies. Between all of us. Kim, you, me..."

"Don't forget Andy," Donna said. "Mike, you haven't told him about your dad yet. He knows something's up, but he can't figure out what. That's why he's acting the way he is, rebelling and all. You can't just keep him holed up here or at the community center the way you've been doing."

The trouble with Donna was she always said what she was thinking. Michael dug the hole deeper, the physical activity doing nothing to relieve the tension in his muscles. He really did believe that Franklin Turner had been bluffing about having contacted Andy. But he couldn't be sure about the future, and that was why he had to protect his son. Sometimes protecting another person meant not telling the whole truth. Michael wasn't happy about it, but he saw no other choice.

"Andy's a child," he said. "That's different."

Donna placed a hand on her stomach and studied it. "So you think we should be completely aboveboard with our murder suspect. Tell her who we are and invite her over for tea."

"I'm saying that you've made the situation worse. It's bad enough that I kissed her."

"You what? Oh, Lord, Mike, where did you kiss her?"

"In a warehouse." He set the shovel aside and pulled the burlap away from the shrub's roots. They looked anemic and scraggly.

Donna groaned. "Oh, no. We're not talking some innocent little peck on the cheek here, are we? Mike . . . you kissed her on the *mouth*, didn't you?"

"Hold the bush," he said.

Donna set her Coke down with a thump. "I don't believe it. You've spent the last half hour telling me how I've botched things, how I've behaved unpardonably, and now it turns out you *kissed* her. That makes me look like a saint!"

He'd decided that the kiss was pertinent information he ought to share with his partner. He'd hoped that would help him to get some perspective on it. So far no revelations had occurred to him, and all his partner could do was babble about it.

"The bush," he said.

Donna lumbered to her feet and waddled over to him. She grabbed hold of the shrub, hoisting it upright.

"Rule number one in the detective's handbook," she said. "Never kiss a suspect on the mouth."

"Put the bush right there," he said, ignoring Donna's remark. "That's good."

"Nothing is good. Mike, don't you realize? Maybe she really did kill her husband. And you're getting involved with her."

"I'm not involved." He wished he could convince himself. He dumped a bag of peat moss over the roots, then began shoveling dirt on top of that.

"Sure, she's a likable person," Donna said, as if arguing with herself. "She *seems* on the up and up. But that doesn't necessarily mean a thing."

He tamped down the soil. "You can let go now."

Donna stepped back and observed his handiwork. "Definitely the ugliest bush I've ever seen," she said gloomily. "Mike, what are you going to do?"

He stared at the shrub. "Water it. See if it grows."

"Mike, you know I'm talking about Kim."

His gaze strayed next door. From here he had a decent view of Kim's drive. Her Jag was parked there; from observing her habits, he knew that she didn't like to use the garage. In half an hour or so she'd be leaving for her exercise class. Yes, he knew her habits, all right. But did he know the things that really mattered?

Donna was watching him with a worried look on her face. "Mike, you're getting in deep, aren't you?"

He thought about Kim: her beauty, her pride...her aloneness. And he didn't have an answer.

At first Michael didn't even recognize Melissa Jacobs—didn't spot the young girl beneath all the hair and makeup, the two-hundred-dollar dress and the high-heeled shoes. In fact, he'd walked right by her several times without realizing who she was, pretending to be just another browser at the Oasis Flower Boutique.

He'd heard she was working here; he'd tracked the information down from a friend of a friend of a friend of a friend. Melissa was a clerk at a flower store downtown . . . she was living with some man . . . he had a family on the side . . .

Maybe that was to be expected. A lot of teenagers ran away from home in order to hasten the demise of their childhood. They were anxious to shed the protective shells of their parents and live like adults, drink like adults, smoke like adults, make all the same damn mistakes as adults.

Michael had to suppress the urge to grab hold of young Melissa, tell her what a godawful brat she was being and drag her home to her parents. But things were never that simple.

"Hello," Michael said in his best customer-needs-assistance voice. "I'm looking for—"

"She's mad at you, huh," Melissa said in a conspiratorial tone. "Go with the mums. No woman can stay mad long with an armful of mums."

Melissa came and stood beside him, running her hands through a tub of purple mums. Her actions were gentle and confident, as if she enjoyed what she was doing. Yet her eyes looked tired, and Michael wondered if her new life was all it had been cracked up to be.

"You sure seem to know what you're doing there," Michael said. "Like you've been handling flowers all your life."

"Thanks," Melissa said. "It's something my mother taught me. Mom always did have a way with plants. Roses mainly."

"And she passed the gift to you," was Michael's response. "That's how it should be, people's special talents handed down to their children." Perhaps he was taking things too fast with this Melissa. He knew from experience you should never get too personal too quickly when you were trying to get information out of someone, or trying to gain their confidence. And right now that was what Michael needed from Melissa. If he had any hope of ever reuniting this runaway with her parents, he needed to gain her confidence.

Melissa didn't say anything, but her lips puckered slightly, making her face look every bit as young as her sixteen years, despite the makeup. Michael decided to change the subject. "Hi," he said. "My name's Michael Turner. And you were right—there is a woman angry with me, and her name's Kim. Is everyone who comes in here trying to smooth a ruffled relationship?"

Melissa's face brightened noticeably. "Pretty much, if you want to know the truth. Oh, sure, we get the usual birthdays and anniversaries and such. But mainly people buy flowers when they've done something wrong and someone's mad at them. It's a shame really, but at least it allows stores like this to stay in business. Shall I wrap some of these up for you? A dozen if you've worked late and missed dinner two nights in a row, two dozen if she's found out you wrecked the car, and three dozen if it's major trouble—you know, an affair, you quit your job to join a circus, that kind of thing.''

Michael gazed at Melissa. He couldn't help but like her. She had an easy way about her, a sweet demeanor and a sense of humor. It was hard to imagine such a nice young girl out on her own, involved with a married man.

''How about a single solitary mum. Can that be arranged?''

''Wow. You never said you were trying to seduce her. Let's see . . . yes, here's the one. I'll wrap it up special . . . for Kim.'' Melissa disappeared around a counter. And that left Michael wondering what the hell his life had come to, when a runaway in one case he was working on was wrapping a flower for a suspect in another.

KIM PACED OFF a section of the warehouse. She couldn't say exactly why she was doing it. Somehow it just felt like a good idea to know the dimensions of this place.

What would she do with it, though, if she really did buy it? Michael had asked that question and she hadn't known what to say.

Michael Turner. She had come here seeking peace of mind, but there was nothing peaceful about thoughts of Michael. Even now she felt that swirl of emotion inside her. Confusion, desire, yearning—without even knowing what it was she yearned for.

She wanted to banish Michael from her head—and her heart. Already she had let him come too close to her. It was right in this warehouse that he'd kissed her, standing almost in this exact spot. . . .

"Fool," she whispered fiercely to herself. But the memory of his touch lingered. Only yesterday he'd come to her house with a flower in hand—a single chrysanthemum, the lovely kind that was such a deep pink it seemed almost purple. Michael had left without saying a word, but the flower remained another taunting reminder of him.

She paced off another section and tried to think about something else. Discarded bits of paper rustled under her feet. Michael was right—this *had* once been a furniture warehouse. From what Kim had been able to learn, the company had gone out of business more than twenty years before, and no one had used the building since. It seemed such a waste. The brick was solid, the windows only in need of a good cleaning. She would sweep out all the debris, and then...

Then what? It was so frustrating, being drawn to a place and not knowing why. Kim bent down, rummaging through the old papers on the floor. She already knew that most of them were sales invoices, as if someone long ago had dumped out the contents of a file drawer. Kim picked up one of the invoices at random. It listed a table, some chairs, a cabinet. She wondered what had happened all those years ago, when the furniture company had failed and closed its doors. She picked up another invoice. A sofa, an armoire, a rolltop desk.

It was then the idea began to take shape in her mind. She knelt there, hardly daring to move as the first excitement went through her. A spark of inspiration—she couldn't call it anything else. It made her smile. But was it workable? Was it really something she could do?

A scrabbling noise came from one of the far corners. It was a very faint sound. Kim glanced up, instantly wary. For all she knew, the place had mice.

She listened, remaining immobile as she crouched there. And then it came again, louder this time, a rustling. Kim realized she had made almost that exact same sound herself when she'd walked across the papers on the floor.

She rose silently to a standing position and strained to see through the dimness. The windows were so streaked with grime that they allowed little sunshine to enter. The corners of the room lurked in shadows.

Kim's mouth had gone dry. There it came again. Did she only imagine it was the noise of someone's foot sliding across the floor, almost a taunting sound?

She glanced toward the door. It seemed very far away just now, the warehouse suddenly too large, too filled with secrets. But she took a step and then another toward the door, willing herself not to panic.

The sliding sound came again as if in echo to her own steps. Heart pounding, Kim once again measured the distance to the door. Still much too far away. Should she make a dash toward it or move cautiously? If only she had a weapon of some kind . . .

The rustling, sliding noise came closer. And Kim saw no choice. She sprinted full-out across the warehouse.

Someone tackled her from behind and she went crashing to the floor. A hand jammed over her mouth, shoving her head back. She struggled wildly, but her attacker had her pinned. Now her heart pounded as if to burst. She tried to scream, just as fingers squeezed around her throat.

CHAPTER TWELVE

SHE COULDN'T BREATHE. Nothing else mattered right now but that terrible lack of air. The hand at her throat felt as if it were made of iron, crushing her windpipe. She clawed at it, frantically twisting her body. And still she couldn't breathe, a painful pulsing inside her head. Terror surged through her, and fury. She struggled all the more.

From somewhere very distant she heard a crashing noise, and the pulsing in her head seemed to crescendo. But no—it was the sound of footsteps racing toward her. And suddenly the hand left her throat. Like a miracle, her attacker leapt away from her and vanished.

Gasping, she started to raise herself, a wave of nausea washing over her. She heard a voice speak urgently—Michael's voice, wonderfully real.

"Kim! Kim, are you all right?"

She couldn't speak, her throat raw, but she managed a nod.

"Stay here," he commanded. And then he was gone, chasing across the warehouse. She fought her way to her knees, the nausea threatening to engulf her. Darkness clouded her eyes at the same time. *No!* She wouldn't give in, wouldn't faint. She knelt there, shaking, forcing her head to clear. She took in great gulps of air, as if she would never get enough. The breath burned inside, and still she needed more.

She didn't know how many minutes passed—she didn't care, as long as she could breathe. But then she heard footsteps moving toward her again. Michael? She couldn't take the chance it wasn't him. Scrambling to her feet and fighting another swell of nausea, she headed toward the door.

"Kim." It *was* Michael. She stopped and he took hold of her. It appeared he had reached her just in time. She leaned against him, partaking of his strength. At last she tried to speak.

"Michael...who...?" The words rasped in her throat.

"I don't know. He got away through one of the windows in back. No sign of him outside. He's good, whoever he is. Are you sure you're all right?"

The thought came unbidden: she'd be all right as long as she was in his arms. It seemed a weakness, clinging to him like this, but she couldn't let go.

He smoothed the hair back from her face. "He must've been waiting for you inside. Otherwise I would've seen him."

She didn't know what he meant, and at the moment she didn't care. "Hold me," she whispered. "Just...hold me."

"I am. I'm here."

She felt the warmth of his body against hers, and that was what she needed. In spite of the stifling air of this building, she was so very cold. She trembled in Michael's arms.

"Kim, I have to ask you... Did you get a look at him?"

"No." The words came with difficulty. "He grabbed me from behind. And I think... I think he was wearing something over his face, but I can't even be sure of that."

"It's okay," he murmured. "We'll figure out what's happening."

Suddenly she wanted more than his comfort. She turned her face, her mouth finding his. She was awkward in her haste. Her throat still hurt, everything hurt, but still she kissed Michael, demanding he kiss her back.

He didn't answer that demand. Instead, he moved his lips only gently against hers and then broke the contact between them.

"It's okay," he repeated, his tone oddly impersonal.

The emotions churned inside her, more a tumult than ever—unmet desire, this craven need to have Michael go on holding her. But at last she had the will to pull away from him and stand on her own. It was unfortunate that her legs threatened to buckle underneath her.

Michael steadied her. "Easy," he said.

"I'm... fine. Just delayed reaction." It terrified her to think what would have happened if he hadn't been around today.

"Michael," she said, the pain in her throat finally starting to subside a little, "why are you here? I want to know what's going on."

He didn't speak for a moment. "Maybe I'm just watching out for you," he said at last.

"Somehow I don't think so." She bent to search for her purse; she'd dropped it when she'd been attacked. She located the purse, only to realize that its contents were strewn on the floor. Why couldn't she have kept the damn thing closed? Suddenly that felt like a monumental mistake, as if keeping her purse snapped securely would have prevented everything else from occurring today. She realized she was being irrational—more delayed reaction, she supposed. Knowing as much didn't make her feel any better. She groped for her wallet, her comb, her keys.

Michael bent down to help.

"I'm fine," she said. "I have everything."

"Kim, it's normal to be shook up by something like this." He sounded too reasonable, too reassuring, and her anger spilled over.

"Is that true?" she said mockingly. "Is *anything* normal about this? Maybe being an ex-detective, you know all about it. Maybe events like this were commonplace in your work. Obviously you're very adept at calming the hysterical victim."

"No," he said, his voice suddenly harsh. "Nothing like this is commonplace. If something had happened to you, something worse... I don't even want to think about it, Kim."

She heard the intensity in his words, and somehow she wasn't ready for that. She scrambled to her feet, bringing her purse with her, and headed toward the door. It was a relief to find that she could walk perfectly well on her own. When she emerged outside, all she had to do was get into her car and drive away from this place—away from Michael. Maybe then she could think, figure out what to do next.

She'd barely unlocked the car before Michael took her keys from her. "I'll drive you home," he said.

"That won't be necessary."

"You don't have any choice," he said. "Donna can pick up my Jeep later."

Kim glanced around, but there were no other vehicles on the street. "Where *is* your Jeep?" she asked.

He waited just a fraction too long before answering. "Around the corner. Out of sight."

"Dammit, Michael, tell me what's going on!"

"Get in and I'll explain." He sounded curt. Before she knew it, Kim was ensconced in the passenger seat of her own car, Michael taking the wheel. But he didn't start the engine. He just sat there beside her, staring out through the windshield. Kim studied his profile. Every line was severe, uncompromising. Even the dark hair falling over his forehead hinted at some implacable quality inside him. A troubling thought occurred to Kim: a woman could break herself against such a man.

"I followed you here today," he said. "I'd already told you—it's not a good idea to come to this place alone."

"You followed me...and you parked around the corner so I wouldn't see you?" A strange prickle went along her spine, but she was indignant more than anything else. "Why the subterfuge, Michael?"

"I decided to take a look around," he said, ignoring her question. "I checked the outside of the building and didn't find anything unusual. Which means your attacker was already waiting for you inside. He knows your schedule—he's been watching you."

She heard the cold certainty in his voice and she didn't like it. "You can't know any of this. Besides, I don't follow a set pattern."

"Everyone follows a pattern," Michael said, his voice emotionless. "It's easy for someone to discover what you do and when you do it without your knowing."

She thought about the gray sedan following her that day, but she wanted to reject the implications. "You make it sound so deliberate," she burst out. "Someone watching me . . . I hate that! Maybe he really was just the local neighborhood creep lying in wait for anyone—"

"Does that seem logical?" Michael's voice still had a disquieting lack of emotion.

"This time you truly are frightening me," she said.

"I want you to see how serious the situation is."

She closed her eyes, and suddenly it was upon her—the memory of that hand jerking her head back, then tightening around her throat. A rush of adrenaline went through her, as if even now she had to fight for her life.

"Of course I know how serious it is." She tried to keep her voice from shaking.

"I just want you to be safe, Kim."

He was doing it again, sounding impersonal, his tone distant. She could too easily picture him as a police detective, gravely explaining the situation to some hapless victim, offering reassurances but remaining objective all the while.

She wanted more from him. She wanted him to take her in his arms and blot out the terrible thing that had happened.

"I think I should go home," she said, managing to keep her voice quite steady, after all.

He started the car then, and they drove away from the warehouse. They traveled in silence for some time, but Kim found she couldn't contain herself.

"Michael," she said, "maybe you could explain at least one thing. Why does your assistant—your *research* assistant—carry a gun?"

He glanced at her briefly. "Donna certainly has been talkative."

"She didn't say anything. I saw it."

Michael didn't speak for another long while. Kim was feeling more and more wound up. What would it take to get an answer from him, a *real* answer, for once?

"I can't tell you everything right now," he said at last. "I just want you to trust me."

"You haven't given me a lot of reason to," she pointed out.

"Maybe that's what trust is. Believing even when you don't have a lot of reason to." He spoke almost as if to himself. But his answer didn't satisfy her. She didn't want blind faith. She wanted Michael to stop being so mysterious and tell her everything. And then, after that, she still wanted him to take her in his arms.

She would have laughed at herself, but it seemed her entire body hurt. A shock to the system, that was how it felt. This intensified longing for Michael's touch had to be part of the shock. If only she could get home, crawl into bed and shut out the world for a little while, she'd be able to cope. With Michael. With everything.

Meanwhile, he sat beside her, handling the Jaguar smoothly and skillfully. His hand looked powerful and masculine on the gearshift knob. Surely he wouldn't use that power to hurt. And if she could believe that much about him, it was a measure of trust. A beginning at least.

Kim leaned back wearily in her seat. That was the joke right there. Because she didn't trust beginnings. She already knew how deceptive they could be.

The distance between the warehouse and Kim's neighborhood was more than a matter of miles. It had to do with attitude. The warehouse was the sort of place that got left behind. You moved on from there if you were lucky. Now, as Michael turned down the shady avenue leading to her own street, it struck Kim just how different this area was—permeated with an aura of self-confidence. This was the sort of neighborhood people aspired to; it was an end in itself. If you made it here, you settled down and didn't think about moving anywhere else. You congratulated yourself on being safe and snug at last.

But maybe it wasn't all that safe. Kim thought about the accident with the window. She didn't believe in coincidence, and she knew Michael didn't, either.

When he pulled into her driveway, she tried to give no sign of her unease. "I guess I should thank you, Michael. For...saving me. It sounds so inadequate, but you were certainly there when I needed you, and—"

"You're staying with me tonight," he said.

Somehow he always seemed able to spark an argument in her. "That's ridiculous," she protested. "I'll be fine. I'll lock myself in and turn on the burglar alarm—it's a very good one." She wondered if she was trying to convince herself or him.

"You can pack a bag and bring it over to my place," he said inexorably.

"Do you always try to take charge of people's lives?"

"When they've just suffered an attack—yes."

Suddenly she couldn't argue with him anymore. She knew she wouldn't feel comfortable in her own house tonight—forget crawling into bed and shutting out the world. But why did Michael Turner have to be so clinical about the whole thing? He offered her refuge as if it was the same he'd do for anyone.

"All I really need is my toothbrush and a few other things," she said reluctantly. "I'll be right back." She got out of the car and went to her front door. It was no surprise to find Michael right on her heels. He was certainly being protective. She could honestly say that as long as she was with him, she didn't fear that anyone would try to attack her again.

Once inside, she climbed the stairs, Michael right behind her. When she went into the bathroom, he poked his head in and glanced around.

"Aren't you overdoing it a bit?" she asked as she opened the medicine cabinet.

"What do you think, Kim?"

"I'm glad you're here," she admitted. "After all," she added hastily, "you *are* an ex-policeman, and you certainly seem to know what you're doing...."

"Right," he said gravely. He disappeared, and she could hear him prowling around in her bedroom across the hall.

Undeniably, his presence made her feel safe from physical harm. But in another way it disturbed her, threatening the solitude she'd created in this house. She could hear him sliding open a closet door.

"Lord," came his voice. "You have enough clothes in here to outfit a small town."

With her toothbrush and makeup kit in hand, she crossed the hall to the bedroom. "There was a time when I went overboard," she said defensively. "I was ... frivolous."

"And you're not anymore?" The humor in his tone was unexpected.

"Everyone needs a little frivolity," she said. She took a small overnight case from the closet and set it on her bed. In went the toothbrush, the makeup kit and a pair of men's pajamas from the bureau drawer.

She saw Michael looking at the pajamas. "They didn't belong to my husband, if that's what you're thinking," she said. "I bought them for myself. They're just more comfortable than the ... female variety."

"You don't have to explain, Kim."

Now she could swear he was perusing her king-size bed. "I didn't share it with my husband," she said involuntarily. "He slept ... elsewhere."

Michael didn't say anything in response, just stood there looking at her. She felt the blood heating her face. Why had she confessed this deficiency in her marriage? It made her feel vulnerable, exposed, as if Michael could divine all the secrets of her heart. "Anyway," she went on hurriedly, "I'm almost ready."

"Take your time," he said. "I'll check the other rooms." With that, he disappeared into the hall again.

Kim grabbed some underwear and stuffed it into her case. Now all she needed was a change of clothes for tomorrow. She decided to forgo the selection in the closet, packing, instead, her favorite shorts and a light cotton blouse. She snapped the case shut, listening to Michael as he opened doors in the other rooms. He certainly was thorough.

After a few moments he came back. "No sign that anybody has been here," he said.

"You expected a break-in?"

"Just considering all the possibilities," he said.

Suddenly she wanted to get out of there. "I'm ready. Let's go."

They walked across to the house next door. Michael sat her down in the living room, then pressed the button on the wall. The wet bar magically appeared. He poured two brandies and handed one to her.

"I really am okay," she said.

"Kim, it takes a while to recover from something like that."

She couldn't argue with him now and she sipped the brandy. Although it burned her throat on the way down, it felt good...warm...relaxing. Settling deeper into the sofa, she examined evidence of the two bachelors: a pair of socks cast willy-nilly on the floor, a laptop computer residing on the carved chest, a basketball wedged in a corner. Little details, the kind that said a place was lived in. Kim had never liked overly neat and fussy houses; a certain amount of clutter was necessary.

Michael went into the kitchen to make a phone call. He could have used the phone in here—Kim surmised that he wanted privacy. She heard the low murmur of his voice, the words indistinct. She sipped more brandy, feeling its warmth bloom inside her. Slipping off her sneakers, she folded her legs up on the sofa. She tried to tell herself not to get comfortable here, but it was too late; already she felt the tension drifting from her. It was a very welcome sensation after the day's trauma. The afternoon had mellowed, sunlight spilling into the room like liquid gold. Kim felt as if she could sit here forever, cradling the brandy, listening to the deep murmur of Michael's voice.

A few moments later he came back into the room. "Andy won't be back tonight," he said. "He's bunking at Doug's—a friend of his from the old days. He'll be fine."

"You sound like you're trying to convince yourself," Kim said. "Michael, aren't you just a little overprotective of your son?"

He sat down across from her. "I have to watch out for him. No one else can do it."

"He's eleven years old," Kim pointed out. "He needs to start proving he can look out for himself a little. That's why he made his getaway to the park."

"He has no excuse for that," Michael said. "He was instructed to stay with Donna—no exceptions."

"You sound almost like a military commander."

"Having a kid will do that to you."

To Kim, his words could only imply one thing—*she* didn't have any children, so who was she to judge? She sat up a little straighter, the brandy no longer making her feel so warm and relaxed.

"I'm sure you told Donna to keep Andy away from me. That's it, isn't it? I'm the reason you're so damn...overprotective."

He didn't bother to deny her words. He just sat there, gazing off to some unknowable distance, his expression brooding. Kim leaned forward and set her glass down. She thought about returning to her house and despised her reluctance to be alone over there. It had come to this—she would rather be with a man who distrusted her than face her fears on her own.

At last Michael spoke. "I've already told you, Kim. When I look at a situation, I consider all the possibilities."

"I don't understand," she said flatly. "Me harming Andy—how can that be one of the possibilities?"

The look he gave her was constrained. "The situation is more difficult now. We know that someone is trying to harm you."

She could no longer sit still. She stood, moving restlessly about the room. "I still don't understand. How can you have so little faith in people? So little trust?"

"Kim, think about it. If you had a child, wouldn't you err on the side of caution?"

She hated his words, hated the yearning they invoked in her. But she couldn't deny them.

"Yes," she said at last, reluctantly. "If I had a child... I would do everything I could to keep him safe."

"Come sit down again," Michael said.

She ignored him and for a long moment stared out the living-room window. She could see her house from here—the gracious lines of adobe, the slope of the red-tile roof. It was a beautiful place, but right now it seemed to belong to a stranger. She had fought so hard to make it her own, something more than another Bennett stronghold. Had the fight been worth it? Had she succeeded?

Finally she did go sit down, curling her legs up on the sofa as before. She studied Michael. "I know you care about Andy more than anything. I don't suppose I could respect you otherwise."

"Respect," he echoed, his voice hard. "Don't be too quick to respect anyone, Kim."

"You're being cynical again," she said. "Do you realize just how much Andy takes after you? Both of you are so determined to barricade yourselves behind the Turner skepticism."

If he was impressed by her insight, he kept it well hidden. "We're off the subject," he said. "Andy's friend Doug—his father is with the police. I spoke to him just now on the phone and told him about your attacker. He's sending a patrol car down to the warehouse to really look the neighborhood over. Unfortunately I don't think they'll find anything. It's up to you and me to figure out what's going on."

Michael was using his clinical tone again, the one that had no doubt been very effective when *he* was with the police. Kim disliked it more and more.

"I have no idea why someone would want to hurt me," she said. "Unless one of the Bennetts sent someone to frighten me into selling my shares."

Michael didn't respond; he merely looked thoughtful, as if considering what she'd said.

"That was a joke," she told him. "My mother-in-law may be many things, but she's no terrorist."

"The other Bennetts—are you so sure about them?"

"Don't be ridiculous," she protested. "It really *was* a joke, Michael."

He leaned forward, his expression intent now. "Kim, you need to tell me everything you know about your husband's death."

She felt an iciness creep over her and wished they could talk about anything else. The brandy seemed like a good idea, after all. She picked up her snifter and took a long swallow. Unfortunately it could not reach that secret coldness inside her.

"I don't see how it matters," she said. "Besides, I don't know anything. Toward the end, Stan and I...we hardly exchanged confidences. I don't know what was going on in his life."

"There must be something," Michael persisted. "It's important, Kim."

"What are you trying to say? What happened this afternoon, it's related to Stan's death somehow?"

"Like I keep telling you. We have to consider all the possibilities."

Kim stared into Michael's dark brown eyes, sensing the turbulence he always kept under restraint. She couldn't prevent another tingle of apprehension going through her.

"Think back," he said. "Tell me about the night your husband died."

She closed her eyes briefly, trying to resist Michael's command. But that night was with her again. She couldn't avoid it, couldn't escape.

"I was already thinking about a divorce," she said, her voice barely above a whisper. "I'd told Stan that we needed to talk. He promised to come home at a certain time. He didn't." Kim took a steadying breath. "Finally I called his office. The phone rang forever and I was about to give up... but then he answered. He didn't even bother to invent a good excuse for not coming home. And I could tell that someone else was there with him. I just knew..." She didn't want to remember any more, but Michael would not leave it alone.

"How did you know someone was with your husband?"

"I didn't *really* know," she said, gazing into her empty brandy glass. "It was just a sense I had. An in-

stinct. That Stan was with another of his women." She
gave a humorless laugh. "I wasn't very rational after
that. I seem to recall throwing the telephone down,
some dramatic and completely useless gesture. I knew
for sure then I'd ask him for a divorce. The next
morning...that's when the police came and told me he
was dead." Kim listened to the sound of her own voice,
surprised she felt so little emotion. Even the humiliation was gone. Her husband had cheated on her, not
for the first time, and then he had died. It seemed sad
but distant.

Michael uttered something under his breath, something that sounded like a curse, and now he was the one
who stood restlessly.

"Kim," he said, "that wasn't in the police report."

She frowned at him. "You've read the report on my
husband's death? Why?"

"It doesn't matter right now," he said impatiently.
"But what you've just told me isn't in there."

Trust Michael to keep her off balance. "I explained
everything to the police," she said. "How I'd called
Stan and how he was still at the office. Very well, I may
have omitted the part about throwing down the telephone, but—"

"The report didn't say anything about your husband being with another woman." He spoke with that
cool lack of emotion, but it was enough to spark the
anger inside her.

"It was only a feeling," she said. "I didn't have any
proof. Besides, when I told the police about Stan never
coming home that night, I could tell exactly what they
were thinking. They reached the same conclusion *I* did.
They didn't need me to spell it out for them." Her voice
was trembling and she struggled to subdue it. She re-

membered the two detectives who had interviewed her, and the way they hadn't quite looked at her when she'd described her husband's habit of staying late at the office. They had seemed embarrassed for her, had seemed to pity her. Well, at least she didn't have to worry about that with Michael Turner. Clearly he wasn't wasting any pity on her at the moment.

"You told me before you didn't believe it was an accident," he said. "Your husband getting drunk, climbing into that car... trying to drive home."

"Who said he was headed for home?" she countered, tightening her fingers around the brandy glass. "It's more likely he was on his way somewhere else. Anywhere else."

Michael would allow her no peace. "But you still believe he was murdered. Who could have wanted to hurt him?"

"I don't know," she said, feeling inexplicably drained. She just wanted to be done with it. "Stan had his faults, but he rarely drank too much. Why he did that night—who knows." She leaned back tiredly, waiting for Michael to pursue her with more of his merciless questions. But he surprised her. He came over to her, took her glass, filled it with more brandy at the wet bar and returned it to her.

"I'm going to fix you dinner," he said, still in the same cool, emotionless tone. And then he disappeared into the kitchen.

CHAPTER THIRTEEN

KIM SWIRLED the brandy in her glass and reflected on the irony of her situation. She and Michael had just discussed the fact that her husband had been quite drunk on the night of his death, and now it seemed *she* was drinking too much. Certainly the brandy was affecting her, tingling through her body, luring her with its false warmth.

She could hear Michael opening and shutting cabinet doors—forceful sounds. He didn't seem like someone accustomed to being in the kitchen, rather, like someone who would get the job done, whatever it happened to be. And a new irony struck her: the fact that one minute Michael could be questioning her so relentlessly, and the next he could be preparing her something to eat.

It was evening now, the sunlight drifting toward dusk, soft shadows enveloping the room. Feeling a strange sense of unreality, Kim slid from the couch and went into the kitchen. She found Michael tearing the carton from a serving of frozen lasagna and tossing it into the microwave. A few other empty cartons were scattered on the counter.

"I've wondered," she said, "whether you were the type who cooked your son three-course meals or sent out for pizza. Now I know."

Michael shrugged. "Andy and I have worked out a system. We take turns using the microwave."

"Modern technology is wonderful, isn't it?"

He gave her an appraising glance. "Any better ideas?"

"Not for you, no," she said. "I can't picture you slaving over a hot stove." Truly there was nothing domestic about Michael's appearance. Against her will, Kim's gaze traveled over him. He was wearing a shirt of some soft, well-worn material, the sleeves rolled halfway up his arms. But the softness of that shirt only emphasized the lean strength of his body. Kim suspected he had not been the type of police detective to sit behind a desk. And here was irony yet again—Michael had changed his profession to do exactly that.

"How's the book going?" she asked. "And don't tell me you're still having trouble with your heroine."

"I am having trouble with her." He sounded gruff.

Kim sat down at the kitchen table, and several minutes passed while she considered the facts. "Michael, how much of this book of yours, this mystery novel, have you actually written?"

He didn't answer, and that was answer enough.

"You're not a writer at all, are you?"

Again no answer. Michael's expression had closed, the lines of his features obdurate. But now it was her turn to search for the truth.

"You haven't really left the police force, have you?" she asked, hearing the calmness in her own voice. "And neither has Donna—that would explain the gun. You're both still detectives, aren't you? Undercover, of course."

"Don't jump to conclusions," Michael said. The beeper on the microwave went off. He pulled the lasagna out, along with another entrée—something that looked like breaded fish. He should have stopped at the lasagna.

"You've read the report on Stan's death," she said. "It's only logical to assume you're still with the police. Dammit, Michael, why won't you tell me the truth?"

"You're wrong about my being a policeman," he said, his voice carrying utter conviction—and a tinge of regret. "I'm no longer with the department." He divided the lasagna and the fish onto two plates and carried them to the table. Kim wasn't hungry, and she was tempted to push her food away.

"You should eat," Michael said as if sensing her intent. "You're probably still suffering aftershocks."

Aftershock—that was a good word for everything to do with Michael Turner. There were always repercussions, unintended consequences—such as sitting here in his kitchen, wondering what it was that he was hiding.

She tasted the lasagna. It wasn't bad. Perhaps Michael was telling the truth about no longer being with the police. Kim thought about everything Donna had revealed that day in the park.

"Your assistant says you were dedicated to your work—almost too dedicated. And then something changed. Something about a case where someone got hurt."

She saw the way his face tightened.

"Donna has been talking too much lately. Seems to be a result of her 'pregnancy.'"

"At least I know the truth about that." Kim set down her fork and rubbed her forehead wearily. "What happened, Michael? If you really aren't with the police anymore, what changed? Obviously you didn't leave because of some overwhelming desire to be a writer."

He didn't seem to be eating his own food. "You've accused me of being too curious, Kim. But now you're doing the same."

The tension was building inside her again, all the unanswered questions in her life swirling in confusion. She ate a few more bites, but every motion was automatic.

"Something wrong with the fish?" Michael asked.

"Just the usual problem with instant food. The picture on the box doesn't always measure up to what's inside."

He took a bite of the fish himself. "It always tastes like this."

"How could I forget?" she said. "You've learned not to have high expectations."

"If I remember, that's a talent you want to acquire."

Now she did push her plate aside. "At least I don't have to worry about your providing a romantic, candlelight dinner," she said. "You sure aren't trying to sweep me off my feet, are you?"

"No," he said gravely. He looked the fish over more critically now. "It's not the best," he conceded. "Andy and I don't seem to notice these things when we're on our own. Maybe we should start paying more attention."

"I don't know," Kim said. "Being a connoisseur isn't everything you'd expect, either."

Michael gazed at her with disconcerting thoroughness. "Was your husband a connoisseur?"

Kim wished she'd never broached the subject. "Yes," she said after a moment. "In that way he was discerning. Good food...romantic music...and, yes, candlelight. He knew how to set the stage." Kim had fallen for every detail, not realizing how practiced Stan was. But that was a word that would never occur to her in describing Michael—practiced. She had the feeling that if he decided to make love to a woman, he would be straightforward about it. Elemental. He would use no devices, no tricks. He would simply...make love.

Kim stood, grabbing her plate and taking it to the sink. "Look, it's nothing personal against your cuisine. I'm just not hungry right now."

Michael came to stand beside her, taking the plate from her. "Relax," he said. "I'll get rid of the evidence."

She was too aware of his nearness. Here they stood, side by side in front of the sink, something that should have been prosaic. Instead, it seemed a situation fraught with unknowns.

She retreated to the other room. After a few seconds' hesitation, she poured herself more brandy and sat down. Drinking on a virtually empty stomach—not the greatest idea in the world, but right now she couldn't think of a better one. She heard the clatter of dishes from the kitchen—more forceful sounds. After a short time, Michael joined her. He pulled a chair toward the small computer sitting atop the carved chest.

"I have some work to do," he said. The suggestion was clear: she ought to find a way to keep herself occupied. A few books were piled on the chest, and she picked one up at random. It happened to be, of all things, a mystery novel.

She glanced speculatively at Michael as he booted up his computer.

"Andy likes to read those," he said. "I find them too unrealistic."

"That makes perfect sense," she said. "A mystery writer who finds mysteries . . . unrealistic."

"You don't believe I'm a writer, remember?"

He certainly seemed to be writing now, tapping away at his keyboard. Kim felt an almost overwhelming temptation to peer around and see what was on the screen. With an effort, she controlled herself.

She tried to concentrate on the mystery novel. Unfortunately the mystery of Michael was far more compelling. Her gaze kept straying to him over the top of the book. He worked with concentration, behaving as if he had completely forgotten her presence. His features were set in those grim lines, his hair falling over his forehead. What did she really know about him? She felt confident of only two facts: Michael Turner was a man of uncompromising loyalty when it came to his son, and he would be equally uncompromising tonight in protecting Kim from physical harm. But emotional harm . . . that was something else again.

Kim stood abruptly. "It really has been a stressful day," she said. "I think I'll turn in. Just tell me which room—I'll find the way."

Michael stopped typing and considered her thoughtfully. "You do look tired. But I won't oblige you to wander the house on your own. I already gave you a lousy dinner, after all. The least I can do is tuck you in . . . so to speak." Now he looked discontented, as if he regretted even the hint of impropriety in his jest. Without saying a word more, he retrieved her case from a corner and escorted her up the stairs. As they

walked down the hall, she caught glimpses of two bed-
rooms. One had an Atlanta Braves poster on the wall—
Andy's room, no doubt. The other had only bare walls
and a rumpled, unmade bed. Was that where Michael
spent his nights? Restless nights, from the look of it.

He opened a door for her near the end of the hall.
"Guest room," he announced. Kim peered inside and
saw her mother-in-law's undeniable touch: desert hues
of sage and sienna, just as in the rest of the house. Sophie had never learned that there could be too much of
a good thing.

The mattress in the room was bare. Michael and Kim
both studied it. "Be right back," he said. He vanished
down the hall, then reappeared a few moments later
with a pile of wrinkled sheets in his arms. "Clean," he
said. "I don't mind washing the stuff, but folding
laundry is a bit much—for an ex-cop, that is, and supposed mystery writer. And this is one area where Andy
definitely takes after his old man—he's never folded a
sheet in his life."

"Just leave them here," Kim said. "I'll make the
bed." But already Michael had taken a sheet and was
flapping it over the mattress. She went to the opposite
side and helped smooth it down. It was much too big.

"Hell...king, queen... Can't they label this stuff?"
said Michael.

"No matter. We'll just tuck it in." It seemed odd to
be making a bed with Michael. She glanced at him to
see if he found it peculiar, too, but he simply seemed to
be giving the task his usual forceful concentration.
Soon they had the bed in order, with the too-large
sheets and a pillow in a wrinkled case.

"You've really done quite enough," Kim said.
"You've been the perfect host."

"In other words, you'd like me to get lost."

If only it was that simple. The truth was, she wanted to be near him. No matter how he unsettled her and provoked her, she wanted to be with him.

"I think it would be best if I did spend some time alone," she lied.

He went around the room, checking the windows. "All secure," he said. "I'll be in the next room if you need me."

"Michael, you don't think anyone would try to get to me here . . . ?"

"No, I don't, but you already know I believe in being prepared for any possibility."

"Yes, I know," she murmured.

"You'll be safe, Kim, with me. I'll make sure of that."

She believed him. It was the ache of longing and need inside her that had her worried.

"Good night," he said.

"Good night, Michael."

He gazed at her, the expression in his eyes unreadable. And then he left, not quite closing the door behind him, the sound of his footsteps receding down the hall.

Kim sank down on the bed. It was barely dark outside; she never went to sleep this early. Why did she feel so tired?

Maybe her fatigue was a normal reaction, after what had happened today. Whatever the case, she certainly felt drained by her experience.

This guest room had its own small attached bathroom. Kim brushed her teeth, washed her face—all the bedtime rituals that had become second nature to her, but that seemed strange in Michael's house. Correction: her mother-in-law's house, occupied by Michael. Certainly he had left his own imprint on the place, a masculine aura that intruded even here.

After a moment's hesitation, she slipped off the tights she'd worn for her exercise class—it seemed aeons ago—and folded them neatly over a chair. She started to pull off her T-shirt but thought better of it, crawling into bed still half-clothed. Not that she didn't trust Michael Turner. But the thought of lying between the man's sheets wearing nothing at all didn't seem conducive to sleep. None of her thoughts about Michael seemed conducive to sleep.

Then she remembered that she'd packed her pajamas. Good. Pajamas were so... respectable. Crawling out of bed again, she went to her case and rummaged through it. She stripped and slid the pajamas on next to her bare skin. It had never seemed a sensual activity in the past; now, however, thoughts of Michael Turner jumped to mind even as she buttoned the pajama top.

She got back into bed, yanking the sheet up under her chin. The room was pleasant, temperature well modulated by the house's climate control. But Kim's temperature refused to modulate. She felt disturbingly warm as she lay here in Michael's bed.

It was only the guest-room bed, she reminded herself fiercely. And Michael was only her next-door neighbor, watching out for her. Nothing more.

But she knew it wasn't that simple. Michael Turner had something to hide. Until she knew what it was, she couldn't feel genuinely safe with him. Not in the way that really mattered.

She switched off the bedside lamp. Because the door was slightly ajar, she could still see a sliver of light from the hall. She found that comforting—and wished she didn't need the comfort. Turning her head on the pillow, she closed her eyes. In spite of her fatigue, she was so keyed up she couldn't believe she'd ever be able to rest. And yet, miraculously, sleep came.

IT WAS HAPPENING all over again. She couldn't breathe. Those fingers were tightening around her throat, taking air away from her. Taking life...

Kim tried to scream. Gasping, she awakened with a jolt. It had been a nightmare, she told herself. Only a nightmare. But she felt completely disoriented, not remembering at first where she was. When she groped for the bedside lamp, she couldn't find it.

The sliver of light in the doorway widened to reveal a tall, masculine silhouette. Kim's heart pounded. Making a sound of protest, she started to scramble from the bed.

But it was Michael, moving to sit beside her, reaching out to hold her. "It's all right," he said. "Everything's all right."

She couldn't stop shaking. She leaned into his arms, pressing her face against his chest. "I don't know what happened," she whispered.

"You were calling out in your sleep. Crying, almost."

"It felt so real," she said. "I couldn't breathe. It was such a horrible feeling."

"It's over," he murmured, smoothing the hair from her face. "You're here...with me. Nothing can happen to you."

His voice was deep and rich, sending a warmth all through her. And gradually she became aware that his skin was bare next to hers. She had her cheek pressed against the hard muscles of his chest, and she could feel the steady rise and fall of his breath. When her heart began pounding this time, it was for an entirely different reason.

He shifted position, turning on the bedside lamp. In the cascade of light, she saw that he was wearing his jeans, nothing more. It appeared that he'd pulled them on hastily. They were zipped, but the top button was undone. A dark swirl of hair went down his chest, disappearing beneath that button. The warmth seemed to radiate all through Kim.

She pulled away a little, trying for some dignity. However, there was nothing dignified about sitting here in her pajamas, blathering about a nightmare.

"I'm fine," she said. "It's just like you said—aftershocks. Nothing more."

"It's okay, Kim. You don't have to minimize it. What happened to you would have shaken up anybody."

"If you hadn't been there, Michael, if you hadn't come in time..." How odd that her voice should be so calm, while her body trembled. Michael drew her close again.

"It's okay, Kim," he said. "It's okay."

His cheek brushed against hers. She waited, not daring to hope...needing him, not daring to let it show. She stayed in his arms, motionless now, the trembling gone deep inside.

And then, at last, he kissed her. His lips were so very gentle on hers, as if he feared hurting her. She didn't want gentleness. She wanted to feel his strength, his power. Twining her hands in his hair, she deepened the kiss, bringing him closer to her.

He understood. His arms tightened around her, and with a low groan he gave every response she required.

No longer uncertain, no longer waiting, she leaned back against the bed, drawing Michael with her. The warmth inside her flared. It was the warmth he gave to her with every touch, every caress. His hands moved against her, tender and strong at once.

"Michael," she breathed against his mouth. "Oh, Michael..."

He lifted his head to gaze at her, his eyes very dark, almost black. An unspoken message passed between them. Kim nodded, ever so slightly, and Michael brought his mouth to hers again.

It felt so good, being here with him like this, the two of them stretched out on the bed. But too much was in the way: the sheet tangling against her legs, the cotton of her pajamas, the denim of Michael's jeans—all barriers. She pulled the sheet off. Michael kissed her throat now, finding the pulse that throbbed there. His hand moved underneath her pajama top, more skin to skin, and she sighed at the rightness of it. She helped him, reaching to undo her buttons, sliding the material away from her body, revealing herself to him.

She heard the intake of his breath as he gazed at her. "You're beautiful," he said as he touched her, his fingers cupping her breast. Then he bent his head over her, kissing her, his mouth and tongue intimate against her skin.

She drew in her own breath. "Michael..."

He seemed to understand, sensing her hesitation. He held her close. "What is it?" he asked, his voice husky. "Tell me."

Shame had come over her, chasing away the warmth. How could she tell him? How could she say it? But the old hurt festered, preventing the closeness she longed to share with Michael. Every instinct told her she had to get it out in the open, away from the secret corners of her heart. Perhaps it would ruin everything, yet she saw no other choice. She couldn't go on without telling him.

"Michael . . . it's been a very long time for me. Too long . . ."

"It doesn't matter," he said. "We'll go slowly."

She needed to explain. "It wasn't just my husband's affairs," she said, her voice low. "Even before I suspected Stan was unfaithful . . . he couldn't seem to make love to me anymore. As if something was wrong with me."

Michael tilted her chin with one finger, gently obliging her to look at him. "There's nothing wrong with you," he said. "From the first moment I saw you, Kim . . . I've wanted you. I've desired you."

She tried to believe him, to see herself as a desirable woman. But she'd had too much practice believing exactly the opposite.

"There must be something defective in me," she said, her voice dropping even lower. "All those affairs . . . Other women could satisfy Stan—but never me."

Michael brought her closer, fitting the length of her body to his. "Let me prove you're wrong," he murmured. "Can you trust me, Kim?"

This time she gazed fully into his eyes. She felt as if she hovered on the edge of something both terrifying and wonderful. To believe, to trust without knowing each step ahead . . .

"Michael," she said, her voice unsteady, "there's only so much I can risk—" She stopped, unsure how to go on. But again he seemed to understand.

"It's been a while for me, too," he said wryly. "But I must have something we can use." He gave her a lingering kiss, then slid away from her. "I'll be right back."

Kim pulled the sheet up around her, watching as he left the room. Never had she felt so vulnerable. She listened to the sounds of Michael opening and shutting drawers somewhere across the hall. At last he came back to her, a small condom packet in hand.

She stared at the packet. "Does it always have to be this awkward?" she grumbled.

"If we start trusting each other...maybe it won't be awkward at all."

She gazed into his eyes. "Yes," she whispered, hardly knowing what she said.

A few moments later Michael lay beside her, his jeans tossed carelessly on the floor. His caresses began again. Masterfully, tenderly, his hands moved against her back, her hips. The warmth flamed inside her with every touch and she moaned softly, arching against him. Yet doubts assailed her. Would he see her only as ridiculous? Would he laugh at her efforts to entice him?

She hadn't spoken her fears out loud, but he answered them. "Kim," he said, his voice thick, "you're driving me crazy. Everything you do..."

She arched toward him again, and his fingers worked under the waistband of her pajamas. He tugged them downward.

"Beautiful," he murmured, his gaze as intimate as any caress. "You're so lovely, Kim."

She had felt unwanted for such a long time. Could it be this simple to believe something different? Because she could no longer deny the look in Michael's eyes, the wanting she saw there.

Even so, she felt oddly frantic, as if he would lose interest in her unless she hurried. She touched him, and his face went taut.

"Kim, you're driving me wild."

"Please, Michael," she said, her voice shaking.

"We can take it slow." He framed her face with both hands. "We don't have to rush."

"Yes, we do—please, Michael." The entreaty came almost on a sob. She was on fire with her yearning— not to be satisfied, but to satisfy. And once again, he understood. He entered her, deeply and completely. And he no longer held himself back. He rocked above her. She wrapped herself around him, accepting him, lost in the joy of giving him pleasure. The light from the bedside lamp played over his face, disclosing every nuance of passion. He made no attempt to disguise what he was feeling and for that she was intensely grateful. She needed to see him now and to know that *she* was the one taking him toward fulfillment. She moved under him, enticing him . . . inciting him.

He looked deep into her eyes as he came, his shudders echoing inside her. She clung to him, wanting to experience every measure of his enjoyment. She didn't look away from him, not for a second.

Afterward he lay beside her, his skin damp with perspiration, that curl of hair falling over his forehead. She touched his hair, smoothed it back, saw how it fell stubbornly forward again. She smiled dreamily, feeling replete, and wondering if she had ever felt quite this way before.

"Kim," he said, his voice still husky. "You are desirable. Damn desirable."

"Yes," she answered, without even a doubt.

They lay tangled together for long moments. Michael was naked, while she wore that pajama top—unbuttoned of course. It felt utterly natural to be like this with him, a sense of belonging and contentment taking her over. She never wanted the moment to end, but then Michael stirred.

"It's your turn now," he said, a seductive glimmer in his eyes.

"What do you mean?" she asked. "I don't need anything more. Besides, it's not important."

"Your own pleasure... not important?"

She ran a hand over his shoulder. "I didn't mean it quite like that. I just meant... well..." She flushed, wondering how many confessions she had to make in one night. "I haven't had the best experience with that, either.... Even in the beginning, when my husband and I *did* share a bed, everything always happened so quickly...." She couldn't—wouldn't—explain any more. In spite of her problems with Stan, she felt sad they'd been such a failure as husband and wife—and at the same time she hated that failure intruding here with Michael. Perhaps the perfect moment was already ruined, too fragile to endure.

Michael, it seemed, felt differently. "This time we go slow," he said, provocatively tugging away her pajama top. And then the kisses began. Languorous, tempting... ravishing. He trailed his mouth down her body, and she moaned with the unexpected delight, burying her hands in his hair, pressing close to him. Michael led her to the brink of pleasure. She skated near it, then retreated, all at his command. She had never known anything like this, giving herself up to someone else so completely, trusting herself to let go of control.

As he kissed her mouth, his fingers slid gently inside her, and she realized the gift he was offering her. He was concentrating solely on her fulfillment. There could be nothing more private between them, nothing more trusting. Suddenly she was lifted on a wave of intense, startling pleasure. Sensation rippled all through her as Michael touched her and kissed her. Then, as he held her close, she knew what true happiness meant.

CHAPTER FOURTEEN

MICHAEL AWOKE from a dream that he'd done something foolish. He couldn't remember exactly what it was, he just knew it was stupid—very stupid—and he felt guilty, as well as foolish. In the early-morning haze of too much brandy and too little sleep, for a moment he just rubbed his eyes and considered how odd dreams could be. Then he raised himself on one elbow and glanced around the room. Dear God! There was a naked woman lying next to him. He'd had sex with Kim Bennett! And not only had he had sex with Kim, he'd had *great* sex with her.

Sex with a suspect! Yes, that qualified as stupid, extraordinarily stupid. Michael was certain that Donna would back him up on that one. What had he been thinking? Or had he been thinking at all? That was the problem. Where Kim was concerned, Michael didn't seem to be considering the consequences of his actions. Kissing her...escorting her to a little family get-together...feeling guilty about all the lies and deceit...and now, sex.

As if becoming aware of Michael's gaze on her, Kim stirred in the bed and drew the sheet up near her shoulders. That was a disappointment. In the warmth of the Arizona dawn, Kim had been sleeping with the sheet barely covering her thighs. What beautiful skin the woman had, with those sensual freckles here and there. And her body...

Michael sat up, disgusted with himself. Not only had he compromised practically every principle he had been taught as a detective, he was still ogling the woman. It was as if he couldn't get enough of her.

Now she stirred again and opened her eyes. She had pretty eyes, too. Pretty eyes, a sexy bottom, and her breasts...

"Good morning," she said.

Michael pulled the sheet up over *his* waist now. He had also been sleeping in the raw, and he didn't want Kim to see his interest piqued so early in the morning.

"You know," Michael said, "if you weren't so desirable, last night wouldn't have happened at all. You might have escaped this house with your virtue intact."

That half smile came to Kim's mouth. Michael had come to look forward to seeing it.

"My virtue," Kim said, still smiling. "No one's been concerned with my virtue since Tommy Baker at the drive-in theater in the twelfth grade. And as I recall," she continued, "Tommy was more interested in me losing my virtue than retaining it."

Michael ran his hand over Kim's shoulder. He couldn't help himself. He just had to touch her. "Tommy Baker, huh? I dislike the guy already. Did he succeed, this Tommy Baker of yours?"

"Certainly not," Kim said with apparent delight. "Why, it wasn't even his car. *I* drove us to the theater. No way was I going to make love in the back seat of my own parents' car! Besides, Tommy wasn't all that hot."

Kim's mouth had gone all crooked now in mock disgust. She had a nicely expressive mouth. Michael had to suppress the urge to kiss her all over again. "A drive-in theater and Pinetop, Arizona," he mused. "Despite Tommy Baker not being that hot a prospect, sounds like you had some good times in Pinetop."

Kim's expression became guarded.

"I know I probably shouldn't ask, Kim," Michael said. "But that evening with Sophie, it made you mad as hell when she mentioned your mother's problems."

Kim rolled over onto her stomach. "Always the detective, Michael? Always curiosity and distrust first?" She pulled the sheet loose from him and, standing, wrapped it around herself like a Grecian robe. Unfortunately that left Michael feeling a little too exposed.

Kim paced around the room. "I never told Sophie about my mother," she said. "Do you know how she found out? When she realized Stan and I were getting serious, she had me investigated. Can you believe it? She hired a private investigator and sent him to Pinetop to dig up anything he could about my background." Kim stood still and gave Michael an accusing stare. Maybe he only imagined the accusing part, but he felt guilty, anyway. Guilt—one of his more constant emotions these days.

Of course, he'd seen the report that private investigator had made eight years ago right before Kim's wedding to Stan Bennett. He'd read all of Sophie Bennett's efforts to trash her future daughter-in-law.

And now Kim stood there regally in her sheet. She managed to look imposing even with her hair tumbled and her skin flushed. She also managed to look incredibly sexy. Michael's interest in her was very readily apparent, and he debated once again how to cover himself. He couldn't see any sign of his jeans.

Kim started pacing again, the sheet trailing behind
her. "If Sophie had just *asked* me, I would have told
her all about my mother. I was that eager to belong, to
find a new family. I needed someone to confide in. But
no, Sophie went behind my back."

"Kim, you don't have to talk about it if you don't
want to," Michael said. "I shouldn't have brought it
up. Maybe it's something to keep to yourself."

She turned toward him, holding the sheet against her
body. "No," she said in a strong voice. "Sometimes
keeping things hidden only makes them worse. You
create problems, instead of facing them. That's what
happened with my father and me. We both tried as
hard as we could not to talk about what was going on
with my mother. We thought *not* talking would make
the whole sorry mess go away."

Michael wanted to go to her, hold her in his arms as
he'd done last night. She'd probably think that all he
wanted was more sex. Yes, he did want to make love to
her, again and again. But he also wanted to erase those
shadows from her eyes, that haunted expression he had
seen too often.

She sat down on a chair in front of the bureau, her
head bowed. "My mother was very young when I was
born," she said, smoothing a fold in the sheet. "She
had to marry my father because she was pregnant, and
then she had to work with him in the restaurant, struggling to help support us. She wanted more, but she
didn't understand how to go about getting it. My ear-
liest memory of her is seeing her cry."

Michael listened without making a move. It was as
if Kim were weaving some sort of spell, going back to
her childhood to seek forgotten memories. All he could

do was let her talk. It was clear she needed to remember.

After a moment she went on, her voice remaining steady. "When I was a teenager—that was the worst time. Because by then my mother had perfected all the little subtleties. She'd help me choose a new dress and then a few days later she'd start telling me how unflattering it was. Or she'd cut my hair herself, and then say what a mistake it was—she'd made me look ugly. She'd laugh about it, try to make it a joke. It was as if she wanted me to hate her—hate her and compete with her somehow. She started to be proud of the fact that she looked so young, that people would mistake us for sisters, not mother and daughter. Only I was supposed to be the homely one, she the pretty one."

The sheet tightened under Kim's hand, and now her voice wasn't quite as steady anymore. "It wouldn't have been so bad if it had stopped at that. But something more was wrong with my mother. It wasn't just lost dreams or motherhood too early. She was . . . unstable. That was how one doctor put it to my father. Pop took her to another doctor after that, but he never really wanted to talk about it. He just ignored all her small, petty cruelties. I think he believed that I could handle it, that I was stronger than her, so I'd come out okay. He always acted like it was something temporary, Mom acting the way she did—the hatefulness, the depressions, all of it. Like one day we'd wake up and the problem would just disappear."

Michael had known the outline of the story before, known that problems with Kim's mother had taken the small family very near bankruptcy. But now Kim was filling in the picture, making it vividly human. And Michael could see the pain in her eyes.

His jeans were strewn half under the bed. He pulled them on and went to Kim. He knelt beside her, taking her hands. They felt cold in his.

"You can stop now," he said. "You don't have to remember any more."

She scarcely seemed to hear him, although she curled her fingers around his. "She killed herself, Michael. Don't you see? That's how it ended—the problem gone, after all. And deep down, I believe Pop and I felt relieved. How can that be? How can you feel relief when your own mother kills herself? What *kind* of person feels that way?"

"A normal person," he said, "with normal emotions."

"No." She pulled away from him. Standing again, she readjusted the sheet, drawing it over her shoulders, and now it looked like a shroud. Her face was bleak. "In spite of the way she tried to make me hate her, what she really needed was my love. And now it's too late. It will always be too late."

The years-old investigative report on Kim stated that her mother had died of a drug overdose—possibly accidental, possibly suicide. The report, however, revealed nothing of the pain left behind: the recriminations, the sorrow, the regrets.

"You couldn't have stopped it from happening," Michael said. "You didn't have that power."

"I should have loved her more," she whispered. "Love should be powerful enough."

"Sometimes it isn't." He knew all about that, but he couldn't tell Kim. He didn't know how to get through to her.

Maybe that was because he'd started with deception. Kim herself had said it—keeping things hidden only made them worse.

"There's something you need to hear," he said. "You'd better sit down again." He took her toward the bed, and she sank onto the edge of the mattress. She stared at him.

"Michael, that look on your face... Does it repel you so much, what I've told you?"

"It's not you," he said. "It's me." Where did he start? He couldn't think of a good place. "Kim," he went on, "last night you wondered whether I was still a police detective. Well, you got only half of it wrong. I'm not with the police anymore, but I am a detective."

She simply gazed at him, waiting to hear the rest. But that was the hard part—telling her the rest.

"I'm a private detective," he said. "Donna and I are partners in our own firm."

She continued gazing at him, as if she didn't want to understand. "Michael—"

"You need to hear all of it. Donna and I were hired by Sophie to investigate the death of her son."

Kim stood up and slowly stepped away from him. "What are you saying?"

"We were hired to investigate you, Kim."

She had gone very pale. "Sophie hired you..."

"I'm sorry, Kim." The words sounded hollow, inadequate.

"Damn you." Her voice shook. "Well, at least I can no longer blame you for not trusting me. All along you've believed I murdered my husband."

"It's not that simple."

"Oh, it's not?" she asked mockingly. "Am I supposed to feel grateful because maybe you've had some doubts about my guilt? Just tell me, Michael. Was getting me into bed all part of the job?"

He got to his feet to stand beside her. "You know it wasn't," he said in a low, intense voice.

"I don't know anything! Except that I've been a fool. How you must have been laughing at me. You and Donna, playing your little games."

"It's never been a game." The impossibility of what he was trying to do struck him. He was trying to use words to patch a rift—one that he himself had caused. It was as if he'd led Kim onto a fault line and then made it shift underneath both of them.

Still clutching the sheet to her, Kim grabbed her overnight case and the clothes she'd draped over a chair. She headed toward the bedroom door. "What an idiot I've been," she said, her voice brittle now. "I actually started to trust you."

"Kim—"

"Save it, Michael. And from now on, just do me one favor. Stay the hell out of my life."

IT WASN'T UNTIL MICHAEL found himself doing sixty up the wrong side of the street that he began to question the prudence of his actions.

"He'll be fine," he muttered to himself. "Donna's there, and she'll have things under control." Despite these reassurances Michael punched the gas even harder and laid the Jeep into a four-wheel drift.

"A right on Roma. Only two more blocks to go."

Unfortunately those two blocks were laced with traffic, and Michael found himself having to swerve in and around the slow vehicles, his hand on the horn the entire way.

"What I wouldn't give for the old siren," he said grimly when he had to put two wheels on the curb in order to avoid swiping a silver minivan. "There it is now, just up ahead."

His destination was the community-center gymnasium, and Michael almost got a firsthand view of the place's interior as he jerked to a stop only inches from the front door. In a flash he was out of the Jeep and in the building. Donna was standing by the bleachers, dribbling a basketball.

"Where the hell—"

"Easy, Mike. He's in the locker room. Looked a little queasy to me after I explained things to him. Guess I got a little too rough."

"And Andy?"

"Outside," said Donna, "although he's really pissed off at me, Mike. He knows that's his granddad in there and he wants to see him. Wouldn't listen to a word I—"

"Later," Michael said. "I'll deal with all that later. First things first."

"Now, Mike, calm down. You know how you get." Donna had taken hold of his arm and was trying to impede his progress toward the locker room. But she had taken her shoes off in order not to scuff the basketball floor, and she merely slid behind him in her stockings. "Mike," she said, "you're always telling me you don't ever want to be like him. Well, listen, if you go in there now, like this—"

He stopped to scowl at her. "It's my son we're talking about, Donna. *My* son. I'll kill that son of a bitch before I let him anywhere near Andy."

"Now, now, Michael. Is that any way to talk about your old man?"

Michael turned and found Franklin Turner standing before him. His father looked tired today, tired and spent, like some used-up scrap of iron ready for salvage. His five-o'clock shadow was at a quarter to six, and his once-elegant suit looked as if he had been sleeping in it pretty regularly. Michael refused to be moved.

"I warned you, old man. I made things very clear. You were to stay away from Andy. So what the hell are you—"

"Mike—" Donna was at his side again, holding on to his arm "—don't do it like this."

Michael felt the anger all through him. But he saw the concern in Donna's eyes and knew she was right. He tried to control the anger. He tried to remove himself from it mentally. He tried to let it exist as something apart. That was the trick he'd learned: to separate himself from the anger just long enough to get his perspective back.

"It'll be okay, Donna," he said. "I'm going to stay here. I'd like you to go see to Andy."

She stared at him hard, and then, as if reassured, she gave a brief nod, then she left Michael and his father alone.

"The locker room," Michael said, his voice even. "We can talk there."

Frank gave a shrug that was half weary, half cocky. "Sure, son. Whatever you say."

At this hour of the afternoon the men's locker room was empty, caught in the lull between the morning rush of kids and the nighttime gathering of adults. Franklin Turner sat down on one of the benches, adjusting the crease of his pants as if it actually mattered.

"That's some bodyguard you've hired for your kid," he remarked. "Donna, she says her name is. Only she doesn't seem to believe in ladylike introductions." He winced a little and pointedly rubbed his shoulder.

Michael sat down on the opposite bench. The anger was receding, leaving him with a heavy coldness inside. That he could manage. "I told you to stay away from Andy. He's got nothing to do with you."

"He's my grandson." How plaintive Frank sounded. That was something new; in the old days he'd resented sounding anything but in charge.

"What do you have pictured?" Michael said, his tone emotionless. "Sunday afternoons in the park with Andy? Fishing trips? Maybe a little camping thrown in?"

Frank looked regretful. "Okay, so I never did any of those things with you, Mike. Do you still hold it against me?"

It occurred to Michael that the human mind had an amazing capacity for selective memory. Did Frank believe it was only a little parental neglect he should carry on his conscience? Had he forgotten the rest of it?

Michael studied his father. "No reason to drag this on. You'll stay away from Andy. No second chances."

Frank straightened his threadbare cuffs. "It's a little more complicated than that. Today Andy knows he has a grandfather. He's going to be pretty upset with you for keeping me from him."

Michael recognized the cunning expression in his father's eyes. Frank always had enjoyed knowing he held the advantage.

"So he'll be upset," Michael said. Now he saw a flicker of something else in the older man's eyes—just an instant of uncertainty. It was quickly replaced by Frank's usual confidence.

"I know you, Mike, maybe even better than you know yourself. You've gone overboard trying to be a good dad—trying to be the opposite of me. So you can't tolerate the thought of your own son hating you. That would be history repeating itself."

How cool Frank sounded. If he felt any remorse at all, he didn't show it. Was it really possible to forget all the harm you'd inflicted? But maybe you had to forget in order to live with yourself. Maybe remembering could destroy you.

Michael looked his father over again. Yes, the signs of wear seemed deeper today, as if Frank was using himself up little by little. He seemed old in a way that went beyond years.

Frank stood. His skin, already etched with wrinkles, grew blotchy with anger. "Don't pity me," he said. "I didn't come back for that." He straightened his jacket, then the knot in his tie. "I taught you to respect me, Mike. I taught you well. Things haven't changed that much."

The human mind *was* truly selective. Because Franklin Turner had taught his son a lot of things—and respect hadn't been one of them.

"You can't keep me from Andy forever," Frank said. "He won't let you."

Michael didn't say anything and a moment later he watched his father walk away. Frank almost had it recaptured: the aggressive stride of twenty years ago. But the signs of age were undeniably there—the sag in the shoulders, the sparse hair, the crumpled skin. Supposedly you could feel sorry for a man who'd been so ill-used by time.

But Frank was wrong about one thing. Michael would never waste any pity on him.

A SHORT WHILE LATER Michael emerged from the back of the community center, where the old basketball court was. He didn't see his father anywhere; hadn't expected to, not with Donna standing guard. He looked across the court and saw his son sitting cross-legged on the cement. Even from here, Michael could see the stony expression on Andy's face.

Donna shot a ball toward the hoop, but missed. It probably wasn't her fault, though. The hoop hung askew, the netting on it torn. No one had bothered to dismantle this court after the new gym was built, and it stayed here like a relic.

Donna came over to Michael, the basketball tucked under her arm. "How'd it go?" she asked.

"Don't worry. He's intact."

She dribbled the ball. "He can be a nasty old guy, can't he? But still..."

"There's nothing you can say to change anything, Donna."

"Okay, okay, I won't butt in. I just wonder how you're going to explain all this to Andy."

Michael looked over at his son again. Andy was tugging a weed that grew from a crack in the cement, seemingly engrossed in the task. "I'll figure something out. But meanwhile, we have another problem." He paused. "The Bennett case."

Donna held the ball in front of her as if experimenting with yet a new form of pregnancy. "Mike, I don't like the sound of this. What on earth did you do now? You didn't kiss her again, did you?"

"Kiss her?" he muttered. "If only it was that simple."

She stared at him in obvious dismay. "Mike...please tell me that what I'm thinking isn't true."

"I never know what you're thinking," he said sourly.

"It *is* true." She dragged him off to the side, even though they were already well out of Andy's earshot. "Mike, for crying out loud, you're involved with this woman! Do you realize how crazy that is?"

He'd asked himself the same question plenty of times since awaking that morning. "We're not involved in the strictest sense of the word," he said. "She told me to go to hell before breakfast."

Donna got a suspicious look on her face. "There's more, isn't there?"

He'd always appreciated Donna's astuteness; he couldn't blame her for it now. "I told her about us," he said. "About Sophie... She knows we're investigating her."

Donna let out a squawk. "Mike! You just blew the case."

"Except for one thing. I don't think Kim Bennett killed her husband."

Donna shook her head. "She could have rigged that incident yesterday, hired someone who'd pretend to attack her. Anything to make herself look innocent."

Last night, when Michael had called Donna and told her about the attack, she'd been a lot more sympathetic. "I thought you wanted to believe in Kim's innocence, too," he reminded her.

"That was before you told me you *slept* with the woman. For all you know, she seduced you in order to get you on her side."

It hadn't been like that. Kim had been vulnerable and he'd taken advantage of that. He couldn't see it any other way and couldn't excuse himself. He hadn't intended to make love to Kim...but it had happened, and he took full responsibility for it.

Michael figured he'd already told his partner everything she needed to know. "Listen," he said, "you'd better go back to the house and tail Kim if necessary. We need to watch her more carefully than ever now—she could be in very real danger."

"Right," Donna said sarcastically. "At least you've made the job easy for us. She knows we're watching her. We won't have to try to stay out of sight."

"I'm counting on you," Michael said. "Nothing can be allowed to happen to her."

Donna gazed at him. "Mike, you really have it bad, don't you?"

He wished he knew how to answer that. He wished he knew how to explain exactly what it was he felt for Kim Bennett.

CHAPTER FIFTEEN

ANDY CONTINUED to sit stony-faced at the edge of the basketball court. As Michael approached him, he didn't even look up.

Michael sat down beside him. "I know you're ticked off at me," he said. "We'd better talk about it."

Andy pulled at another weed. It would be quite a load, Michael thought, suddenly finding out you had a grandfather you never knew existed.

"Maybe I should have told you about him before," Michael said. "But I was fifteen years old the last time I saw him. I guess I figured I'd never see him again."

Andy's head came up sharply and he gave Michael an accusing stare. "He said you didn't want to see him."

Michael didn't have any guidelines for something like this. How much should he say? How much should he leave unspoken?

"Andy," he tried again, "a lot of things happened when I was young, just about your age. A lot of bad things that . . . yes, I would like to forget."

Andy continued to stare at him, no sympathy in his dark brown eyes. Michael tried another tack.

"I think your grandfather wanted to forget, too, and that's why he left all those years ago. Sometimes it's better for families when they separate."

"Sure," Andy muttered. "Just like you and Mom, right, Dad?" His tone was belligerent.

"No," Michael said. "Your mother and I may have our differences, but we both care about you very much, Andy. The situation with your grandfather—it was something else entirely."

"What happened?" Andy asked cautiously, as if reluctant to show too much interest. But he *was* interested—there could be no doubt of that. For the first time in his young life, he'd been presented with a hint of family history. It was just too bad the history was tainted.

"There are some things I can't tell you," Michael said. "You have to trust me that I have good reasons."

The expression on Andy's face indicated he wasn't into trusting Michael these days. If anything, the wariness had grown.

"He's just an old guy," Andy said. "And he looks sad."

Michael wondered if Frank had rehearsed that look, that sad look. He wouldn't have put it past him. Frank had said he didn't want pity, but maybe he would do anything to gain his grandson's affection.

"Andy," Michael said very quietly, "people aren't always the way they appear. For your own sake, you have to trust me on this one thing. Your grandfather—he's not a good man."

Andy gave Michael a skeptical glance. "What did he do, Dad? Kill somebody?"

There was more than one way to kill another person, particularly a person who loved you.

"Just believe me, son. That's all."

Andy stood up, stuffing his hands into the pockets of his shorts. He looked small and fragile and defiant. "You don't have to keep everything a secret," he said. "I can handle it."

How could he explain? Michael wondered. No one should have to handle the memories he carried inside him.

"Your grandfather's not a good man," he repeated. "You *will* have to trust me on that, son. You don't have any other choice."

The wariness never left Andy's expression, and it was all too clear that he didn't trust Michael at all ... didn't trust his own father.

"SURELY THEY COULD DO better than this!"

Despite the spacious-sounding name—Adobe Acres—the condos now occupying Kim's perusal were clustered together like frightened children. And as far as the adobe part was concerned, Kim had her doubts about that, too. All the walls were too precise to be adobe, too straight, too uniform, too bland.

Kim parked in a space marked Visitors Only, grabbed her purse—a somewhat awkward proposition, considering the little surprise she carried in there today—and went off in search of building 44G. The grounds of the place were as unpleasant to Kim as the pseudo-adobe walls. They were covered with that itchy Bermuda grass she detested so much and evergreen trees, trimmed so neatly they reminded Kim of that damn shrub of her husband's—the shrub now in the care of one Michael Turner, private eye.

Just the thought of Michael tightened the knot in Kim's stomach. A writer of mystery novels—forget it! Not even close. From the first time she'd seen him, she'd sensed something not quite right about his supposed persona. Little did she realize she'd have to have sex with the man in order to find out the truth!

Sex. Such a short, compact word for such a complicated set of circumstances. Sex with Michael last night had been the most physically fulfilling encounter in Kim's experience. Granted, she might not be what most people would consider a well-traveled woman as far as sex was concerned. But she knew what she liked. She liked Michael Turner. She liked him in bed...touching her...bringing her pleasure. She liked it a lot.

Kim stood still, there among the huddled, meager little buildings. The thought of Michael could do that to her—stop her right in her tracks. And she could no longer deny the truth. It had been more than just sex last night. She'd felt a bond with Michael, an overwhelming closeness of body and soul. No matter that with the morning and Michael's confession, the bond had been irrevocably broken. She'd felt it, and the memory of it stayed to torment her. It was as if, for a few brief and lovely moments, she'd been allowed a paradise of fulfillment. Now she was cast out.

Kim made a great effort to focus on the task before her. She walked on, making a right at a particularly brown patch of Bermuda—did this complex never water its grounds?—and headed down a narrow sidewalk squeezed between two buildings. "Let's see," she said to no one in particular, speaking out loud simply to give herself courage. "Building 29...building 36...building 44. These people count as badly as they tend their grounds."

Taking the steps up to the entry of the eight-plex, once again the thought crossed Kim's mind that for men as wealthy as Stan and Roger Bennett, they'd possessed rotten taste in hideaways.

Condo G was at the back, the last door on the left. Kim paused outside. She already had the key in her hand—the small tarnished key she had found in Stan's files. So why was she hesitating? Surely it had nothing to do with her feelings about the harm Stan had done to their marriage in this seedy place. Surely it had nothing to do with any sense of impropriety about coming here.

The key slid into the lock easily, but before Kim even had the chance to turn it, the door opened of its own accord.

"Roger!"

Her brother-in-law grabbed her by the sleeve of her blouse and yanked her into the room. Then he slammed the door behind her, shot the lock into place and peered through the peephole.

"Dammit, Kim. Damn, damn, damn. What are you doing here?"

Kim pulled herself free of the man's grasp. "What am *I* doing here? Roger, you can't be serious. Isn't it every woman's right to visit the lair where her marriage was violated over and over again?" Kim folded her arms across her chest and paced around the room. She could scarcely describe what she was feeling.

"Imagine my surprise," she said acidly. "I was finally going through some of Stan's files—it seems he was very meticulous with his record keeping—and I found out everything about his lease on this place. Your name was on it, too, Roger. How about that?"

He chose to ignore her sarcasm, his eye still pressed to the peephole.

"I wonder why I even came here," Kim muttered. "But you know something? I think sooner or later Stan *wanted* me to find out about this place. Maybe he was proud of his nasty, secret little life here. Well, I'm obliging him. I've come to see it for myself." Her gaze swept the room. "Even the furniture is tacky," she said contemptuously. "What's the matter, Roger, did you and Stan lose the numbers of your interior decorators?"

The sofa was a cheap plaid with overstuffed pillows, the tables were indisputable veneer, and the lamps cast only light, no elegance. In fact, the whole room looked as if it had been furnished with a single check written to some bargain-basement bazaar.

Roger Bennett shook his head. "Kim, Kim...you don't waste money where it's not needed. Didn't Stan teach you that much? The women we brought here wouldn't know champagne from light beer. They were happy enough to...enjoy our company."

Kim felt sickened. She'd always known about Stan's hero worship of his older brother, the way he'd tried so futilely to be as charming, as successful as Roger. It seemed that he'd also tried to match Roger's sexual prowess. How many women had Stan brought here in his empty attempts to stroke his own ego?

"The two of you must have had a difficult time keeping your schedules straight," she said. "I suppose it's easier for you now. You have this wretched place all to yourself."

Roger continued to be fascinated by the peephole. "If you'll only be quiet, please. I don't see anybody yet. But that doesn't mean—"

"Go ahead, Roger, say it. Or let me say it for you. 'But that doesn't mean Michael Turner or his partner didn't follow me here. Doesn't mean they're not lurking somewhere outside the door.' That's right—I found out about Sophie's scheme. I'm sure you were in on it—hiring someone to investigate me.''

Now Roger did turn to face her. In fact, he gave her a practically lethal dose of those Bennett blue eyes. Stan's eyes had been like that, too, able to dazzle you at first. But Kim had learned all too quickly to see through the sparkle to the pettiness beyond.

''It was a stupid idea, anyway,'' Roger said with callous nonchalance. ''I knew you couldn't have been the one to kill Stan. You're more the suffer-in-silence type, Kim, than the revenge type. I mean, look at all you went through when you were a kid, and you never did anything about it. Never even tried to run away from your enchanting mother.'' Roger smiled and seemed to be waiting for the effect of his words. Kim, however, refused to show any response.

''If you think I'm innocent, then why the detectives? Surely Sophie listens to her favorite son's advice?''

''But that's just it,'' Roger said with another smile. ''I never told Mother how I really felt. Hell, hire a detective, I said. Hire two. Get someone to watch her night and day. But I was thinking more along the lines of gaining some leverage over you, Kim. I figured that sooner or later we'd need something on you. All those Bennett shares...''

Kim felt an unpleasant foreboding. ''Then it *was* you who attacked me in the warehouse.''

''Warehouse? What are you talking about?''

He looked genuinely puzzled, but that didn't mean anything. ''Never mind for now,'' she said. She glanced about once more. ''I only wish I knew—'' She stopped herself, but Roger seemed to latch onto her words.

"Poor Kim," he murmured. "Wondering why Stan did it. Wondering why he came here when he had a beautiful, willing wife just waiting for him at home." He spread his hands. "You were always *too* beautiful for my brother, Kim. You intimidated him. He could hardly believe a woman like you would even look at him. But that's not a sentiment exactly conducive to intimacy, is it? Feeling inferior to your own wife. Feeling inadequate. No wonder he went looking elsewhere."

Kim's stomach churned and she knew only that she had to get out of this place. She strode toward the door, but then she noticed a pair of shoes tucked to the side of the plaid sofa—a pair of woman's shoes. She studied Roger in disgust. "You're still using this place, aren't you? In fact, you've got a woman here right this very moment." Kim marched over to what appeared to be a bedroom door and pulled it open—revealing a very startled and flustered Norie Bennett.

Norie sprang back, but it was obvious she'd been listening at the door. When she spoke, her words tumbled over each other. "Why, hello, Kim! I was just about to come and talk to you. I mean, *I've* just found out about this little Bennett hideaway myself. Can you believe it? I'm here to make absolutely sure Thad isn't involved. The very idea of Thad with another woman..." Her voice trailed off, as if she couldn't even tolerate the thought.

"Get real, Norie." Kim looked her sister-in-law over. Norie's linen blouse was just a bit rumpled, the collar not quite straight. "I never thought of you as the unfaithful type," Kim said. "Somehow you've always seemed too skittish for adultery."

Norie gave her an offended glare. "You can't possibly think...Roger and I...of course not! Such an idea is beneath you, Kim. I'm only here so I can talk to Roger. I want to find out exactly what's going on with this family."

Norie was playing her part just right—all wounded innocence. Too bad for her that Roger came into the bedroom and began chuckling.

"It's no use. Kim's found us out. We're guilty of exactly what she's thinking."

"Damn you, Roger—"

"That's what I like about you, my dear sister-in-law. You're fiery underneath that very proper exterior."

Norie sank onto the bed as if defeated and buried her face in her hands. "I didn't want to do it," she mumbled. "You have to believe me, Kim. Roger—he blackmailed me into it. That's the only word for it. Blackmail!"

"You seemed perfectly willing a short while ago," he said.

Norie began to cry. She was subdued about it, nothing overdone. Kim could almost believe the tears were real.

She supposed she ought to be more surprised—repelled, even. Certainly it had been a shock to find Norie here with Roger. But now all Kim felt was numb. More than anything, she just wanted to leave this place and forget it had ever existed.

She couldn't leave just yet, though. She pulled out the manila envelope she'd stuffed in her purse. Standing over the bed, she opened the envelope and shook out its contents: a thin gold bracelet, a length of satin ribbon, a single jade earring, a blurred photograph of a pretty young woman.

Kim had captured the attention of both her in-laws. Norie stopped crying and gazed suspiciously at the items Kim had scattered on the bed. Roger observed them with interest, also.

"Trinkets," he said. "But they don't seem your style, Kim." He picked up the satin ribbon and wove it around his hand.

She became impatient. "I found this stuff in Stan's files, along with the key to this seedy little place of yours. Just tell me who the girl is in the photograph."

A slow grin came over Roger's face. "Ah...good old Stan. Of course. These are his mementos. The girl in the picture—I don't remember who she is. Just another woman. But who cares? That's not the point."

Norie sifted her fingers through the items on the bed, looking oddly mesmerized. "They're souvenirs?" she said.

"Exactly." Roger sounded smug. "It seems my little brother took my advice, after all. I told him how amusing it is to keep some small remembrance of each...encounter. But as usual, he didn't get it quite right. The souvenir needs to have some particular significance for the lady in question. It needs to be something so important to her that giving it up is...a bit incriminating. But that bracelet, for example—what meaning can it have?"

Kim didn't want to hear any more. Now she truly felt sick. Stan had kept relics of each affair—trophies. He'd hidden them away, perhaps to gloat over his conquests.

Norie took the gold bracelet from the bed. "I can just imagine," she said, her voice strangely vacant.

"Suppose that Stan had an affair with a woman—any woman—and he coaxed this bracelet from her. Suppose that it was something her husband had given her, and now she has to pretend she's lost it. Suppose the husband doesn't believe her." She gazed at Roger with some obscure sort of challenge.

He shrugged expansively. "Nonsense. Stan really had no imagination about the enterprise. Look at this ribbon—why, it's harmless, and it almost seems sentimental. The same goes for the earring and that photograph. All sentimental tokens. Stan missed the point entirely."

Kim took a steadying breath. "I understand. It's all about power, isn't it, Roger? You sleep with a woman—that gives you a certain power. Only you want more. And so you have to take something of hers, something important. What next? Do you threaten to expose her, threaten to use the so-called souvenir to ruin her life? But maybe even that's not enough power."

Roger lifted his hands in a gesture of self-deprecation. "You give me almost too much credit. It's an idea that works well in theory, but not always in practice. That's the challenge—to keep refining it. I tried to teach Stan all about it, but he never quite understood. He was a bit dense, my kid brother."

Norie rose to her feet and confronted Roger. The tears had left smudges of mascara on her pale skin. "You have it, don't you?" she said. "I know you have it." Her voice shook, and Kim had the uneasy feeling this was no longer an act.

Roger gave Norie a placating pat on the arm. "I told you we'd discuss it later. No need to involve Kim, is there?"

"Later—it's always later with you. I've done my part. I want it back, Roger."

This time he gripped Norie's arm. "I said this isn't the time or the place."

"No. It's only the time and place to seduce your own sister-in-law." Norie gave a laugh that sounded on the verge of hysteria. She struggled against Roger, but his grip on her arm only tightened.

Kim stepped toward the two of them. "Let her go, Roger."

"Maybe I'm enjoying my power right now," he said. "You accused me of that—enjoying power. Why shouldn't I prove you correct?" He shook Norie as he held her, and she let out a gasp.

"You're hurting me!"

Kim glanced around. She saw a lamp on the bedside table—cheap again, but at least it was metal. It would have to do. She took the lamp, yanking the cord from the socket, and came toward Roger with her makeshift weapon.

"Let her go," she repeated.

Roger grinned. "You'll actually try to brain me with that, Kim? I didn't know you had it in you—"

A crashing noise came from the front of the condo, and a second later Michael's partner, Donna, was in the room. With her pillow tucked under her shirt she looked very pregnant—and very competent. She grabbed hold of Roger, twisted him away from Norie, flung him down on the bed and shoved her knee into his back. She patted him down, obviously searching for a weapon.

"Now," she said, "let's discuss exactly how to treat a lady."

With Roger's face pressed into the mattress, his voice came out muffled. "Sorry, but I don't believe we've actually met."

Donna glanced at Kim, then Norie. "Are you all right?"

Norie gave a bewildered nod. "Don't you think... It might not be so good for the baby, you know."

Donna grimaced. "Trust me, the baby's fine." She addressed Roger again. "I'm going to let you go now. Try anything else, though, and—"

"I get the idea," came Roger's muffled voice.

Donna released him. He struggled to a sitting position, doing his best to appear jaunty but not succeeding. He seemed just a tad shaken.

Donna was still in charge. "I'm giving you a minute to leave," she told him. "I want you to get in your car and drive away. No questions, no explanations."

He looked peeved. "This does happen to be my place—"

"Thirty seconds."

Roger smoothed his ruffled hair and headed toward the door. "I believe you take your investigative duties too seriously, Miss... whatever your name is."

"Ten seconds."

Roger's good humor vanished entirely. He stalked into the other room, and Kim heard a few expletives.

"You've kicked in the damn lock!"

"Five seconds," Donna called out to him. After that, it was only a moment before a car engine could be heard cranking to life outside the window and then racing away.

Norie pressed both hands to her face. "Thank goodness you came in time. I'm terribly afraid of what might have happened."

"No need to be melodramatic," said Donna. "But I think you should get out of here, too... Norie, isn't it? Norie Bennett? And if you're smart, Norie, you'll never come back."

Norie looked stricken. "Thad must never find out about this! It really was blackmail, Kim. Roger has something of mine—something that means a great deal to me. And he said he'd only give it back if... if I did what he wanted."

Kim almost felt sorry for her sister-in-law. "You gave Roger one of those so-called mementos, didn't you? Don't you realize? That's the last thing he'd return. Whatever it is, it gives him power over you."

Norie pressed her hands together, almost as if entreating Kim. "He has to give it back to me," she said. "Or else... everything will be ruined..."

"What does he have on you?" Donna asked. "It's always better just to get it out in the open."

"Not this," Norie said, her tone unexpectedly bitter. "Never this." Suddenly she seemed in a hurry. She went into the other room, found her shoes and slipped them on. "Goodbye, Kim," she said. "I'm sorry about...I'm just sorry, that's all." She left quickly, as if afraid Kim would say something else to her.

Now Donna and Kim were alone in the Bennett hideaway. Kim glanced at the cheap furniture and the ugly carpeting.

"They didn't even bother to make the place inviting," she said. Her sense of revulsion was so strong that now she really did have to get out of here; she couldn't stay another minute. Emerging into the hot sunshine, she began walking toward her car.

Donna caught up with her. "I heard most of it," she said.

"Of course," Kim said, and just kept on walking. "You and Michael, you're experts at that, aren't you? Eavesdropping on other people's lives."

"Sometimes it doesn't take much expertise," Donna said imperturbably. "You just have to stand outside a window. But we're only doing our job, Kim. And maybe we can help you out of this fix."

"I'm not in a fix." Kim frowned at the parched Bermuda grass as she walked by.

"Why did you come here, then?"

Kim wondered if Donna always asked such annoyingly direct questions. But she didn't know what to answer. At first she'd been impelled by a curiosity to discover just how completely her own husband had betrayed her. But now...now she'd learned things she'd far rather not know.

She stopped on the narrow sidewalk. "Why do people do anything?" she said. "Why did my husband try to emulate every wretched thing about his brother? Why was he so despicably weak?"

Donna stood in the middle of the brown Bermuda grass. "In my line of work, I see too many people like that. Weak, small inside, trying to make themselves into something important. I can't explain it. Human nature...it's beyond me. But maybe we all do crazy things." She placed a hand on her rounded stomach and gave a sigh.

Yes, that was the problem. Everyone had weaknesses, and right now Kim despised her own: she'd married a man not worthy of her love and respect. She'd been deceived by his charm, awed by his wealth, flattered by his attentions. She'd fallen for every bit of it.

Never could she allow that to happen again.

CHAPTER SIXTEEN

THE NEXT MORNING Kim knelt in her living room and turned a chair carefully over on its side. It was a valuable piece, early-1800s rustic style, colorfully stenciled with decorations of fruit and vines. After almost two centuries, the clusters of plump grapes and rosy apples looked as fresh as if they'd been painted yesterday. Kim examined the chair's underside, running her fingers along the wood of the legs. She wrote down a few observations on her ever-present notepad.

Today she wanted to forget the way Michael Turner had deceived her. She hadn't seen him since their reckless night together, yet every moment of it seemed emblazoned on her soul. If only she *could* forget making love with him—

The doorbell pealed and Kim gave a start, dismayed at how quickly her imagination got carried away when it came to Michael. She scrambled to her feet and went to squint through the peephole. This reminded her too much of Roger Bennett. He'd done the same thing yesterday—peering out that peephole of his little love nest, worried that someone would find out just how sleazy the Bennett men really were.

She continued gazing out her own peephole. She didn't see anyone at first, but then lowered her gaze and saw a mop of dark, curly brown hair.

She opened the door and regarded young Andy Turner, hovering on her porch. He had the look of someone about to go darting off.

"Hello," she said.

He gave her an unenthusiastic glance, as if he'd been forced to ring her doorbell. His hands were stuffed deep into the pockets of his baggy shorts, his feet looking too big in those basketball shoes. She saw all the ways he resembled Michael: the curl of hair over his forehead, the dark eyes that gave away so few secrets, the cynical expression. And once again came the inconvenient reactions: longing, tenderness. To have such a son as this...

"Well," Kim said briskly, "I didn't expect to see you of all people. Don't tell me your father sent you."

"No." Andy began inching toward the porch steps.

"I guess your dad still doesn't want you hanging around here," Kim said. "He as much as told me that."

Andy paused, scuffing a foot back and forth. "Now he's telling me to stay away from my grandfather, too."

"Really." Kim didn't want to get involved in any aspect of Michael Turner's personal life. She'd had enough of the man—but meanwhile, his son was skulking about her front porch. "You ought to make up your mind," she said. "You can come inside or go away—either one. But you'll have to make it quick because I'm busy."

Andy hesitated for a moment. Then he ducked into the house.

She led the way back to the living room and surveyed the chair she'd tipped over on its side. "I'm done with that one," she said. "Why don't you set it to rights while I start on something else? Carefully," she added. "It's an antique."

Andy set the chair back on all four legs with somewhat less than the proper reverence, then watched her as she advanced purposefully on the colonial Williamsburg desk in the corner. "What are you doing?" he asked, his tone conveying boredom, as if he didn't really care what she was up to.

She started tugging the desk away from the wall. "Help me out here and I'll tell you."

Andy took hold of the other side, and together they pulled the desk toward the middle of the floor.

"That's fine," Kim said. She knelt down behind the desk, running her fingers over the back of it. She liked the satiny, age-old texture of the wood.

"You said you'd tell me," Andy said. And this time he sounded as if he wanted to know.

Kim sat back on her heels. "I'm learning about furniture," she said. "All kinds of furniture. How it's put together and why it looks the way it does. Why some pieces hold together for centuries, and others fall apart if you so much as poke them."

"Wow," Andy muttered. "Major excitement."

Kim drew her eyebrows together. "Don't be a smart aleck, Andy. Different things are exciting to different people. And for me, right now it happens to be furniture."

"Why?"

"Why what?" she murmured distractedly as she reached up and fiddled with the rolltop of the desk.

"Why is furniture exciting?" He sounded extremely skeptical.

"Why is anything exciting?" she countered. "I mean, what gets your blood pumping?" She knelt down again, peering underneath the desk.

Andy sat on the floor beside her. "I don't know," he said. "I like basketball, I guess."

"Don't go overboard on the enthusiasm." Kim tapped the side of the desk experimentally. She didn't know what type of wood it was made of. There were so many things she didn't know yet, so much to learn. During the past several years it had been a heady sensation, buying beautiful items for her home. She'd purchased any number of valuable antiques just because she liked the way they looked. Now, however, she was requiring herself to go deeper—to think about why a chair or a desk or an armoire was valuable, what made it special and distinctive. Craftsmanship was important of course, but it was more than that.

She glanced over at Andy and saw that he appeared glum. "You know what makes furniture so interesting?" she said. "Take this desk, for instance. It's been around for more than two hundred years. I try to picture who might have used it before me. A gentleman in a powdered wig, a lady in a bustle..."

Andy didn't seem as captivated as she was by the thought. "Like I said—" she smiled "—everybody gets excited by different things. With you, maybe it *is* basketball."

That subject didn't seem to thrill him, either. He sat there looking very intense, and again Kim was reminded far too much of Michael.

"My grandpa came to see me," Andy said. "Except I didn't even know I had one. My dad never told me, and that's weird. Everything's weird."

Kim wouldn't have minded a friendly discussion about basketball. This grandfather talk was something else again—a private matter of the Turner males. "Andy, this is a subject you ought to take up with your father. Not me."

Andy scrambled to his feet, and now he looked embarrassed. He seemed ready to bolt for the door, and Kim was sorry she'd been so abrupt with him. It was obvious he was troubled.

"Listen," Kim said, "I need a break from all this furniture stuff. I have some more lemonade in the fridge. More of those cookies, too."

Andy frowned. No doubt she'd offended his dignity again, offering him something as childish as lemonade and cookies. But he did follow her into the kitchen.

This time they both seemed to know what to do. Kim took out the can of lemonade concentrate, opened it and dumped it into a pitcher along with some water. Then she handed the pitcher and a large wooden spoon to Andy. He looked beleaguered, but he began stirring, anyway. A short while later they were seated at the kitchen table with two glasses of lemonade and a plate of hazelnut cookies. Kim still hadn't been able to bring herself to give up those Bennett cookies.

Andy ate two in a row. He'd clammed up, no doubt sorry he'd mentioned anything about his problems in the first place. If any discussion was going to take place, it would be up to Kim to initiate it. She felt very reluctant, but the nagging thought remained: Andy needed someone to talk to right now, and it appeared she'd been elected.

"So tell me about this grandfather of yours," she said as casually as possible. "What's he like?"

Andy stared into his glass. "He's old. And kind of creepy. But he didn't say a whole lot because Donna jumped him."

Kim could picture that easily, considering the way Donna had handled Roger Bennett. Nonetheless, it was still a puzzling statement. "Why on earth would Donna jump your grandfather?" she asked.

"My dad doesn't want me to talk to him. I think he did something really bad a long time ago. Like maybe he murdered somebody."

Kim was startled. "Did your father tell you that?"

Andy squirmed uneasily. "No. But I can tell it's something bad. Maybe my grandpa had to go away all those years so he could hide from the police or something. Or maybe he was in jail."

"Andy, why don't you just ask your father what this is all about?" It seemed the only reasonable solution.

"I already did," Andy said. "And he won't tell me."

It sounded overly dramatic: a grandpa on the lam and Michael refusing to talk. Kim suspected a great deal of youthful imagination was at work here. Nonetheless, Andy seemed both disturbed and fascinated by the subject of his grandfather.

Lacking experience with children, Kim felt hopelessly inadequate. "Andy, you just have to trust your father," she said at last.

"That's what *he* keeps saying," he muttered.

Once again it struck Kim—the difficulty the Turner males had with each other. Michael and Andy were very similar, both of them grand cynics, and maybe that was part of the problem right there.

"I don't know a lot about your father, Andy," Kim said thoughtfully, "but I do know one thing for certain. He cares about you more than anything else in the world.''

Andy gave her a disbelieving glance. It just didn't seem right. Why couldn't Michael and Andy sort out the problems between them? Surely any misunderstanding could be surmounted by the affection they shared. Because that was another thing—for all young Andy's sarcasm and skepticism, Kim was convinced he loved his father very much.

It was frustrating to see something in need of fixing, but not know how to fix it. Kim reminded herself that it wasn't any of her business—whatever needed working out between Michael and Andy. Why couldn't she just leave it alone? Why did she have to worry about two people she had no claim on?

The doorbell rang again. ''Let's hope it's not one of my crazy Bennett in-laws,'' Kim said. ''*That* we don't need.'' She went down the hall and peered out the peephole. It wasn't one of the Bennetts—it was worse. It was none other than Michael Turner. Just the sight of him made her pulse race. Dark hair, dark eyes, that lean, powerful physique. He gazed straight back at the peephole, his face grim.

Kim retreated a step or two. Glancing over her shoulder, she saw that Andy had followed her. ''It's your father,'' she said. Andy's face immediately seemed to close up, as if he was retreating deep inside himself. Kim felt frustrated all over again.

''I'm sure you're not supposed to be over here,'' she said, ''but your dad's not an ogre. He's not going to chew your head off.''

Andy didn't say a word. He stuffed his hands into the pockets of his shorts, looking stubborn and watchful, as if he had to make sure no one got too close to him. He looked, in fact, just like his father.

Kim grumbled under her breath and pulled open the door. Michael stepped inside.

"Thought I'd find you here, Andy," he said in a calm voice. "Donna and her mother are waiting for you."

"Great," Andy mumbled. "I get to go shopping for baby clothes again."

"I hear there's a movie in the offing, too."

This didn't appear to sway Andy. Kim wondered what it would take for the boy to let his emotions out—the happy, as well as the sad. But he was gazing at her now somewhat intently, as if trying to send her an unspoken message.

It was there again—the unexpected affinity between Andy and her. Because somehow she knew exactly what his silent request meant. He was asking her not to tell his father what they'd discussed.

It was unfair to expect this of her. She didn't want to be a keeper of secrets, especially where Michael and Andy Turner were concerned. But she could tell it meant a lot to Andy. She saw the hint of anxiousness in his eyes.

She gave the briefest of nods, and that seemed to release Andy. He sped past her, past Michael. Kim glanced outside and saw that Donna's van was parked in her driveway. Donna put her hand out the window and waved. Kim didn't wave back. She noted that an older woman sat in the passenger seat—Donna's infamous mother-in-law, no doubt. Kim couldn't help wondering how things were going in the fake pregnancy department. She watched as Andy clambered into the back of the van and as Donna drove off. All of which meant that Kim was now left alone with Michael Turner—the man who had made love to her only a few short nights ago.

She could feel her skin heating up at the memory and she cursed the treachery of her thoughts.

"So you're the one on surveillance duty now," she said caustically. "I really ought to make it easier—I could print up my itinerary for you."

He observed her gravely. "You ran out on me the other morning."

Her skin flamed all the more. "We don't need to discuss it. As far as I'm concerned, the whole thing was a terrible mistake, but it's over."

He didn't seem to be paying any attention to her at all. He went out to the porch, retrieved a paper sack he'd left there and brought it into her living room. Kim trailed after him.

"Don't mind me," she said. "Don't wait for an invitation—just march right in."

Michael set the bag on top of her Williamsburg desk. He pulled out a single flower wrapped in tissue, another purple-pink chrysanthemum, and handed it to her. She had to resist the urge to bring it up to her face, to brush the petals against her skin. How could a single flower affect her so? But Michael was rummaging through the sack again.

"You left some things behind," he said, and then he pulled out her pajama top.

Kim snatched it away from him. "You didn't have to bother—"

He brought out her pajama bottoms, dangling them from one hand. Kim snatched those away, too. She felt utterly mortified.

"Very well," she said. "You've made your delivery. Goodbye."

He gave no sign of leaving. He stood in her living room, tall and masculine in his polo shirt and jeans. Kim's gaze traveled over him. She remembered him peeling off those jeans...

With a small moan, she turned and sank into one of her armchairs.

"So you feel the same way," he said. "You keep thinking about it. And you keep wanting more."

No one could rile Kim like Michael Turner. She could hardly believe what he'd just said. "Wanting more?"

"Yes. I keep wanting more, too." His voice held the huskiness that sent a quiver through her. Why did she have to feel this way—aching for his nearness, his touch? She pressed her arms tightly against her body as if that would contain all her rioting emotions.

"What we did was wrong," she said. "Wrong in just about every way possible."

"I know."

"So why are you here, Michael?" she burst out. "I told you to stay away from me! I meant it—I still mean it."

Picking up his paper sack, he folded it in half. "I'm investigating the death of your husband," he said. "I have to follow through on it."

"Of course," she answered disdainfully. "I'm sure Sophie has you on a very generous retainer. You wouldn't want to give that up."

"You know that doesn't have anything to do with it," Michael said in the calm tone she could find maddening. "But it's very probable someone did kill your husband."

"How could I forget? I'm the prime suspect."

"No, Kim," he said in that controlled voice. "I don't believe you killed him. I *do* believe you're in danger, though. It's likely that if someone did murder your husband, he's after you now."

His words were ominous. "Even if someone did kill Stan, why come after me? What could be gained?"

"I don't have all the answers yet. Until I do, I don't want you running around like you did at that condo, poking your nose into trouble."

The man was infuriating. "Look," she said, "if my life *is* in danger, I'm not going to wait around for someone to attack me again."

"You should have told me about the Bennett hideaway, not gone there on your own." Michael tossed the paper sack aside and sat down in the armchair across from hers. They were matching Queen Anne wing chairs, meant to be shared by a cozy couple before the fireplace. But Kim and Stan had never been cozy together, and she saw no hope of ever achieving that state with Michael Turner. The sensations he evoked in her were too confusing.

"That was a personal matter," she said stiffly. "Believe me, when you're discovering the many ways your husband cheated on you, it's something you like to keep to yourself."

"From now on, you won't be keeping anything to yourself," Michael said inexorably. "You'll be sharing all possible information with me."

"Dammit, Michael—"

"I won't allow anything to happen to you," he said, and now she heard the intensity in his voice. "I'll keep you safe with or without your cooperation."

It wasn't what she'd expected to hear. As usual he'd found a way to keep her off balance. He made it seem as if keeping her safe was very important to him.

She gazed at the fireplace, swept clean and empty. Because of the warm Arizona weather, few days during the year justified logs crackling on the hearth. The marble mantel and the Delft tiles of the fireplace were luxuries—yet further proof that the wealthy could afford whatever they pleased. In the beginning, she had allowed herself to be caught up in that sort of privilege. She'd been impressed by it.

"I don't know anything else," she said after a moment. "Not about Stan's death, not about any of it."

Michael leaned forward, resting his elbows on his knees. She was beginning to recognize that brooding expression of his. "Your husband's investment firm was in trouble at the time of his death, Kim. Did you know that?"

Kim also recognized Michael's clinical tone, the one that said he was all business. It made him seem so remote, so removed from her. But wasn't that best? She couldn't allow herself to forget that he'd been hired by her mother-in-law.

"I wonder what version you got from Sophie," she said. "But here's the way it really was—Stan's business was always in trouble. He had such grandiose dreams of the deals he'd put together and somehow they always fell through. Sophie had to keep funneling money to him. She complained, but she did it."

"Yes, I know. But when your husband's deals fell through, people lost money. No doubt some of them weren't too happy about it."

Kim stiffened. "And you think it had something to do with his death?"

"I'm just considering—"

"—all the possibilities," she finished for him. "Yes, yes, I know!" She stood and walked over to the Williamsburg desk, running her hands along the satiny old wood. But her enjoyment in it had faded. Bennett money had purchased these antiques—Sophie's money, when it came right down to it. Kim needed something of her own. She was on her way to finding it and she couldn't let anything stand in the way.

"I have things to do," she said. "And you really have overstayed your welcome, Michael."

He ignored this comment. "Donna informs me you found that key of your husband's among his papers. I'd like to go through those files."

Kim stared at him incredulously. "Forget it. I already told you—I want you out of my life."

Michael stood, his expression impassive. "You'll get me out all the sooner if you cooperate. You'll also be a lot safer."

His words chilled her. She couldn't deny one thing: when she was with Michael, she felt that no physical harm could come to her. Only her emotions were in danger.

"I've already gone through Stan's files myself," she said. "I didn't find anything else that seemed important."

"I do this kind of thing for a living, Kim."

How could she forget? He was a professional. He had been from the very beginning—working to gain her trust because it suited his job.

She thought it over for a long moment, trying to be cool and distant about the whole situation. At last she gave a curt shrug. "A lot of Stan's papers are at his office, but some are in his study upstairs. I suppose you can start with those." She went toward the stairs. Michael reached them the same time she did, and suddenly they were standing close to each other.

She stared at the soft blue material of his polo shirt, already knowing the softness was deceptive, concealing as it did the hard muscles of his chest. But there was another unyielding quality in Michael, something that showed in the sternness of his features. It seemed he would let nothing prevent him from accomplishing what he believed was right and necessary. Was that how he'd been able to deceive Kim so expertly—he had believed it right and necessary?

She raised her gaze slowly to his and saw the storminess in his dark eyes. Unbidden, the memories of his touch cascaded over her. And she knew the truth—if he touched her now, she wouldn't be able to resist him. She would succumb to her own pathetic longing, the need to have Michael always near.

His gaze imprisoned hers. They remained together like this for a long, shimmering moment, and she saw the desire revealed in Michael's expression. Regret, too.

But then his rigid self-command took over. He didn't touch her and his expression grew dispassionate once more. "I need to look at those files," he said. He went on up the stairs, leaving Kim to follow. Leaving her, too, with that unfulfilled aching of need.

CHAPTER SEVENTEEN

MICHAEL WATCHED as Diane Bennett, wealthy heiress and senior vice president of Bennett Industries, erased the blackboard. The job was taking her forever, because she pushed the eraser in such small, neat circles. She worked earnestly, as if she found the menial task a privilege. At this rate, she was going to be all day. Michael glanced at his watch. He saw Kim glance at her own watch. Obviously they shared the same thought. Michael caught Kim's eye and gave a faint smile. She didn't smile back. What else had he expected? All morning she'd treated him with cool politeness, making it clear she didn't want anything more between them. If *he* wanted more, he really was a damn fool.

This morning he'd been as efficient and professional as possible while he'd gone through Stan's files. Keeping his concentration hadn't been all that easy, what with the lovely widow Bennett hovering beside him. But he'd found something of interest, something that needed follow-up, and now he and Kim were sitting here together at the back of the classroom.

At the front, physics professor Jack Hutchinson stacked his lecture notes together. He wore a narrow tie and a short-sleeved polyester shirt that strained across his middle. Again he gave the impression that he might be more comfortable wearing overalls, tinkering in his backyard rather than teaching college students. Michael and Kim had listened to the last half hour or so of the lecture; Jack Hutchinson appeared to be a proficient but hardly stellar instructor. He'd gotten the job done, yet added no pizzazz to the material. Michael had seen a few students struggling to keep their eyes open. He'd started to doze off a little himself. Diane Bennett, however, had sat in the very front row and gazed at Jack as if enthralled by every word.

Now, at last, she finished erasing the board. She turned and glanced toward Michael and Kim, giving them both a grudging perusal.

"I think this is our cue," Michael said in a low voice to Kim. "She's giving us permission to approach." He tried another brief smile. Again Kim refused to smile back. She led the way to the front of the classroom, walking in that proud way she had. Michael watched her slender back, the gentle curve of her hips emphasized by the short fashionable skirt she wore. Whenever Kim was around the Bennetts, she seemed to favor clothes more daring and sexy than the ones she usually chose—as if she wanted to flaunt her existence before them. Diane Bennett looked almost dowdy in contrast, wearing navy slacks and a prim blouse; perhaps she considered this the appropriate attire for playing adoring assistant to her professor boyfriend.

"Jack has an office hour right now, from two to three," Diane informed Kim and Michael in a hushed tone. "That's when he's supposed to see students."

Jack spoke up. "Hardly anyone comes to see me," he said. "If you want to talk, we won't be interrupted."

"If students *don't* come, it's their loss," Diane said loftily. "They're missing an opportunity." She picked up the file with his lecture notes and held it to her.

Jack looked half embarrassed, half pleased by Diane's solicitude. "My office is right down the hall," he said. "Come along."

A few moments later he ushered Kim and Michael into a small, cluttered room with barely enough space for a desk. Clearly Jack Hutchinson was not the top man in the physics department. It wasn't just the small office, but the fact that he was teaching a summer-school course. Professors higher up in the pecking order got to take their summers off. Diane Bennett, however, treated him as if he were the university president. She sat down in a chair squeezed close to his and gazed at him attentively.

Kim and Michael sat down on the other side of the desk. No sense in wasting time—Michael got right to it.

"Dr. Hutchinson, we've discovered that—"

"Jack, please. Whenever anyone calls me Dr. Hutchinson, I feel like I should be taking somebody's pulse."

"A doctorate in physics is every bit as legitimate as an M.D.," Diane said righteously. "Don't underestimate yourself, dear."

Jack looked more embarrassed than ever. "Anyway, what can I do for you?" he asked Michael.

"We've discovered that you were a partner in a real-estate investment with Stan Bennett. We've also discovered that you lost quite a bit of money as a result."

Before Jack could so much as open his mouth, Diane said indignantly, "What on earth is this all about? It's bad enough that Jack lost the money, but now to be questioned about it—"

"They haven't asked any questions yet," Jack cut in mildly.

"Dear, your private financial matters are no one else's concern." Diane stared at Kim and Michael with displeasure.

Kim gave a shrug. "You know how it is, Diane. I keep finding out these interesting little tidbits about my husband. Gets me curious to find out more."

"I don't like what you're implying," Diane said. "Everything about Jack's investment was entirely aboveboard. It was my brother who ruined the deal. *Your* husband," she added, as if to suggest that somehow it had been Kim's fault, too.

"I'd like to explain the matter to Mr. Turner," Jack said. "I don't have anything to hide."

"Of course not, dear, but don't you think it would be wiser—"

"Stan approached me with an offer that seemed reasonable," Jack said. "He was looking for people to invest in a housing development. It was my own fault that I didn't check out the contractor myself."

"Stan was the one who should have been careful," Diane protested. "What a joke he was, styling himself as a venture capitalist. Jack, if only you had let me know what you were doing, I could have warned you about Stan."

"It's done," Jack said. "No use feeling sorry." He spoke in that same mild tone, but Michael detected a flicker of resentment in his eyes. Was Jack Hutchinson upset about the money he'd lost? Or was Diane simply getting on his nerves?

"Any chance you'll recoup your investment?" Michael asked.

"None," Jack said, almost curt now.

"That's not necessarily true," Diane put in. "I've talked to my mother about it. I think it's only right that Jack be recompensed for Stan's poor judgment—"

"We've been over it," Jack said. "I don't want your family's money."

"We're talking about *your* money," Diane answered. "It's only fair that something be done. I'll get Mother to come around, just wait and see."

The resentment was now clear in Jack Hutchinson's expression. But when he gazed at Diane, there was also a perplexed affection there. Michael didn't envy the guy.

He'd heard everything that was necessary, though. Standing, he reached across the desk to shake hands with Jack. "Appreciate your time," he said.

"If there's anything else you need to know, just ask." Jack sounded too congenial, too willing to divulge information. He probably didn't make a whole lot on his professor's salary; losing money would be something he didn't take lightly. Michael didn't buy his "done is done" attitude.

"See you later," Kim said to her sister-in-law. Diane didn't answer. She just kept glancing at Jack with a worried expression, as if wondering whether or not she'd said the right thing. Michael didn't envy her, either.

A few moments later Michael and Kim walked along the palm-shaded university mall. Kim seemed deep in thought, keeping herself separate from him, so he took it upon himself to initiate the conversation.

"Too bad for Hutchinson getting caught up with the Bennetts like that."

Kim shook her head. "He's too apathetic. He behaves as if he invested that money without thinking it through, and he lets Diane get away with mothering him even though you can tell it irritates him. People that passive, sooner or later they're bound to explode.''

"Maybe he already did explode.''

Kim glanced at him. "You think he killed Stan out of revenge and then decided to go after me, too? No, don't tell me—anything's possible, right?''

Michael was having a difficult time concentrating on the Bennett case. It had something to do with the way Kim looked in that skirt, her legs long and graceful. Her hair fluttered in the breeze, the golden strands eclipsing the brown. There were any number of coeds strolling by on this campus, but Michael couldn't spare them his attention. Kim was lovelier than any of them.

"Diane's the one who's really in trouble,'' she said. "I think she's far too much in love with Jack. The worst thing she can do is get Sophie involved—yet that's exactly what she's doing. Sophie's always found a way to wreck Diane's love affairs. What's to stop her from doing it this time?''

"Couldn't say.'' Michael had an urge to take Kim's hand as they walked along. It would be just a small gesture, nothing major, but he had a feeling Kim wouldn't see it in quite the same light.

"One time Diane was in love with someone at Bennett Industries. A rather high-up someone, too—the marketing director, I think it was. You'd hardly think that was scandalous, but Sophie managed to dig up some dirt on him. And Diane, instead of telling Sophie to go to hell, broke off with the man.''

"Hmm.'' Michael had a good vantage point from which to study Kim's profile, and he could see that dusting of freckles across her lovely nose. Why was it the freckles that always got to him?

"The point is, Michael, Sophie has a habit of interfering. But why am I telling *you* that? She's paying you to interfere right now. She can't think of anything she'd rather do than put me away for life."

This was probably the worst time to do it, but Michael took Kim's hand. He wanted to touch her any way he could. The surprise was that Kim didn't pull away from him. Her fingers curled against his.

"Oh, damn," she said under her breath.

They kept on walking, hands clasped. "It won't disappear," he said. "You know that, don't you?"

"I don't want it," she said in a low, fierce voice. "I don't want to feel this way." After a pause, she went on, her voice tight now. "You saw how Diane was. So enraptured, smothering the man with attention. She behaves as if the relationship is everything to her."

"Kim," Michael said, "you don't seem like someone who could get so wrapped up in a man you'd lose yourself."

Her fingers moved restlessly in his grasp. "But I already did that, don't you see? With Stan. When I met him, my mother had just died and everything seemed so terrible. I thought he would sweep me away from the pain..." Her voice caught.

Michael drew her aside, away from all the college students milling past. He was beginning to understand a lot more about the shadows haunting Kim, and he wished he knew how to banish them forever.

"So you made a mistake once. The same thing doesn't have to happen a second time."

She gazed at him, her eyes the blue of summer storms. "So what do you suggest, Michael?" she asked mockingly. "We should make love again?"

It was an idea that had occurred to him more than once. It had occurred to him a lot.

He knew she could read the thought in his eyes; a rose color stained her cheeks. "It won't solve anything," she said. "And not just because of me. You're always watching for something, Michael. You're always...on guard. I don't know why. I can't explain it. But it's there. It's between us, and it won't go away."

Regret went through him. He wished it could be different, but she was right.

Always he had to remain on guard—not against any outward danger, but against himself.

THAT NIGHT Michael waited at the very bottom of the trellis in his backyard. Darkness had fallen, and the lights in the windows of the neighborhood evoked any number of images: a family gathered for a late dinner, a couple watching a movie on TV, a teenager locked in his room against adult intrusion. Kim's windows were bright, too, all through the house; maybe she needed to chase away the darkness. Michael didn't like thinking of her in there alone. Hell, if he could have his way, she'd move in with him and Andy for protection. She'd have her own room, of course. She had already made it pretty clear that she didn't want to share his bed.

They'd had only that one night together. Perhaps, if he hadn't told her the truth about himself, they could have had more nights. Kim, in his arms...

He'd already tried to stop thinking about it. Discipline and self-control were things he'd come to rely on in himself—part of the watchfulness Kim had mentioned. But when it came to her, his thoughts knew no discipline. He kept imagining every womanly thing about her.

A few moments went by, and then Michael heard a rustling above him. The trellis creaked and then seemed to shudder. Another few moments, and Andy dropped to the ground. Michael reached out a hand and put it on his son's shoulder. Andy yelped in surprise, whirling around.

"Dad!"

"One and the same," Michael said. He couldn't read his son's expression in the darkness, but he didn't need to. He knew what would be on Andy's face: defiance, maybe a little confusion. Certainly wariness.

"How did you know?" Andy asked at last.

"I'm a detective, remember?" Michael wondered how to proceed. He wasn't happy with the decision he'd made; it was, in fact, one of the most difficult he had ever faced. He just didn't see any other choice.

"Andy," he said quietly, "I won't try to talk you out of it. Evidently this means a lot to you . . . so I'm going to drive you over there. We'll go together to see him."

Andy didn't say anything, but Michael sensed the unspoken—his own son's distrust.

"It's not a trick," he said. "If you really want to see your grandfather, that's where I'll take you." Michael walked around the side of the house and climbed into the Jeep. Nothing happened at first, but then Andy opened the passenger door and clambered inside. He hunched in his seat, still not saying a word. Michael started the engine, backing out of the drive. His headlights swept across Donna's van. She was parked right in front of Kim's house, and she flashed her own headlights at him as he went by.

He drove in silence, his hands gripping the wheel. He told himself to take that deep breath, to step away from his anger. It was harder than usual to distance himself. When he'd learned that Frank had actually called the house and talked to Andy on the phone . . .

Yeah, he had been pretty angry about that. And he had come up with a whole lot of ways to deal with the situation—ways that his father would have understood. And that was what had stopped Michael, knowing too well how his father would have understood those dark impulses.

So here Michael was with his son doing the civilized thing, even though Frank didn't deserve it. For Andy's sake, he just didn't see any other choice. He had to keep reminding himself of that.

"Rule number one," Michael said. "If you don't want me to find out what your plans are, don't write your destination on the notepad by the phone."

Andy squirmed, but showed a remarkable capacity for silence.

"Maybe you wanted me to find out about tonight," Michael said. "I don't blame you. Could be pretty scary going there by yourself."

At last Andy spoke, the defiance all there. "I'm not scared."

"Sometimes it's smart to be scared," Michael said. "It makes you think things over and find a better way to do them."

"You said I couldn't see him. How was I supposed to know—"

"Even I can change my mind, Andy—if it's the right thing to do." It sure as hell didn't feel right, but Michael just had to keep telling himself there was no other choice.

The motel was on the far side of town, and anger stirred in Michael all over again. How had Frank expected Andy to reach this place tonight? A young kid traveling alone. As usual, Franklin Turner had only been thinking about his own needs, his own wants.

Michael pulled into a parking space. The motel was a lot like Frank: putting up a front of respectability with its turquoise-painted doors and small white fence around a scraggly flower border, but already on the inevitable slide toward shabbiness. Michael climbed out of the Jeep, waiting for his son to follow. Andy hung back as they approached room number 18.

Frank didn't open until the second knock. He didn't seem surprised to see Michael, as well as Andy, at the door.

"Come in, come in," he said genially. "A real family get-together." He ushered them into the motel room, with its two sagging twin beds. "Sit down," he said. "Make yourselves comfortable." He sounded as relaxed as if he were presiding over a luxurious drawing room. Michael remembered this Frank from his childhood: magnanimous, lord of the manor—even though there'd been no manor, just a lousy one-bedroom apartment.

Michael sat down on one of the beds. After a second's hesitation, Andy sat beside him, trying to scoot close without making it look too obvious. His young face was tense. Michael wanted more than anything to reach out and put a reassuring arm around his shoulders. But he knew he couldn't do that—not now. He had to allow Andy at least a semblance of dignity, as if they were two equals here to confront their long-lost relative.

There was a tray of plastic cups on a small bureau. Frank made a show of tearing off the wrappers, filling the cups with water at the bathroom sink. He handed one each to Michael and Andy.

"There," he said. "We're fine now." He sat down on the opposite bed. "This is what I've wanted all along, just the three of us together." He raised his plastic cup in a toast.

Michael didn't raise his cup in return. Andy didn't seem to know what to do.

"My son . . . my grandson," Frank said, every inch the patriarch. He wore an argyle pullover sweater, a bit ratty but the type you'd expect kids to give as a present on Father's Day. Hell, why hadn't Frank gone all out and provided himself with a pipe and a pair of slippers?

Michael felt the anger rising inside him like a tide. *Easy,* he told himself. *Back off.* With an effort of will, he achieved the necessary distance. For Andy's sake, he simply waited.

Frank gave his grandson an encouraging smile. "You're awfully quiet, Andy. Tell me about yourself. I suppose you're enjoying your vacation from school."

Andy shrugged uneasily, not saying anything. From long experience, Michael knew all the different meanings of Andy's silences. This one conveyed uncertainty rather than the usual defiance. Frank didn't seem to notice.

"I know you like to play basketball," he said. "Are you going to try out for the school team?"

Again a shrug, and Andy moved imperceptibly closer to Michael.

"I'll let you in on a secret I bet your father doesn't even know. I played basketball when I was a kid, too.

I was pretty good. Maybe you got your talent from me.''

Silence. Frank's smile became a little forced.

''I'm your granddad. You must want to know all about me. Go ahead—ask me a question. Anything.''

Andy picked at a thumbnail and seemed incapable of speech.

''Okay,'' Frank said. ''I'll tell you a little about myself. I've traveled a lot. Even went to Mexico for a while. I like to travel, see new things. Keeps you fresh—remember that. I'm passing down a piece of wisdom to you. Make sure you see plenty of new places in your life.''

How well Michael remembered all those moves they'd made during his childhood, Frank always believing he could make a big splash as long as it was someplace new. Eventually the three of them—Michael, his mother and his father—had ended up in Tucson. Mere chance had brought them here. Frank could have chosen any other place just as well for yet another new beginning.

''Kid, you have to talk to me sometime,'' Frank said, an edge to his voice. ''I'm your granddad.''

Andy went on picking at his thumbnail and now he was leaning right up against Michael. ''Did you have to run away from the police?'' he mumbled.

Frank laughed, a somewhat unpleasant sound, dry and papery. ''What's your dad been telling you about me? I never did anything wrong, Andy. Never had the police after me. That's pretty dramatic, don't you think? Where'd you get your imagination?''

Andy looked miserable, and Michael knew he couldn't stay in the background any longer.

"Tell Andy the truth," he said, his voice very controlled. "Tell him why you left all those years ago."

Frank made an obvious effort to be the expansive patriarch once more. "Son, that's history. Both you and I know that. What's important now is to go forward, be a family. It's all I want."

"Tell him," Michael repeated.

Frank stood, going to the bureau and setting down his cup. "It's a pretty low thing, isn't it, Mike? Trying to turn my own grandson against me." He looked old tonight, jaw seeming to sag even more than before, those unhealthy pouches under his eyes.

"Tell the boy," Michael said, his voice harsh. Andy slid away from him, a frightened look on his face. Michael hated seeing that, hating scaring his son, but again there was no choice. All three of them were moving toward some unknown but inescapable destination.

Frank gave his unsavory laugh. "You asked for it, son. I'll tell Andy. I'll explain that you were the one who locked me out of my own house that night. Yelled at me to leave and never come back. So I obliged you. Gave you what you wanted."

Andy had slid to the very edge of the bed, as far away from Michael as he could get. This did not escape Frank's notice, and his smile turned slyly triumphant.

"That's right, Andy. Your dad was the one who didn't want anything more to do with me."

"Tell him why," Michael said.

"What's to say? That you were an ungrateful little bas—an ungrateful little kid? Is that what you want him to hear?"

"Tell him what you did to her."

A flicker of doubt showed in Frank's eyes. "I never meant to hurt her. You know that, Mike."

"Then why were you always hitting her?"

"I never—"

"Yes. I want you to remember." Michael rose and stepped toward his father. His hand curled into a fist, but then, slowly, he relaxed it. He just stood there, realizing how odd it seemed: he was taller than his father now. Taller and stronger.

Frank stared down at his own hands, as if seeing them for the first time. Like Andy, he looked frightened. "I never meant to hurt her," he repeated. "It's just . . . she'd make me so crazy. The things she'd say, that way she had of looking at me—the damn cowering. Like she actually *wanted* me to hit her . . ."

"She never wanted that," Michael said, disgust roiling inside him. "I never wanted it, either."

The Frank of Michael's childhood showed through, just for a flash. "You deserved it. You needed discipline."

"Not like that I didn't."

Frank stared at his hands again. "There wasn't any other way," he said, the plaintiveness in his voice. "I had to do something. The two of you, always making me crazy . . ." He went over to the bed and sank onto it again. He gave Andy a glance that seemed suddenly disinterested. "I think you'd better leave," he said. "Get out of here, kid."

Andy remained immobile, hunched on the other bed, staring at his grandfather.

"Leave," Frank repeated. "Don't you get it? Your dad's right about me. I'm not a very nice person. Not a very good person." Something inside him seemed to crumble then. He leaned forward as if in pain.

Michael felt what he thought he could never feel—pity for his father. He didn't know what to do with the emotion.

"Dad," he said. He couldn't remember the last time he'd used that word to address his father.

Franklin Turner looked up at him, anguish in his face. "Get the hell out," he said. "Give me at least that much."

Michael understood. No matter how his father had hurt him in the past, maybe he did deserve to be left with a little dignity. Yes, Michael could give him that much.

"Come on, son," he told Andy. "We're going." He guided his son out the door without looking back.

A few moments later they were both seated in the Jeep again. Andy huddled on the passenger side; in the unsteady light from the motel sign, he looked very small and fragile. Michael wondered how much harm this evening had caused him. But there was no turning back from it.

"The hitting started when I was fairly young," he said, speaking carefully. "My mother and I, we tried everything we could. We tried to keep him happy, but nothing seemed to work. There was always some failure in his life he couldn't contain. He took it out on us."

Andy's silence seemed to fill the air, almost a tangible thing. Michael knew what this silence meant: revulsion at what he was saying. But it had to be said.

"By the time I turned fifteen, I was big enough to try protecting her. One night it got particularly bad, and yes, I did throw my father out of the house. I did tell him never to come back. It almost seemed a miracle when he didn't. But my mother, your grandmother . . .

her spirit seemed broken after that. Sometimes I blamed her for not being a stronger person, for not fighting back. But there's something my father did teach me—blaming somebody else is never the answer. Your grandmother died before you were born. It's just too bad you never got to know her.''

There. It was finished. At last there was nothing more to say. But Andy's heavy silence continued to fill the air. And Michael still didn't know the answer. He still didn't know what harm had come from this night.

CHAPTER EIGHTEEN

"MICHAEL, DON'T TELL ME she's mad at you again!"

Michael had only just entered the Oasis Flower Boutique, and already Melissa was picking out a single purple mum for his purchase.

"Well, Melissa, what can I say? I guess I'm just an aggravating sort of guy. No one seems happy with me these days." There was Kim, who appeared to despise the very sight of him, after he'd made love to her and then turned out to be a private investigator; Andy, who despised him for destroying his illusions about his grandfather last night; Donna, who still thought going to bed with a suspect was the ultimate no-no; *and* both his employers—Sophie Bennett and Luanne Jacobs, neither of whom thought he was handling their cases worth a spit.

"Nonsense," Melissa said. "You're a nice guy, Michael. If people are unhappy with you, why... I'll bet it's more to do with how they feel about themselves than how they feel about you."

Michael had been in the flower shop several times now, and each visit he had made an effort to get on friendlier terms with Melissa and gain a little of her confidence. So far he thought he'd been fairly successful. Was it too early to put it to the test?

"You know, Melissa, speaking of people not being happy, I ran into a woman I know today, a woman who's very, very sad. So sad, in fact, she's practically given up hope."

"Hope for what?" Melissa asked. She already had Michael's mum nicely wrapped in tissue, with a few leaves and the tip of the bloom left out for display.

"Just hope," he said. "Hope of ever being happy again. You see, Melissa, she's lost her daughter—at least that's what she fears. Her daughter ran away some time ago. Hasn't been heard from since."

Melissa stared at him with her tired eyes. He could tell she knew who he was talking about. He could tell she was adding things up, realizing who he probably was and what he was doing here. The girl was smart—real smart. He was almost certain he'd spoken too soon.

"Gee, what a shame," Melissa said as she rang up his total at the cash register. "That'll be five dollars and twenty-five cents, Mr. Turner. You might want to consider opening up an account with us—all of a sudden you seem to be one of our best customers. Then again, I kind of doubt we'll be seeing much more of you."

Michael was being dismissed. Damn. It *had* been too soon. He laid some money on the counter and picked up his flower.

"It's just that, if the woman could hear from her daughter, talk to her, know that she—"

"Cut the crap, Mr. Turner," Melissa said, after glancing around to make certain they were alone in the shop. "My mom sent you to look for me. You know it and I know it. Well, you've found me, so what happens next? You drag me back to her and I'll just run away again, first chance I get. Except this time I'll make certain no one—not even you, Michael—will ever track me down."

She looked scared now, scared and unsure.

"No, Melissa," he said, "I won't take you back to your mother by force. I haven't even told her where you are—only that I've found you and you seem to be okay. A little bit worn down, perhaps, but okay." He was stretching the truth there. Sure, Melissa was all in one piece; she had a roof over her head and enough to eat. But that didn't mean her new life was healthy in the ways that really counted.

"You see, Melissa," he went on, "your mother loves you so much she wants you back by any means possible. But she still thinks of you as a child. She still believes she can force you to behave as she wishes, to live at home and finish school and everything else. She hasn't yet realized you've decided to be an adult."

Michael stopped there before he said too much. He really wanted to tell Melissa Jacobs that she was on the verge of ruining her life—that she ought to go home, where she belonged, back to the safety of being a kid again. Granted, her parents were the type who doted on her too much, putting their own unique pressures on her. But that didn't change the fact that she was still only a teenager and she needed her parents' love and guidance.

Michael didn't say any of these things, because he knew how useless it would be. If he treated Melissa like a child, she would definitely run again. Right now she gazed at him with her tired, defiant eyes. It bothered the hell out of him that he'd seen that same type of defiance in the eyes of his own son.

"Look," he said. "You've made your choice to try to live an adult life. There's a reason your parents can't accept it, though. And that's because, where they're concerned, you're behaving like a child—hiding like a child. You know what being an adult is? It's accepting that your parents, no matter how good or bad they might be, are part of your life. It means acknowledging the connection you have with them, at least letting them know you're okay. If you choose to be an adult, Melissa, you have to take the whole thing. You can't just pick the parts you like. So call your mother. You don't have to go see her. But quit acting like a child. Pick up the phone and call her."

He studied Melissa one last time. Nothing about her expression had changed. She gave absolutely no sign that anything he'd said had an effect on her. There was nothing more he could do. He took his single purple mum and left the flower boutique, leaving behind a girl who had grown up much too fast.

MICHAEL HAD BROUGHT another flower today. It was a single purple-pink bloom, so fresh that dew still seemed to sparkle on the petals. No explanations, no romantic trappings of any kind—just a single mum. Kim couldn't explain the impulse that had made her carry it along with her this afternoon everywhere she went. Of course, Michael and Andy Turner seemed to be coming along with her, too, as if they had both decided to be her personal bodyguards.

Now Kim had led the Turner males to a secondhand shop. She knew that ninety percent of the furniture in secondhand shops was absolute junk. It was the other ten percent that enticed her, the promise of finding something unexpected and wonderful. And only a moment ago she *had* found something wonderful: a small library stepladder made of varnished oak, every joint fitted perfectly together. She knelt beside it, running her fingers over the wood, learning the shape and feel of it. She couldn't believe her luck.

"It's just a ladder," said young Andy Turner as he hovered beside her.

"Not just any ladder," she told him. "This is something special. Can't you just see it with the varnish stripped off, refinished, presiding in a room full of books?"

Andy appeared highly skeptical. But just then Michael came up to the two of them.

"I found some old jigsaw puzzles," he said. "They're pretty interesting. Maybe you'd like to have a look at them, Andy—on that table, over there."

Andy ducked his head and went to the other side of the shop—in precisely the opposite direction Michael had pointed. The Turner males were having even more trouble than usual with each other today. There was a new tension between them; Andy didn't seem able to look at his dad. He didn't even bother with the sarcastic remarks anymore.

Kim felt the too-familiar ache inside her, the wish that somehow she could make things right between Andy and Michael. How foolish that desire was. Couldn't she remember that she was an outsider? Andy already had a mother, off in England somewhere—a mother who'd be coming back at the end of the summer. Kim had no real place in the boy's life. She was just the neighbor lady.

She tried to concentrate on her stepladder again. But Michael was here beside her, and that meant every part of her was alive to his presence. Her gaze lingered on him. She saw the bold, stern lines of his face, felt the sense of watchfulness that never seemed to leave him. She wished that she could tell him to relax. He could take a break now and then; he didn't have to be on guard all the time. Well, maybe she *could* tell him that much.

"I don't know why you're here with me," she said. "No one can attack me in this place."

"We have to be careful," he answered. "If only you'd move in with Donna until—"

"Donna's life is complicated enough, what with her mother-in-law making plans to turn the guest room into a nursery." Holding her flower, Kim sat down on the ladder. It had broad steps that would be perfect for taking a seat and browsing through volumes found on a shelf. She could certainly picture it in a library somewhere. It made her feel safe, musing about different pieces of furniture and where they could end up. Such ordinary thoughts seemed to preclude the possibility of anything bad happening again. If only she could cling to them.

But she could find nothing ordinary in the way she felt about Michael Turner. She brushed her fingers over the chrysanthemum. Michael inspired a tumult of emotion in her, making her yearn for something she had to struggle to describe: a sense of belonging, perhaps, a knowledge that she had finally arrived at her true home.

How foolish she was! Because, in spite of all her warnings to herself, in spite of the way he'd deceived her, she was falling in love with Michael. She had let him into her heart, and she didn't know if she could ever get him out again.

She bowed her head over the solitary flower. The longing inside her seemed too immense, too painful. If only she could run away from it somehow. That was the problem, though, wasn't it? How did you run away from your own heart?

She gazed at him, knowing that was a mistake. Surely her longing, her terrible need, would show in her face. But she couldn't stop looking at him. She took in everything about him: the dark hair curling stubbornly over his forehead, the deep brown of his eyes, the laughter lines he didn't exercise often enough, the way his body looked so lean and powerful in his polo shirt and jeans faded to an old blue. She couldn't picture Michael in new jeans. Nothing but soft denim for him, a softness that disguised his implacable strength.

"Oh, damn," she whispered, pressing a hand to her throat, feeling the pulse beating there. The wanting inside her was so sharp and poignant she couldn't even seem to catch her breath. All the while Michael gazed back at her, and she knew he saw her longing. She knew it because his features seemed to tighten against it.

He sat down across from her in a 1960s tubular chair; made all of steel in abrupt angles, it seemed to suit him. They were alone in this little corner, Andy wandering aimlessly at the far end of the shop.

"Kim," Michael said, "there's something I want you to know. When you told me about your mother, the problems you'd had with her—it felt too familiar, I suppose. My own father was . . . physically abusive."

She listened to the detached way he said those last two words. She tried to imagine what it could have been like for him, but she failed. Her mother, for all her faults, had never raised a hand in anger. The small, persistent cruelties had been emotional, never physical.

"I'm sorry, Michael," Kim said inadequately.

He gave a curt shrug. "I'm just trying to make you understand something. For a long time, I hated my father for what he'd done to my mother and me. But I always wondered if, deep down, I was just like him. My job with the police—that just confirmed the idea. Getting violent is too easy when you seem to have an excuse—you're trying to apprehend someone, he resists, and the urge comes out."

She could tell how difficult it was for him to talk about this. The lines of strain along his jaw and forehead were unmistakable. All she could offer him was what he had once told her.

"You don't have to talk about it anymore."

"There isn't much more," he said brusquely. "One homicide case Donna and I worked, another police detective was shot. I didn't know at the time that he was going to be okay. When I tackled the guy who did it . . . let's just say I got rough. And that's when I realized that I had to change my line of work."

Kim leaned forward. "Michael, you're being so hard on yourself. The situation you're describing—you'd have to be a little rough, just to get the job done. I know you by now. And I know you couldn't do anything really wrong . . . anything really violent."

"I wish I could be so sure," he said grimly. "When my father came back into my life, my first impulse was to use my strength to hurt him—the way he used to hurt me.''

"But you stopped yourself, didn't you?" she said. "I know that you did. Oh, Michael, that's the answer. Your father couldn't stop himself, but *you* did." It seemed so simple, so clear. Michael was strong, a man who had learned to control harmful impulses. Other men, like Roger and Stan Bennett, were the weak ones. Not Michael. Never had Kim felt such a conviction that she was right about something.

If only she could convince him. But his expression had closed, and everything he'd said seemed a warning for her to keep away. The ache inside her grew. How would they ever reach each other, with so much between them?

Paying close attention to Michael, she only gradually realized that Andy was once again hovering nearby, the expression on his young face solemn and intent. She wondered how much he'd heard—and she hoped, with all her heart, that he would understand his dad.

THE FOLLOWING AFTERNOON Kim dialed her father's number and put the phone to her ear. Andy sat beside her at the edge of the pool, trying to look bored but not succeeding very well. He had his feet dangling in the water, a towel over his shoulders, a scuba mask propped up on his head and a snorkel dangling around his neck.

Once Andy had gotten the okay from Michael to swim in Kim's pool, father and son had made a visit to the sporting-goods store—bought out half the place, by the looks of it. Kim wondered if the venture had brought them any closer together. She hoped so, but then, she'd been hoping a lot of things lately and wondering if any of them would ever come true.

The phone kept ringing and she began to think her father wasn't home. Part of her felt relieved. Was she really ready to talk to him yet? But then he answered, with the words she remembered from her childhood: "Lambert residence, Carl speaking." He was always so precise about answering the phone, as if he didn't want the caller to have any mistaken ideas about the number reached—no fear of surprises.

"Hello, Pop," she said.

"Kim..."

"Yes, it's me."

"Is it my birthday?" he asked, his tone rather too jocular. "Christmas, maybe?"

"No. Believe it or not, I'm just calling to say hello."

There was a brief silence on the line. "Kim, it's good to hear your voice." Now he sounded awkward. And it *had* been awkward, these past eight years since she had fled Pinetop. They'd talked to each other only when strictly necessary and had shared only a few uncomfortable holidays together. The memory of Kim's mother was always present between them, never mentioned but separating them into their own private regrets. The unspoken part, that was the problem. It had to change.

"Pop, I have a complaint," she said lightly. "Those checks I send you, why don't you ever cash them? It wouldn't hurt you."

"I've told you all along," he said. "I'm doing fine. The restaurant business isn't bad these days."

That was what he always said. He clung so stubbornly to that little diner in Pinetop. Why couldn't he let go of it, do something else with his life? She wanted to help him out. Why was he so proud?

"You know," she said, "I was thinking of coming up for a visit. Maybe even a few weeks' worth. You and I, we could just...talk." The word hung there, over the line. Her father knew as well as she did that they'd never been big on talking.

"Sure," he said cautiously. "You know I'd like to see you."

"Maybe we can do a little hiking. The way we did when I was a kid. You're still up for a hike, aren't you?"

"That would be very nice indeed." He sounded courtly and old-fashioned.

"I'll probably get there sometime next week," she said. "I'll let you know for sure in a few days, all right?"

"You're always welcome, Kim. This is still your home."

It had been a long while since she'd felt anyplace was truly her home. She watched as Andy slid into the pool and tried out his snorkel. He swam facedown, the tube bobbing well above the surface.

"I'll be driving up. I'll let you know when." She realized she was repeating herself. "Pop, it's good to hear *your* voice, too. Talk to you soon."

"Yes...we'll talk again soon." He still sounded formal; they'd have to work on that. Kim hung up the phone, placing it on the poolside table. Did she feel better or worse? It was hard to say. After a few moments reflection, however, she settled on better. No matter how superficial that conversation had been, she and her father were on speaking terms, weren't they? And once she was in Pinetop, all it would take was a good heart-to-heart with her dad—one of them opening up for once—and she was certain they'd draw close again.

A heart-to-heart with Pop... Kim was starting to cotton to the idea when she noticed a man standing next to her house just inside the pool fence.

"Oh, Thad, it's only you. You startled me for a moment."

"Yes, yes," Thad Bennett said ponderously, "it's only me."

"Now, you know I didn't mean it like that. It's just with all that's been happening lately, I guess I'm a bit jittery."

"Jittery...yes." Thad moved closer to her, and Kim saw that he looked very preoccupied today—as if he was more weighed down by his thoughts than ever.

"Is everything all right?" she asked. "You look upset."

Despite the heat of the Arizona sun, Thad was wearing a dark suit and a silver-gray tie. All very distinguished, boardroom attire. He looked particularly out of place by the swimming pool.

"I've come, Kim, to tidy things up a bit. I never did like mess—Norie knows that."

The last thing Kim wanted right now was a conversation with Thad Bennett. He always meditated on everything he had to say, drawing matters out interminably. But he really did look perturbed, lost in his own little world. Andy was swimming noiselessly around the pool with his snorkel, and Thad apparently hadn't noticed him.

"Have a seat," Kim said.

Thad shook his head. "I don't believe so. This is not a discussion for sitting down."

Something about his tone made Kim uneasy. She sat up straighter in her lounge chair, glad she'd worn her T-shirt and shorts over her maillot. It made her feel more dignified. Thad brought that out in a person—the need to be dignified.

"What's wrong?" she prodded. "You might as well tell me."

He looked vaguely annoyed. "Don't try to rush me, Kim. You'll hear all of it soon enough—but first things first. Where is the letter?"

She stared at him. "What letter? What are you talking about?"

"Don't be coy. It doesn't suit you. The letter Norie wrote—the one confessing that the child is Stan's."

Kim sat frozen in place, more confused than ever. A chill went through her in spite of the heat. "I don't know what you're talking about."

"Of course you do." He began pacing the patio. "But even without the letter, surely it would have occurred to you as odd, Norie having a third child when the other two were almost teenagers." He spoke matter-of-factly, as if discussing a stranger, not his wife.

"Norie always said she wanted another baby," Kim argued. "She's always loved being a mother. And so, when your son was born—"

"Not *my* son," Thad said, "my brother's child. Stan's. Please try to keep the details straight."

It was impossible—a cruel and horrible joke. Kim had wanted children so badly. To learn now that her husband had fathered a child—and with Norie . . .

"It can't be true," she said numbly. "If she had an affair, it wasn't with Stan. It had to be Roger—"

"Ah, yes, Roger." Thad seemed off on a tangent of his own. "Roger, it turns out, knew all about Stan's affair with my wife. I can just picture Stan bragging about it to his big brother. And then Roger getting into the act. Apparently it was *his* idea that Norie write a letter to her lover rhapsodizing about the son he had provided her. Stan asked for the letter, and Norie, obliging idiot that she is, wrote it. Did she really believe I wouldn't find out about it? Roger does so love to talk about such things."

Kim struggled to her feet, pressing her arms tightly against herself. But the chill remained deep inside. What perversion had twisted all the Bennetts? Why was their wealth, their great success, not enough for them? It seemed they were compelled to destroy each other.

"I've heard enough," she said. "Please go, Thad."

"I will leave, Kim—as soon as you hand over the letter."

"I don't have it. I've never seen it." She thought back to that wretched visit she'd paid to Adobe Acres. Obviously Norie had believed that Roger possessed the letter.

"It's reckless of you to make denials," Thad said almost conversationally. "That's what Stan did at first. Denied that he'd ever slept with my wife." His tone faltered just a bit, but then he recovered. "It wasn't difficult to get Stan drunk that night. In fact, it was easy to make my little brother feel inadequate about himself. All I had to do was start talking about Roger's successes. That was Stan's weak point—knowing he couldn't measure up to Roger. So he kept drinking that night, trying to forget about himself. And afterward...the jammed accelerator—I'm proud of that touch."

"Stop," Kim said. But she wondered if anything could surprise her anymore.

"The letter, Kim. I must have it. I can't have the world knowing that my youngest child...my only son...is my brother's bastard." Thad, even as he spoke, moved with remarkable alacrity. He was upon Kim in a second, his hands closing around her neck from behind. It was happening all over again—the fingers squeezing her throat, cutting off air.

A loud splashing came from the pool, just enough to make Thad slacken his grip for a second. It was all Kim needed. She jabbed her elbow back into his stomach, then hurtled herself forward, yanking her body away from him. There was no time to think, only to act. She raced around the pool, almost slipping on the tiles. Reaching down, she helped Andy haul himself out of the water.

"Run," she yelled. "Go!"

But Michael was already here, tackling Thad and bringing him to the ground. He pinned Thad's arms neatly behind his back. Now Donna came jogging around the side of the house, gun in hand. When she saw that Michael had things under control, she came rushing up to Andy and Kim.

"Are you all right?"

"We're fine. Just fine." Kim was shaking uncontrollably, but she gripped Andy's wet hand in her own. "Quick thinking," she told him. "I've never been so happy about splashing in my life..." Her teeth chattered as if she'd been in the pool herself.

Andy tried to look bored, but couldn't quite disguise his pride.

"He snuck in through the back," Donna said. "By the time I figured it out...well, I'm just glad you're both okay." She jogged over toward Michael, replacing her gun in its holster.

It seemed a very short while later that Thad was handcuffed and escorted into a police squad car. Andy sat on one of the lounge chairs, a towel wrapped around his shoulders, regaling Donna with details of the adventure. Fortunately he seemed to see it as just that—an adventure. Kim wondered why she couldn't stop shivering. Michael had draped a towel around her, and now he took hold of her hand. It was a gesture he might have offered to anyone—so kind, yet so remote. It was like this between them now, as if there was only so much they could give to each other.

"It's over," Michael said. "It's all over."

"Yes," she said dully. "I suppose someday we'll find the letter. Stan must have hidden it somewhere, or maybe Roger really does know where it is. All along, Thad believed I knew. Maybe he was just trying to frighten me that day in the warehouse." She couldn't say the rest of it—that Thad's obsession with his wife's betrayal had taken him into some dark place where he could murder even his own brother.

"Don't think about it anymore," Michael said, that remote compassion in his eyes. "It really is over."

Kim felt no relief, just a terrible emptiness. She knew it would be a long while before she could fully comprehend what had happened here today. But that wasn't what caused this sadness deep inside her. The sadness came from fearing that it was indeed over, everything she and Michael had shared.

CHAPTER NINETEEN

THE NEW OFFICE smelled like paint. Donna had wanted the place redecorated before they moved in, so now the walls were "alabaster white." Michael couldn't tell the difference from ordinary, everyday white, but he didn't tell his partner that. She seemed pretty happy that they were moving to a bigger office suite.

Michael carried a box of files from the Jeep to the reception area. That was something else—they were finally going to hire a receptionist. Business was going well, two new cases in the past week alone. One in particular interested Michael; it involved gathering information for the defense attorney in a murder case. Any evidence Michael uncovered might very well prove the defendant innocent. It reminded him of the old days, when he'd been a police detective and had felt an underlying sense of purpose about his work.

Donna brought in another box and set it down. She glanced around in satisfaction. "Not bad," she said. "Not bad at all. We're going to the top, Mike."

"Don't get carried away," he told her.

"You know what your problem is? You're a pessimist." She paused dramatically. "Guess who called me on my car phone just a few minutes ago. Luanne Jacobs, that's who. She says she heard from her daughter. Nothing spectacular—Melissa just called to say she was all right. Wouldn't give her address yet or anything like that, but it's a beginning.''

Michael thought about Melissa Jacobs, the pretty young girl with her weary, too-mature eyes. He *was* too much of a pessimist to believe that Melissa would turn her life around—leave the married guy, move back home. But a beginning was something—not much, but something.

"I thought you'd be happier about it," Donna said, giving him an astute glance. "I know what your problem really is. You're still brooding about Kim."

The problem was that Kim never seemed to leave his mind. Hell, he even dreamed about the woman.

"Take my advice," Donna said. "Just go to her."

"It's not that simple."

"Sure it is," she argued. "You go to her and admit you were a fool—and that you're in love with her."

He frowned.

"Mike, I'm not a detective for nothing," she said wryly. "Of course you're in love with her. Why else do you think you've been acting so mopey? You're mooning around in the most incredible manner. Anyway, she's not a suspect anymore, so I can't imagine what's stopping you."

Too bad Kim didn't see things in quite the same light. She'd left town a few days ago and hadn't told anyone where she was going. It could be that she'd just wanted to get away from him. Would she ever forgive him for the way he'd deceived her? Then again, would she ever trust any man after Stan Bennett? She'd had it rough in her marriage, no argument about that.

But Michael knew that it went deeper. What about the way he'd messed up his own marriage? Could he honestly say he'd do better the second time around? He'd spent so much of his life being vigilant, making sure he wouldn't turn out like his father. Could he ever let his guard down? Could he give Kim what she needed?

He wished the damn questions would stop plaguing him. Donna, meanwhile, seemed amused by some private thought. She hummed as she moved around the new office. All morning she'd alternated between distraction and an odd giddiness.

"Okay, what's up?" Michael asked. "Did you finally tell your mother-in-law you're not pregnant?"

Donna placed her hand over her flat stomach, a strange little smile on her face. "I could hardly do that. You see, Mike...well, the funny thing is...I just found out that I *am* pregnant."

He regarded her skeptically. "Donna, if this is your idea of—"

"It's the truth, Mike! I'm scared to death about it. I mean, what do I know about kids? But I'm kind of excited, too. Really excited, I guess you could say." She gave a silly grin.

"Donna, congratulations." He meant it. He'd bet his partner would figure out exactly what to do with a kid. She was resourceful. She could handle anything.

Make that *almost* anything. "Mike," she said, a look of growing dismay on her face, "I really *am* in a pickle now. How on earth am I going to explain this to my mother-in-law? Do you think she'll buy a fifteen-month pregnancy?"

Michael didn't even bother to answer that one.

A SHORT TIME LATER Michael pulled up at the community center. He walked to the gym, opened the door and stepped inside. Andy was on the basketball court playing a game of two-on-one with his friends Doug and Eric. Lately he hadn't complained quite so much about spending time with his buddies from the old days. He no longer said that Doug was a jerk, or Eric a whiny ass. Michael supposed that was a sign of progress.

Andy glanced over and saw Michael. Right after that he grabbed the ball, took it down center court and shot it into the basket.

Way to go, Michael said silently to his son. He knew enough, however, not to make a big deal about it. When Andy came toward him a few moments later, he just said, "Good game," and left it at that.

Andy picked up his duffel bag and trailed after Michael as they went outside to the Jeep. Once they'd both climbed in, Michael didn't start the engine right away. He pondered the best way to talk to his son, then decided on the straightforward approach.

"Last night I went to see your grandfather again."

Andy hunched down in his seat, trying to look uninterested.

"It's true he hasn't been a very good person," Michael went on. "Maybe he never will be. I keep trying to figure it out—what makes people the way they are, why they do certain things. I haven't come up with any answers yet, but it won't stop me from trying."

Andy looked as if he was about to make one of his sarcastic remarks, but he didn't say anything. He just let the silence speak for itself. This one said he was listening.

"Anyway, son, I went to see him. And a peculiar thing happened. For the first time in my life, I wasn't angry at him. I just felt sorry for him, nothing else, and I think he could tell. He didn't like it. He said he was going to leave town and he didn't know when he'd be back. He said to tell you goodbye, Andy. And he said . . . he wished he could be a different kind of grandfather."

There. Michael had finished. All he could do now was wait. He knew it was a lot for an eleven-year-old to think about. Not that Andy was a typical eleven-year-old. Sometimes, like Melissa Jacobs, he seemed awfully old for his years.

At last Andy stirred. "I feel kind of sorry for him, too," he said gruffly. Another long silence, and then he glanced over at Michael.

"Dad," he said, "we're not gonna make it to the movies if we just sit here."

"Hey, I did promise you a double feature, didn't I?"

"Yeah, well, only if you use the gas pedal."

Michael revved the engine and pulled out of the parking space. Andy leaned forward and turned on the radio. This time he didn't choose the oldies; he went to a rock station and turned it up loud. Then he glanced at Michael again. And Michael noticed only one thing. The wariness in his son's eyes was gone.

KIM WALKED SLOWLY across the warehouse floor, her feet stirring up the litter of papers. It was really going to be a job, cleaning this place out, getting it ready. But it was hers now. She'd finalized the purchase of the building this morning, and she could get started on renovations just as soon as she pleased. It gave her a heady sense of power. For the first time in her life, she was going to do something entirely her own.

She stopped in the middle of the warehouse. She couldn't deny that Bennett money had bought this place. Her inheritance from Stan had left her quite wealthy indeed, but it wasn't *her* money.

She was struggling to make peace with that, to accept she had a right to her inheritance. She'd genuinely believed herself in love when she'd married Stan, and she'd tried hard to make it work between them. You couldn't put a dollar amount to something like that. All she knew was that Stan had wanted her to have the money; his will had made that very clear. Maybe it was the only real gesture of affection he'd ever made toward her.

But she didn't want to think about the past. She wanted to think about the future—the one she was going to build for herself. With any luck, soon she *would* be making money of her own. She paced across the warehouse floor again, enjoying the spaciousness that heralded all sorts of possibilities.

She heard a rustling sound. Heartbeat quickening, she swiveled toward the door. Someone was silhouetted there, someone tall and lean and powerful.

Now her heartbeat truly accelerated as Michael came toward her. All she could do was stand there and watch him. She felt like someone who had been traveling lost in the desert, only to catch a glimpse of paradise. The past few weeks she'd thought she was doing better—making plans for her new life, getting on with it. But one look at Michael, and she knew how very much she still longed for him. How very much she still loved him.

She turned away, commanding her body to stop its ridiculous trembling. But Michael came around to face her.

"Hello," he said calmly, as if the sight of her had caused no turmoil in *him*. He was carrying a file folder tucked under his arm. In the dim sunshine that came through the grimy windows, Kim saw that his hair fell over his forehead, as stubbornly as ever. His eyes were dark and smoky, making her think all manner of forbidden thoughts about being in his arms.

She turned away again, bending to pick up some of the litter from the floor. "All these old receipts," she said. "Invoices, lading bills, what have you. I guess I'll have to come up with some modern versions."

"Going into business?" he asked casually.

"Yes." She forced a briskness into her voice. "Pretty soon this place is going to be full of furniture again. All kinds of used furniture that I'm going to restore and then sell." She took a deep breath, rushing on. "You can talk all you like about this being a bad neighborhood. I happen to think it has potential. If things go well, I can open up little shops here and there, expand—"

"You're just like Donna," he said, "thinking big. I wasn't going to complain about the neighborhood, though. I trust your judgment."

Trust—the one word that was a sore spot between them. Kim dropped the papers back on the floor.

"You left town for a while there," he said. "I couldn't find you."

"Whyever not?" she came back. "You're a detective, aren't you?" She felt some healthy indignation, remembering how he'd deceived her.

"Sure, I'm a detective, but I've made a decision. From now on, I only take the cases that really mean something to me. And no more undercover work. I've discovered it's not my style."

"You could have fooled me," she said acidly.

"Kim..."

She needed to protect herself against that huskiness in his voice, and she walked away from him. It was just too bad that he fell into step beside her. Here they were, taking a stroll around the warehouse.

"It's no secret," she said. "I spent a few weeks in Pinetop visiting my father."

"How'd it go?" Michael asked, sounding genuinely concerned.

"Half the time we didn't know what to say to each other. But the other half... we actually started to talk about some of the things that matter. Like my mother, how we felt about her." She didn't want to get this personal with Michael. "It was only a beginning," she added quickly, "that's all."

"I'm starting to think that beginnings are pretty important."

"Well, good," she said inanely. Dammit, what did the man want from her? "When I came back from Pinetop, I noticed you'd moved out." That had been a shock, realizing that Michael would no longer be living next door. And she'd hated that it made her feel so bereft. "I'm moving out, too. Putting the house up for sale."

"Too many memories of the Bennetts?" he asked gently.

"That's part of it," she admitted. "I'm going to sell my shares in Bennett Industries to the family. All this time, I've been suspicious of their motives, but you know what? I think it all really does come down to one thing—Sophie wanting to close ranks, no outsiders allowed—" Kim wondered why she was telling this to Michael, yet he always seemed to affect her like this. She found herself wanting to share everything with him.

"Poor Sophie," she said. "When you think about it, her whole life has been destroyed. Finding out that one of her sons killed another..." Kim shivered. "I went to see her and she seemed so forlorn somehow. Not like the old Sophie, making everyone around her miserable. In a way, she's been deserted. Norie's gone off to stay with her parents—she took the children with her." One of them Stan's child, Kim reminded herself. But she no longer felt hurt or betrayed; she only hoped that somehow all three children would find the security they needed. "To top it all off," she added, "Diane and Jack eloped. They're married now—not a thing Sophie can do about it."

Michael seemed to think this over. "Wonder how it'll work out," he murmured.

"Who knows how any relationship works out," she said irritably. "It's always a gamble, isn't it?"

"Sometimes you can stack the odds in your favor."

She'd had quite enough. She stopped and gazed at Michael. "This chat is all very nice, but you must be here for a reason. What is it?"

"I'm having trouble with my heroine again," he said, completely serious.

"Oh, no, don't start that—"

"It's the truth. She won't leave my mind...my heart. Here, read this." He took the file folder from under his arm, opened it and handed her a few sheets of paper.

She stared at them suspiciously. "You're not really a writer."

"You don't know that for sure."

Kim didn't know what to believe anymore. She took the pages and scanned them. "Michael...so I *am* the heroine." After a moment she raised her eyebrows a little. "This isn't bad writing," she said.

He looked a little uncomfortable. "You can be honest. I can take it."

"I *am* being honest. A mystery novel. You're really going to write one?"

Now he merely looked disgruntled. "Thought as long as I'd put up the front, I might as well see what it's all about. I get tired of mysteries that aren't realistic. I'm a detective, so at least I know what I'm talking about. But it's only a beginning."

"You're the one who just told me beginnings are important." She read on, wishing her hands would stop shaking. "Oh, Michael, I don't have that many freckles."

"Kim." The dangerous huskiness was back in his voice. "You're as beautiful as I've described you. Maybe more. I'm not too good with adjectives yet." He took her into his arms, and the pages fell from her hands.

"Wait," she said. "We can't lose them."

"We'll worry about it later." He kissed her, and she could no longer resist. How she'd dreamed of this, his lips on hers, his body so close and warm.

"Michael," she murmured. "Is it too much to hope..."

"I love you, Kim," he said. "I damn well can't live without you. When you left town like that, without even saying goodbye, it made me realize just how much I couldn't live without you."

Happiness hovered just within reach. Did she dare grab hold of it? "Michael, if only I knew where we're headed..."

"It scares me, too, Kim. I told myself I'd never hurt my wife the way my father hurt my mother. But that wasn't enough. I still couldn't make a go of my marriage. Maybe I went too far the other way, shutting everything off. Can I change?"

"You don't need to change." She tangled her hands in his hair, drawing him closer. Suddenly it seemed very clear and simple. In the end, it was always like that with Michael. She could feel the happiness starting; all she had to do was take a chance on it. "You're so hard on yourself," she told him. "If your marriage didn't work out, it wasn't just your fault. Your ex-wife had a little something to do with it, too, you know. Because with me, Michael, you've already proved how very giving and loving you can be."

"I can prove it some more," he said. And with his kiss, he proceeded to do just that.

A tender, passionate while later, they broke apart. The happiness had spread all through Kim, leaving her with a tingling glow. She placed her hands on Michael's chest, breathing a bit unsteadily.

"I almost forgot to tell you," she said. "I love you, too, Michael. As far as Andy's concerned...well, I fell in love with him the first moment I saw him. It just took me a little longer with you.''

''You're willing to take on both Andy and me?'' he asked solemnly.

''Yes. Definitely yes. I know Andy already has a mother, but—''

''He needs you, Kim.'' Michael sounded very intent. ''When Jill comes back, he'll be living with her, but we'll have him on the weekends at least. And maybe next summer...''

''It'll all work out,'' Kim said. ''And who knows? Eventually Andy might have a kid sister or brother hanging around. Think he'd like that?''

''I think it's something we'll definitely have to work on,'' Michael said more solemnly than ever.

Kim brushed that lock of hair away from his forehead and smiled when it fell stubbornly down again. And then she thought she'd try another kiss.

Her new life had begun.

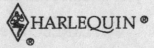

Merry Christmas, Baby!

A romantic collection filled with the magic
of Christmas and the joy of children.

SUSAN WIGGS, Karen Young and
Bobby Hutchinson bring you Christmas wishes,
weddings and romance, in a charming
trio of stories that will warm up your
holiday season.

MERRY CHRISTMAS, BABY! also contains
Harlequin's special gift to you—a set of
FREE GIFT TAGS included in every book.

Brighten up your holiday season with
MERRY CHRISTMAS, BABY!

Available in November at
your favorite retail store.

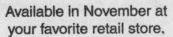

HARLEQUIN ®

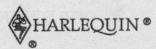

Look us up on-line at: http://www.romance.net   MCB

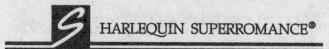

Special Books by Special Writers

MY FAIR GENTLEMAN
by Jan Freed

The Book:
A contemporary, provocative and just plain *funny* story about
changing *your* life—*and* other people's. A keeper!

The Writer:
Jan Freed first burst onto the Superromance scene in May 1995,
and readers can't stop talking about her! Her first novel—
Too Many Bosses—is nominated for three *Romantic Times*
awards, and she's still getting fan letters about *The Texas Way*,
her second Superromance.

"Jan Freed writes with spice and flair! An exciting new voice in
contemporary romance."   —Susan Wiggs

"Jan Freed is a delightful new talent. She has a truly gifted
light touch with characters who still manage to tug at the
reader's heart."   —Alexandra Thorn

Jan Freed's stories are "complex, emotionally satisfying and
intellectually stimulating."   —*Affaire de Coeur*

SHOW11

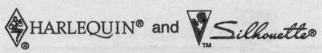

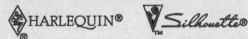HARLEQUIN® and Silhouette®

are proud to present...

HERE COME THE GROOMS™

Four marriage-minded stories written by top Harlequin and Silhouette authors!

Next month, you'll find:

Married?!	by Annette Broadrick
Designs on Love	by Gina Wilkins
It Happened One Night	by Marie Ferrarella
Lazarus Rising	by Anne Stuart

ADDED BONUS! In every edition of
Here Come the Grooms you'll find $5.00 worth
of coupons good for Harlequin and Silhouette
products.

On sale at your favorite Harlequin and Silhouette
retail outlet.

HARLEQUIN®   Silhouette®

HCTG996

REBECCA

43 LIGHT STREET

YORK

FACE TO FACE

*Bestselling author Rebecca York returns to "43 Light Street"
for an original story of past secrets, deadly deceptions—and
the most intimate betrayal.*

She woke in a hospital—with amnesia…and with child.
According to her rescuer, whose striking face is the last
image she remembers, she's Justine Hollingsworth. But
nothing about her life seems to fit, except for the baby
inside her and Mike Lancer's arms around her. Consumed
by forbidden passion and racked by nameless fear, she
must discover if she is Justine…or the victim of some mind
game. Her life—and her unborn child's—depends on it….

Don't miss *Face To Face*—Available in October, wherever
Harlequin books are sold.

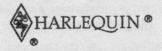

HARLEQUIN ®

®

HARLEQUIN SUPERROMANCE®

Remember the Calloway women—
Mariah, Jo, Tess and Eden?

For all the readers who loved *CALLOWAY CORNERS...*

Welcome Back!

And if you haven't been there yet or met the Calloways...

Join us!

MEET THE CALLOWAY COUSINS!

JERICHO
by Sandra Canfield
(available in August)

DANIEL
by Tracy Hughes
(available in September)

GABE
by Penny Richards
(available in October)

CAL1